Caden's Fate

Kate McKeever

Lyn Su,
Thanks for the
fun! I love Romfest
with you. Enjoy Caden
& Fate. Kate
McKeever

www.crescentmoonpress.com

Caden's Fate
Kate McKeever

ISBN: 978-1-937254-85-8
E-ISBN: 978-1-937254-86-5

Crescent Moon Press
1385 Highway 35
Box 269
Middletown, NJ 07748

Crescent Moon Press electronic publication/print publication: October 2012 www.crescentmoonpress.com

DEDICATION

To my parents, as always.

Chapter One

Evil whispered to Fate in the cool morning air, threatening her composure as she tried to focus on her friend.

"I wish I had your talent." Beth sighed into the coffee cup filled with a double shot of espresso.

Startled, Fate eyed her friend. *How much does she suspect?* She couldn't know about it, surely. Fate never shared her secrets with outsiders. She toned down the voices whispering in her head and smiled. "My talent?"

"To know what to say in situations like this morning." Beth pulled her large Danish closer to her and began to pick at the nuts sprinkled on top of the confection.

"It was a difficult time for the family, what with their mother and wife dying so young." Fate struggled to put something of her *talent* into terms her friend could understand. "I just tried to give them some measure of hope and comfort."

"I know. I wish I could have found some words too. I was her nurse until the end and had nothing to say. You get called in at the last minute and do all the right things." Beth raised tortured eyes to Fate. "I think I'm in the wrong job."

Fate agreed. Working at a residential hospice could be one of the most trying jobs in the nursing field. Yet, Fate's position as a medical social worker fit her, in more ways than one.

"You know, there are other jobs out there." She sipped her own less potent mixture of coffee and cream.

~ ☾ ~

"I hear the rehab wing at the university hospital has openings."

Though they sat at a table in the middle of the city, Fate caught the hint of turning leaves in the crisp dawn air. Underlying it all whispered the ever-present voices, souls calling out to her. And this morning, a feeling of threat hung over the air like smoke.

"Yeah, maybe I'll look into that. I think I'd do well in rehab. More hope, you know?" Beth's eyes held a little more life when she looked up from her food.

Fate nodded. She couldn't imagine being away from the dying, but it wasn't for everyone.

It hadn't been the greatest idea, to sit at the sidewalk tables at the coffee house at five in the morning. The other customers abandoned the crisp air, leaving Fate and Beth alone. Fate realized how vulnerable they were, sitting at their table in the dim predawn hour. Fate's neck grew chilled, as if a cold breeze blew across it, though no wind disturbed the air. Someone watched them. It couldn't be anything else. She could almost taste the evil in the air as she took a breath.

The buzz of warning in her mind grew to an alarming level, blurring the lines between reality and psychic forewarning. A slight noise from the bushes near their sidewalk table caused her to shift in her chair.

Fate leaned toward her friend and whispered, "Let's go inside."

Beth pulled her focus from picking the cinnamon roll to crumbs to glance up at Fate and stare. A minute too long. A man erupted from the bushes. Fate threw up an arm to block the wicked looking blade he thrust toward her. She managed to jar him enough to deflect the blow but gasped as the long knife sliced open her forearm.

Beth scrambled backwards from the assailant. At least the assailant didn't seem to want her friend, as his attention focused solely on Fate The blood streaming

~ ☾ ~

down her arm only distracted her at first, then made her movements slow as she tried to defend herself.

She tried to file away facts, just in case she survived the attack. He dressed totally in black, pants and t-shirt, sported short dark hair and dark, dead eyes. And a serious purpose to kill her, apparently.

"For the soul," he hissed, sending a chill through her. Was she a random target or did he mean to steal *her* soul?

Time slowed with each pass he made at her, as did her attempts to deflect the blows the knife, the blade dulled with more blood. Each stroke of his blade created a red-hot trail of stinging pain.

Beth screamed, pulling Fate's attention away for a split second. A second man, taller and more menacing though he showed no knife, ran toward them. *God.* She hoped he would help. She threw up a hand to dodge another blow.

If this one hit—

But it didn't and no other jabs followed. She took a breath and glanced around for Beth. Their table overturned in a crash as the two men battled in the pre-dawn light, near the edge of the building. Fate scrambled toward the bundle of humanity lying near the wall. Beth huddled in a ball beyond the overturned table, her arms shielding her head, sobbing.

"Beth, did he hurt you?" Fate started to touch her but decided against it. Though her arms were a mass of blood and slashes, she didn't feel any pain. A wonderful thing, adrenaline.

She sat beside her friend and cupped her hand over the gash in her own arm, trying to stem the flow of blood and to prevent it from touching Beth. "We have to call the police. Beth! Do you have your phone?"

Beth just rolled into a tighter ball. Fate glanced over her shoulder toward the scuffle. It wasn't like the movies

~ ☾ ~

at all. The men fought in silence, the only sounds, other than the beating of her heart and ever-present murmurs in her head, were grunts and the dull thuds indicating a fist encountering flesh. An acrid tang of fear filled her mouth.

She needed to find someone to help, but how couldn't leave Beth. She glanced around the coffee shop parking lot. Though cars were parked in several spaces, no one else remained outside. She didn't see her carryall containing her cell phone. And she couldn't focus enough to call for help psychically.

So much for her *talent*.

A sharp movement to her right pulled her head around. Their attacker stood over her. His arm raised and ready to strike. Frozen, she stared into his eyes. No emotion, no crazed wildness, and no drugged haze flickered in his eyes. Just a flat, almost reptilian gaze.

Fate stared at the blade as it swept toward her in slow motion. Eons passed and she waited, too stunned to do more than watch as the knife approached.

The movement outside her bubble of awareness startled her more than the assailant's actions. The other man kicked out, pushing her attacker into the wall and jarring into Beth. A grunt followed a thud as the second man landed on top of the first.

The faint whimper sounded in her head, almost a plea. She couldn't discriminate whether it between a call for help in passing the portal and psychic clutter. In her frenzy to stay alive, she couldn't filter out the sounds, the mess of psychic calls and thoughts she normally dulled.

Fate rolled her head toward the battle but nothing registered. The world receded. The voices. Her constant companions since her earliest memory, faded away to the void.

He'd used two knives, she realized. One, a long one,

~ ☾ ~

utilitarian and silver, nothing out of the ordinary, sliced at her arms. The other appeared to be different, alive. Shorter, with a shine that gleamed from within, it gave off power, evil. Did Death Maidens see their own death coming? She couldn't. And who would escort her through the portal?

***

Caden stared at the dark-haired woman on the stretcher, her body covered with a sheet. *Damn, why didn't I get here earlier?* He stood, ignoring aches and pains from the fight and of the body of the Guard that lay in the street beyond.

The man could have been his brother, for all the similarities in their builds and looks. The only exceptions were that he wore his own hair longer and he sported a short beard and mustache. The most obvious difference, though, the small sun tattoo on Caden's right shoulder labeled him as a Soldier.

When the police checked out the other guy's ID, there would be nothing to find. No name, no job, no social security number. He'd just killed a non-entity, a Guard.

This Guard must have been a novice. He'd broadcasted his intent to kill the woman with no effort to mask his purpose. Caden's interrupted sleep, a vision of murder, jarred him awake instantly, and in time to stop the Guard.

Or had he?

The woman on the second stretcher being loaded onto the ambulance remained unconscious. Blood matted her fair hair and more of it covered her clothing. From the little he'd been able to observe, she'd been hit several times, all before he'd arrived. Hell, if he'd only arrived sooner.

As far as he knew, only one blow landed after his intervention, killing the second woman. Was she the target, or the blonde? No one knew, but still, he'd lost a

~ ☾ ~

soul. The only salve, the Obsidian Guard hadn't gotten the soul either.

He forced himself to relax his stance despite the adrenaline surge. Police officers, emergency response staff and the curious bakery workers and customers that suddenly appeared after all danger passed mingled around him. One or more of them must have called 911, because an ambulance and police car arrived before he could rouse the woman.

He forced himself to remain still, alert. The fact that the cops were present didn't mean he or the survivor were out of danger. Did the Guard still have the blonde as a target? If so, he needed to learn her identity and protect her.

A plain clothes officer approached him, nodding to the uniform watching over the scene, making sure Caden didn't leave.

"Sir, I need to see some ID."

Caden pulled his driver's license, PI license and a business card from his wallet and handed them over. The detective gave the PI license a detailed look and the driver's license a cursory glance before handing them back over and making a note in his book. The business card he kept. "What were you doing around the neighborhood, Mr. Greene?"

"I was on my way to work out, thought I'd get coffee first." Caden motioned toward the coffee shop, now buzzing with onlookers. He briefly outlined what happened between his arrival and the time the police showed.

The detective nodded, "The staff of the shop mentioned the same thing. You aren't under suspicion. You always work out this early?"

"Not every day."

"She's lucky you showed up when you did," the detective murmured as they watched the ambulance

~ ☾ ~

drive off, followed by the second one containing two bodies.

"How's she doing?"

"Lost a lot of blood, but the EMTs said she'll be okay. Looks like her friend bled out."

Caden nodded, he'd seen way too much blood around the other girl to be surprised.

"We'll need you to come into the station and give us a detailed statement."

"Sure. Which hospital did they take her to?" Caden nodded toward the flashing lights in the distance.

The detective eyed him then pulled a sheet of blank paper from his notebook and jotted a name down. "You use this to harass her or give her any grief and I'll be on your ass in a heartbeat, got that?"

Caden half grinned. Apparently, the waif-like woman drew someone else's attention as well. "Got it. Just want to talk to her, see how she is."

The detective narrowed his gaze, staring a moment longer and walked away, leaving Caden staring at the paper in front of him. Fate Halligan, St. Vincent's. He stilled once more before heading toward his car. Nothing disturbed the air, no signs of other Guards rose to his consciousness. Now, he could pursue the target.

***

Fate heard the whispers in her head first. Souls preparing to cross the portal, some quiet and peaceful, others anxious or fearful. Oddly enough, they comforted and assured her she lived. Pain hit her second, throbbing from the cuts scattered across her arms and shoulders. She looked toward the doctor suturing a gash in her forearm then quickly averted her eyes. Even with the local anesthetic, an odd pulling sensation kept her aware of the procedure.

"Lie still, Ms. Halligan. Almost done." The slight

~ ☾ ~

woman dressed in scrubs bent over Fate's arm and
stitched her cuts closed.

"Where am I?"

"Saint Vincent's, Emergency. We'll be finished in a
few minutes then you can rest, okay?"

"My friend—" She started to raise herself into a sitting
position only to be pushed back onto the gurney by the
nurse on the other side of the bed.

"Just relax. Only a few more minutes." The doctor
nodded to the nurse and left the room in a rush. The
nurse began to bandage the stitched area.

Fate knew all the ways professionals used to avoid
breaking bad news. To hell with privacy laws, she
needed to learn Beth's condition.

"How is she?" An unfamiliar voice drew her to glance
out of the corner of her eye toward the curtain dividing
the room into cubicles. She drew a sharp breath as her
vision tunneled into a pinpoint for a few seconds then
widened to encompass two men filling the opening.

One man she recognized, her rescuer. The shorter,
and less intimidating gentleman wore the exhausted
look of a police detective, along with the classic suit and
tie.

"She's lost a lot of blood, but a day in the hospital and
she should be able to go home." The nurse addressed
her comments to the shorter man.

"I have some questions for you, Ms. Halligan, if
you're up to it." The detective approached, the dark man
his tall shadow.

Fate pushed onto her elbows and flinched at the pain
her movements caused. An instant later the darker man
appeared at her side and gently helped her to sit upright.
Fate studied him, taking in his air of authority.
*Shouldn't the detective be the more forceful personality
in the room? This guy took over just by breathing.*

"I don't know who you are." She addressed both men,

~ ☾ ~

though she directed her question more to the dark one.

"I'm Detective Bell, Homicide. This is Mr. Greene, the man who helped you out this morning."

"And you're both with the police?" Fate didn't look the taller man in the eye, not yet. Mr. Greene didn't look like a cop. Tall and muscular enough to be imposing, dark hair pulled back somehow, a trimmed mustache and goatee, dark eyes and a deep tan, he could intimidate any witness he chose to, including her, if she let him.

"He's just here to see how you're doing. Mr. Greene, if you'll wait outside for a few minutes." The detective's notebook out and ready, looked prepared to start her questioning.

Greene nodded, cast a heavy-lidded glance toward her and left the cubicle. Fate waited for the tension he'd brought with him to dissipate. It didn't. "Now, Ms. Halligan, tell me what happened," Detective Bell prompted her.

She spent as few minutes as possible giving him details of the attack, all the while trying to avoid thinking of how close she'd come to dying

"Did you recognize the assailant?"

"No, and I don't think my friend did either. Where's Beth? How is she?"

The detective paused a breath. "She died, I'm sorry."

Fate's eyes stung with her tears but she managed to hold them back. Beth. Hopeful, hopeless Beth, calling to Fate in the seconds before she fainted. "I need to call someone."

"It's already been taken care of. Was she a close friend?" Bell leaned toward her and patted her shoulder with awkward movements.

"Not really. We were coworkers at Weatherly Hospice, and work friends. She has a family, sisters and parents, in the city." Fate pictured the last moments of

~ ☾ ~

Beth's life and grimaced. No one should have to face the end of her life with so much pain.

"We'll contact them. I'll leave you to rest, Ms. Halligan. We'll get in touch, if we need anything else." He left a business card, slightly bent at the edges as though he'd carried it around for a while.

Fate endured the next half hour getting transferred to a private room. By the time the charge nurse left, the weight of the morning's events crashed onto her. For several minutes she fought tears, of sorrow for Beth's early death, of frustration that she couldn't help, and a small measure of self-pity.

She finally laid her head back against the raised bed and turned to the activity that soothed her in times past. She let the voices come to her. She filtered out the calls for help she couldn't or shouldn't assist and allowed the wash of peace that accompanied passing souls to seep into her system.

Beth's voice wouldn't talk to her. She thought of her friend's soul exiting this plane without an escort, no doubt a traumatic journey. She sent an anguished call out to her guide, asking for comfort. Why hadn't she been able to stop the assault on her friend's soul? Intervene, somehow?

No answer came, leaving her with a sense of futility. She'd call Selene and let her know of the attack, but later. After she'd tried to reason out the events, herself.

"Fate."

The deep, almost grating nature of Mr. Greene's voice went to her core. She opened her eyes and turned to stare at him as he entered.

"Mr. Greene, I'm tired—"

"It's Caden. I have a couple questions before you rest."

"I told the police everything I know." *Everything I could tell them.*

~ ☾ ~

"You might have remembered something else." He closed the door securely behind him and advanced toward her. In any other world, he'd be the kind of man you drooled over, she thought. In any other woman's world but hers.

"I haven't. And even if I did, I'd need to tell the police, not you."

He arched a brow and Fate fought to keep the anger from her voice. "I understand I owe you my thanks."

He nodded in acknowledgement and stopped at her bedside. "I'm a securities expert and a private detective. I might be able to help you."

"A random attack? There's no need for help."

"Was it?"

"I didn't know him, and neither did Beth, as far as I know." Fate's voice trailed off as she recalled the attack. Obviously, he'd been after her. Beth was merely an unfortunate bystander.

"Did he say anything?" Caden pressed, his gaze intent on her face.

"No."

"You're sure?" She couldn't hold his stare and lie to him so she fiddled with the sheet covering her.

"Yes." A faint press at her psychic awareness startled her. *Who attempted to get into her head?*

"And the knives he used, what did they look like?"

"Knives, with sharp blades. Blades that cut me and my friend." She glared at him, "Anything else?"

"I couldn't help your friend, Fate. I'm sorry, but I can't change it." He didn't offer empty words of comfort, just acknowledged the fact.

"If you'd protected Beth instead of me—"

"He'd have killed you instead."

"Maybe not, I was defending myself." He scanned her body, his eyes resting on her sutures and bandages a breath longer.

~ ☾ ~

"I wasn't hurt that bad, I held him off." *Who am I kidding? He'd have sliced and diced me even more if Caden hadn't shown up.*

"When you think of something else, call me. I'll be close." He dropped a business card on the bed and exited the room with sure steps.

Fate stared at the closed door until her eyes watered from not blinking. She picked up the card. In bold, simple print read Caden Greene, Greene Securities. Along with the address, the font suggested purpose and capability. The only other symbol on the card, a small sun, the center hollow surrounded by nine sharp black rays caught her attention.

The symbol of The Soldiers of Light.

Oh, God, what have I gotten into?

~ ☾ ~

Chapter Two

"Concentrate, Fate! You're losing your focus." Selene paced the room in front of Fate, her expression fierce.

"I'm sorry." Fate rubbed the ache behind her eyes in an effort to stem the pain of her headache. "I can't get Beth off my mind."

Selene sighed. "Stand up, stretch." Fate's guide came to a stop in front of her. Selene's own slim, lithe form and lineless face belied her age, but pure white hair flowed to the middle of her back in a wave. She lengthened her own body as an example of the position she wanted from Fate and studied her with light grey eyes.

Fate uncurled her body from its Lotus position, stood, and tried to relax. The days since the attack, after intensive questioning from Selene, she'd filled with study and quiet times, allowing her body to heal itself. Now, the only evidence of her struggle, the faint pink of scars, would fade in time.

The training sessions with Selene lasted four hours at a stretch and usually passed in the blink of an eye. Fate's eagerness to learn the craft of taking souls to life's portal always pushed her, made her put forth the extra effort. But, today, she couldn't center.

"Why couldn't I help her soul pass, Selene? Her passing would have been so traumatic."

"You were battling for your own life, your soul's survival, Fate. No one is going to be able to divide focus in a time of crisis. Not even the Prioress would be able to split her powers and save her own soul and that of

~ ☾ ~

another at the same time." Selene went to the large bay window facing the backyard of her home, her back to Fate.

"But I should have been able to sense her passing, her soul's journey to the portal." Fate advanced until she stood beside Selene. She shoved her hair back and sighed. "I've trained for ten years. I should have been able to do more for her. I'm not even sure her soul passed on. What if it was lost?"

Selene patted Fate's shoulder. "You definitely would have felt that. No one with your level of power can ignore the cry of a soul that's searching for the portal. You've said you constantly struggle with your abilities to filter out the voices in your head."

Fate sighed and returned to the exercise mat. As she sank onto the floor, she voiced her frustrations. "We train to hear dying souls, to travel to them and assist them in passing. I don't understand why I can't, why all of the Maidens can't interact more with the souls, choose our own assignments." She cast a sharp look at Selene. "Without a chaperone."

Selene sat opposite Fate, her posture a mirror image as she crossed her legs and assumed a classic meditation pose. "Every Maiden has a different level of power, a different level of need for training. While your potential for power is greater than most, so is your risk of making mistakes."

Fate sighed. She'd heard it all before. She knew better than to interrupt Selene. It wouldn't do any good anyway and probably result in more training sessions.

"You're still as impatient as when you started training at fourteen. You've reached the stage that you're ready to get cases on your own, not observe or assist. And you're close to being ready to take on a case without a teacher, but never one without a Latent."

Fate grimaced. From her experience, a Latent's role

~ ☾ ~

consisted of being only another chaperone.

Selene shook her head. "No, Fate. Understand this. If you misuse your gift, mishandle the assignments or worse, ignore me and strike out on your own, you could end up dead, or worse."

Fate's spine tingled in warning and for the first time since her run-in with the attacker and Beth's death, the voices in her head muted. She focused exclusively on Selene. "I could lose my soul."

"You could do that and cause the loss of other souls as well." Selene leaned forward. "There are people dying in this city every day and our job is to help those who struggle with the journey to eternity's portal. We ease the way for most by calming their fears. But, you have to know, remember from your studies, there are those who resist the journey for more reasons than fear of the unknown or the desire to stay with loved ones. Some fear the retribution on their souls after death. They've lived lives filled with violence and hatred. Their souls are stained and resist the journey."

Fate recalled the stories of souls that defied the journey to the point of violence against Death Maidens who accompanied them. Some Maidens faltered at the portal for an instant too long and lost the battle with the tainted souls, losing their lives instead. "And I'm not strong enough to do battle with the tainted souls," she concluded.

"You're strong enough, but not ready. In time, you'll be able to handle the worst cases I can think of. Not that I'd envy that for you."

Fate eyed her teacher. Selene hadn't been her first Guide, but she'd spent the last five years with the older woman. She trusted the more experienced Maiden to push the limits of training, yet rein her in when necessary. And this looked like one of those times. Fate nodded and took a deep, cleansing breath. "And my Latent?"

~ ☾ ~

The woman paired with her would be her partner for life, an extension of her. The Latent assignment signaled a real beginning of a Maiden's career. The Latent's job to safeguard her Maiden while she journeyed with the dying soul began and ended with the Maiden's success or failure.

"Your latest assignment is to take place this week. You're ready, only one more 'chaperoned' assignment and you'll be rid of me, for the most part." Selene's expression, serene and implacable, didn't change.

Fate smiled, "I don't want rid of you. Just a little more wiggle room would help."

"And you'll get it. But remember, you asked for it."

Fate nodded, "Okay, I'm ready to start again."

"I do have one more thing to ask you about the attack," Selene paused, hesitated as if unsure how to proceed. "You said the man who helped you, saved you, had a sun on his business card. Do you still have it?"

Fate retrieved the card from her purse in the changing room and gave it to Selene. After a moment's quiet scrutiny, Selene laid the card on the mat between them. "Did you recognize the sign?"

"It's the Light of the Sun, isn't it? The Soldiers of Light mark?"

"Yes, he probably has a tattoo as well. Did you give him any information, Fate? Any at all?" A ripple of unease floated between them.

"No, other than telling him that I didn't know the man who attacked. Is he a Soldier?" The Soldiers of Light were legend among the Maidens, menacing, yet a part of the history that each Maiden learned about in depth.

"I suspect he is."

"They've resurfaced?"

Selene allowed a small smile to graze her mouth. "They never left, Fate. Only have steered clear of us, as we avoid contact with them."

~ ☾ ~

"And we avoid them because they try to prevent us from escorting the souls to the portal." This tested Fate's surety in all the rules of the Maidens. *He saved my life and he's the enemy?*

"Only in extreme cases." Selene stood and paced the room, a sign of her disquiet. Fate suspected she regretted bringing up the Soldier. "The Maidens and Soldiers have a history that goes back eons, not only in the odd clashes over dying souls. The maverick Soldier that tries to prevent a soul's passing is worrisome, but not the whole and not in keeping with the Soldier's creed." Selene turned and Fate forced her muscles to remain loose, relaxed under her guide's scrutiny. "Haven't you wondered why we take a vow of non-involvement, Fate?"

Fate shrugged, "Isn't it connected with some ancient religious rite, or something?"

"No, if that was the case, we'd take a vow of celibacy." Selene strode back to the window and stood with her back to the peaceful view. "We take lovers, or at least can have intercourse, if we choose, and for the purpose of having children, of course. But to become emotionally involved, to 'fall in love', has been forbidden for years. Since a Soldier and Maiden chose their love over the souls of men, women, children. Lost countless souls to darkness, to the Obsidian Guard." Selene's voice cracked against the strain of her statement.

"How?"

"The Soldiers of Light have protected souls, souls that aren't supposed to die, from being stolen, in essence. When the Soldier and Maiden chose to value their love for each other more than the lives of others, the souls of others, people who weren't destined to die perished. Souls were lost, never to pass the portal, or to pass it in agony. And since then, for centuries, we've avoided contact with the Soldiers. Any contact."

~ ☾ ~

Fate thought of the pain she felt in losing Beth's soul, of not being able to help. She couldn't imagine a feeling more powerful than that. "Why don't we just avoid men in general?"

Selene's stark expression lifted and she chuckled. "Only someone who hasn't had a good experience with a lover can say that. Remember, until several years ago, the only way to insure we would have children, continue the line that runs in your veins meant taking a lover. Something about the Soldiers, skill calling to skill made them especially attractive to Maidens. The historical records are vague, but apparently, several Maidens and Soldiers mated."

"So, we know nothing of the Soldiers that exist now." Fate stared into space, seeing Caden Greene's dark features studying her.

"I didn't say that. We know what we need to know, what we need in order to protect ourselves. So, if he contacts you, you will let me know."

"Of course."

"Very well, let's start again. Find your center, locate the peace within you..."

As Fate sank into her core concentration, Selene's voice trailed into a murmur, indistinct yet one that registered. Fate allowed her external awareness to depart, all feeling of discomfort from her sitting position, heat or cold, hunger or thirst to slip away. She struggled to bury the image of Caden Greene, his concern when he'd helped her, the energy he emitted. She'd faced the obvious threat in the man who attacked her. Could Caden Greene present a threat as well?

She forced her mind into a deeper level of relaxation until only her inner consciousness remained, her comforting, restful place.

Her awareness opened to seek other Maidens. In this case, Selene's inner consciousness stood waiting for her

~ ☾ ~

acknowledgement. In a soundless voice, she gave
instruction on the passage of the soul. For an untold
length of time Fate struggled with breaking barriers
erected by Selene, each one becoming more formidable
than the last. Finally, Selene called a halt to the exercise
and Fate started to pull away from her Inner Life, just as
she always did at the end of a session.

"Fate." Selene's inner voice halted Fate's withdrawal.
"I need to warn you of something more."

"Is it Caden Greene?"

Fate sensed Selene's surprise. "The Soldier? You only
need to remember to have me near when you speak to
him, if he contacts you again. This is something far more
serious, something that may interfere with the natural
order of life and death."

Selene's announcement rocked Fate's concentration.
Did this mean the end of the Society de la Morte? After
everything the Maiden's fought for?

"Listen closely. I wanted to tell you this in the Inner
Time. There's been a disturbance. We're not sure what it
is, but there's a possibility of the return of an evil that
we haven't encountered in generations. It's in the
history you study..."

Over three thousand years of the Society de la Morte
history to recall, not an easy task. The ancient society,
one rich in oral tradition and then written accounts held
many secrets.

"Are the Soldiers somehow disturbing the balance of
life and death?"

Selene's voice took on an element of surprise again
and Fate inwardly winced. Maybe she hadn't been able
to put Caden Greene out of her mind after all. "Maybe
inadvertently. There's so much you need to know and
not a lot of time to tell you. If it hadn't been for your
attack—. Well, now is the time."

Fate gave in to the urge and displayed the impatience

~ ℂ ~

for which Selene constantly railed at her. "Was the Soldier trying to kill me too?" The act of saving her a mistake on his part?

"I don't think so. As much as they disagree with our purpose, they are the enemies of the Guards."

"The Guards?" A vague memory from one of her studies tried to surface but failed.

"The Obsidian Guards. We thought they were in stasis, not active anymore. A long time ago we battled, the Soldiers, the Society and the Guards. Though after the split between the Soldiers and the Maidens, we united long enough to defeat the Guards. They were severely weakened and went into hiding. Now, I suspect they've regained their strength and numbers enough to start attacking."

"Attacking whom? I don't understand."

"The Obsidian Guard is a group of people whose goal is to steal the souls of people who possessed powers the Guard wanted."

"How is it possible? And the powers they seek, are they psychic or just unusual abilities?"

"Not only psychic powers, but intelligence, creativity, whatever powers or individual abilities make a person unique. In the past, the powers were those of the Maidens. Our society seemed to be a particular target, with our abilities. The leader must have found them more desirable."

"So, you think these Guards have resurfaced?"

"Yes, and are targeting us, as well as other people. I don't know for sure, but I think the attack on you and your friend may have been from one of the Guards."

Fate's effort to tamp down her anxiety failed. Her teacher could tap into her feelings and emotions as easily as reading her expressions. "And the Soldier?"

"I think he sensed the Guard tried to steal your souls and intervened."

~ ☾ ~

"So, wouldn't it be in our best interests to contact the Soldiers?"

Selene paused before answering. "I don't know. Perhaps I need to consult the Prioress."

Fate almost lost her concentration at that point. The Prioress, the founder of the Maidens, dead for over a thousand years. A Guide only achieved contact with her essence, her spirit through intense meditation. The society's history recorded only a handful of such exchanges.

"Wouldn't we be able to handle the Guards on our own? Through our own skills?"

Selene's worry came through loud and clear. "I'm not sure. We haven't dealt with them in hundreds of years. But if anyone can meet the Guards and resist their influence, you can. We might have to rethink our plans."

***

"Damn it, Caden. Don't push so hard." Jake frowned as he rubbed his shoulder.

Caden nodded, "Ten more minutes."

Jake rolled his shoulders and tightened his hold on his sparring staff. "If you can do it, so can I, buddy."

They sparred the requested ten minutes, plus thirty more before Caden got his coworker into a submissive position and called an end to the session. Jake's effort to rise from the mat gave Caden a sense of accomplishment. If he could subdue the ex-Special Forces officer, maybe he could complete his mission. Whatever that turned out to be.

"You're trying to kill me, right? You found out I'm the one the ladies want and you're trying to kill me." On his feet now, Jake bent at the waist, his hands braced on his knees, and panted.

Caden grinned, determined to hide his own battle to slow his heart rate. "Nah. Just putting you in your place."

~ ☾ ~

"My place has always been at your back. But do a three-hour training session again, and I might have to kick your ass."

Caden made his way to the water bottle lying on the weight bench. After giving the top a twist, he drained the contents. "I need your help on something."

"Have to do with GS or more serious?" With Greene Securities for a year, Jake's service with the Soldiers of Light began with his exit from the army, over five years ago. In Caden's mind, no other man could equal Jake's talents, either in martial arts or in the arena of psychic warfare. Though a couple inches shorter than Caden, he weighed more. That extra weight, all muscle from years of bodybuilding and hard work, made the guy an invaluable asset.

"Serious. Definitely serious."

"What's up?"

"A situation came up the other morning and I don't think it was simple violence." Caden went on to detail the attack on the two women and the unnatural spike in his psychic awareness.

"Could it have been the women that sent the message? I mean, both of us have run into the odd Norm with psychic abilities." Jake emptied his second bottle of water and crushed it.

"No, this wasn't someone trying to find a loved one or their Aunt Lucy's lost ring. I sensed an evil intent on something tried to take over."

"You think it the Guard's involved?"

"Oh, yeah.. What he wanted is the question." Caden couldn't voice his concern, even if he could identify it. He just knew, something or someone needed him, needed the Soldiers.

"The Guard haven't shown their faces in a while, why would they choose to attack in public and why now?"

Caden crushed the bottle in his hand. "I don't know

~ ☾ ~

but my gut tells me it's Guard and it's important."

The intercom blipped in before his receptionist's voice chirped, "Mr. Greene?"

"Yeah?"

"You have a call on line three. The client from Simmons wants to know when his system is going to be installed."

"I'll handle it," Jake sauntered from the room, his lazy walk totally at odds with the power he carried when he used his Soldier skills.

Caden headed toward the shower, his mind on Fate Halligan. Where did she figure in the attack? Innocent bystander or target? She'd almost shimmered with power when he met her in the hospital. But were her powers and her soul the reasons she'd been targeted? And what were her powers, specifically?

After he finished showering and dressed, Caden holed up in his office and put in a call to Detective Bell. He often used his contacts in the department to ask a few questions without getting too much of a run around, but he didn't know Bell.

He got transferred easily enough but the detective didn't want to release any info. After several minutes listening to the old arguments about privacy and tainting evidence, Caden gave up and disconnected.

He turned to the computer next. He'd just hacked into the police database when Jake entered. He took one look toward the monitor and shut the door securely behind him. "You know that's illegal, right?"

"Only if I get caught." Caden muttered as he maneuvered through the maze of commands he needed to get to the appropriate files.

He sensed Jake edging closer over his shoulder, his attention finally caught. "Damn, you're good."

"You'd be too if you'd taken the time to learn the skills."

~ ℂ ~

"Nah. I'm the brawn. Anything?"

"No, but that's what I thought. The attacker carried no ID. No fingerprints on file, no identifying marks, nothing."

"Could have been a homeless guy." Jake played devil's advocate.

"Too well nourished, too well dressed, too well armed."

"A lover's quarrel?"

"No evidence either of the victims knew him."

"Well, I quit. What are you thinking?" Jake left the computer area and plopped into a chair on the other side of the desk.

"I'm thinking one of the women might have been a target, and from the thrust of the attack and the fact that he didn't give up until I killed him, I'm guessing Fate, the one who lived."

"So, the other woman?"

"Collateral damage." And a soul he could have saved, if he'd been faster.

"Okay, so we find out as much about the killer as we can before another attack occurs."

"Yeah, and we find out if Fate Halligan has any connection to the Guards and what talent she possesses that the Guard wants."

Jake rose from the chair he'd been lounging in. "You want me to cover the woman?"

"No, I'll do that. You see if you can find out anything about the killer, weapons, background."

Jake stared at him for a minute. "You usually cover the police angle, have more of an in that way. Not to mention the odd skill of illegal hacking." He nodded to the data streaming across Caden's monitor.

Caden knew how the wheels turned in his friend's head. He usually didn't show that much interest in a woman it totally went against his role as a Soldier.

~ ☾ ~

Besides, letting Jake loose with any woman gave him a
tacit approval for a liaison. Apparently, Jake's looks, a
shaved head and deep tan, paired with brown eyes and
muscled build combined to make women flock to him. "I
tried with the detective. Hit a brick wall. You might be
able to slide under the radar and find out something."

"Good deal. I'll touch base with you later." Jake's easy
agreement with him didn't surprise Caden, he just rolled
that way. It also explained why Caden didn't worry
about success. Jake made it to the office door when
Caden remembered the security case.

"Have any problem with the Simmons' case?"

"Nah. I sweet-talked the wife and assured her we'd
have a team out to their house in the morning by eight.
Standard installation, no extras."

Caden nodded. He'd have to devote a couple hours to
paperwork for the securities company and he'd be free
to look into the Halligan case. As he pulled up a file for
securities installation and maintenance on his
computer, he shifted Fate Halligan and her attack to the
back of his mind. As he worked, though, he battled the
constant awareness of her.

Her presence lingered in his mind. They hadn't
touched, other than his checking her pulse as she lay
unconscious, but she'd left something with him.
Whether it was psychic residue of her emotions at the
time of the attack or something more, he hadn't taken
the time to study. It unnerved him, knowing a part of
her remained with him all the time. He'd have to bring it
up with his mentor, if it continued.

He spent the rest of the day reviewing files, assigning
teams to assemble and install security systems for
homes throughout the southeast and ran quality control
on the monitoring unit. He closed a final file, sure of his
cover. He made a couple phone calls, instructing his
assistant on practical matters then let him know he'd be

~ (~

unavailable for a few days.

Donan wouldn't be happy to hear from his old student. Only in dire times of need did Caden turn to his mentor. Maybe by solving the case and putting it behind him, he'd be able to let go of the hold Fate placed on him, the mark she'd left on his soul.

By the time he arrived at the house he'd called home for so many years during his training, Caden convinced himself he'd imagined the connection. No human, other than fellow Soldiers, could tap into his thoughts or emotions. Only a powerfully endowed psychic could have made a connection.

Hidden in a copse of trees, lay the Refuge, Donan's domain. The highest-ranking Soldier alive and Caden's mentor, Donan shared his knowledge readily. His time however, remained at a premium. Caden's precipitous arrival, coupled with the unwelcome link he'd felt with the victim of the attack, held a risk, but one he had to take.

He entered the inner room of the Refuge and waited. No one saw the efficient servants that attended Donan, but his appearance less than a minute after Caden's arrival signaled his mentor's control over everything in his orbit. Donan carried his lean and strong frame with a smoothness that belied his strength. With his long silver hair queued back and his steel grey eyes taking in everything around him, the Soldier leader missed very little.

"Mentor Donan," Caden stood straight and met his mentor's gaze.

"Caden. What brings you here?"

As if he didn't know. There were few sureties in his life, but Caden knew two things. He lived for the Soldiers and no one sprung surprises on Donan.

"A fatality occurred last week."

"And you have questions about it?" Donan walked

~ ☾ ~

toward the chairs situated at the end of the spare room. Caden followed and sank into the easy chair and forced himself to relax. Tension wouldn't help him state his case, wouldn't get the information he needed from his mentor.

"Do you trust me?" Donan's quiet question threw Caden. Could he have been broadcasting that strongly?

"I do, but I'm not sure what to make of the situation."

"Explain."

"I sensed a psychic threat early one morning and responded. When I got to the scene, two women were under attack. I intervened, lost one. When I spoke to the survivor, I got a— a connection."

"A connection?" Donan's gaze sharpened.

Caden inclined his head, "That's the only word I can use to describe it. I don't have a clear link, more like an awareness."

"And the woman. Has she given you any indication of a link?"

"I haven't made contact with her since the hospital."

"And the reason for this?"

Caden stalled, his mind awhirl with the image of Fate Halligan. Her blonde hair flowing over her shoulders, her blue eyes clouded with pain. He refused to acknowledge that her pull could be anything else but that of a victim he needed to protect.

"I wanted to find out more about her, about the attack. I think the assailant was a Guard."

Again, Donan's eyes gleamed then shuttered. "It's been a long time since they showed a presence. What makes you suspect him a Guard?"

"The psychic residue." Nothing left a stain like evil. Nothing like the tinge of awareness he felt from Fate. Her touch wasn't evil, rather like a breeze laden with sensual floral.

Donan's voice filtered through as he requested

~ ☾ ~

entrance into Caden's mind. As he granted the appeal Caden attempted to eradicate the vision of Fate from his mind. He might share his psychic awareness with his mentor but the physical attraction he refused to share with his mentor.

A familiar current ran through his body as he opened his mind to another. As his mentor traversed his consciousness, Caden knew Donan respected his secrets. But understanding that fact alerted him to the fact that Donan *knew* he had secrets to hide. Something he'd never done before.

The present faded, to be replaced by the attack on Fate and her friend. Caden's muscles twitched in memory as he relived his battle. As the scene receded, fatigue set in as if he'd actually endured the fight.

Donan retreated from Caden's consciousness. "I see what you mean. The assailant could have been Obsidian Guard. What did you find out from your background check?"

"No identification, no presence. Classic Guard."

"And the woman?"

"The one killed worked as a nurse at a residential hospice in the city. The surviving woman also works there, a social worker, apparently."

Donan settled deeper into his chair and steepled his fingers. He studied his fingertips, closing Caden out. A classic Mentor role, deep in thought, and Caden took on his own duty, that of waiting.

Finally, the older man raised his eyes from the study of his hands. He rotated his head as in an effort to loosen tension. "There's evidence the Guard has resurfaced."

"To what degree?" Caden shifted in his seat, alert.

"At least four teams are either on the ground in the state or in route."

"The Guard hasn't been that strong in what, over a

~ ☾ ~

hundred years? Why are they here? Is it the girl?"

"Yes. She's important, Caden. I'm not sure why, but we need to find out. And soon, or her life will be in jeopardy, and so will her soul."

***

Fate tossed in her bed, unable to force her mind to rest. Another night of reliving her attack, of wondering if she could have helped Beth, lay ahead of her.

She abandoned her bed for the alcove, her reading area, nestled alongside the stairway leading to the downstairs entrance. Fate dropped into the easy chair and flipped on the nearby floor lamp. She ignored the well-thumbed edition she'd been reading before the attack and flipped through a magazine as she let her consciousness wander.

In the back of her mind, where awareness of other souls lay, the murmurings abounded. Those dying souls that passed quietly, peacefully and with full knowledge of their destinations and a life well spent were the softest, most peaceful. Those were the voices that usually lulled her to sleep in the dark nights.

As a child, before her calling to the Society de la Morte, she'd assumed everyone heard the voices, the whispers in their heads. Only when she started school, when she became the butt of jokes and ostracized for predicting deaths, did she become aware of her *gift*.

Only memories of her mother encouraging her to listen to the voices, followed by the foster mother with vast understanding and acceptance of her gift, gave her enough courage and joy to recognize her talents. When her calling to the Society de la Morte came, her life began to take on new meaning. College, work, everything revolved around hearing the dead, responding to requests for help from searching souls.

She sighed and leaned against the high back of the chair, then closed her eyes. More conflicted souls talked

~ ☾ ~

to her tonight, asking for help, not sure of their destination. According to her Guide, after nearly ten years of training, she still couldn't handle cases independently. Yet, the voices remained.

Tempted to call Selene, Fate wanted to ask for help to calm the voices in her head, but she decided not. If she couldn't handle the voices on her own, she'd never gain Selene's confidence to deal with more difficult assignments.

She dropped her awareness into the morass of voices in her mind. They cried, raged, pleaded. To which she sent soothing assurances that all would be well, a Maiden would accompany them, and if not, another world would await them on the other side. Her mind voice, quiet and calm soon reassured all the voices save one.

The last voice, one full of hate and pain, sounded different from the others. Fate sent a message of hope to the voice.

"Woman, you have no power over me." It wasn't male or female, but a voice filled with hate, enmity and something so dark Fate couldn't begin to label it.

"I want to help you move on," she urged.

"My minions missed you before, but I will get your soul. And your power." Dark laughter grated through her as it faded, leaving her with the cold certainty that she needed more power than she possessed to meet the danger she found herself in.

~ ☾ ~

Chapter Three

Caden wasted little time in tracing Fate Halligan. Her record consisted of one speeding ticket, paid in full fifteen days after receipt. No other legal violations. Her legal guardian had home schooled her after the age of fourteen. She attended the Kingston campus of the state university, and went to work at Weatherly Hospice immediately after graduation.

"No dating, no social engagements other than with coworkers, and no evidence she spent any significant time out on the town. This girl needs to get a life," he muttered as he stared at the DMV photo. Even the grainy picture revealed her fragile, almost ethereal beauty. Blonde hair, crystal blue eyes, porcelain skin. His memory filled in the rest, a lean body filled with gentle curves and long limbs. Not his type, by any means, but something compelled him in her look. He leaned back in his chair. She could be a nice distraction.

The DMV and police department facts were a starting point, but didn't give him enough info. He closed the file then opened a new one. As he worked, Caden sensed a new awareness in the back of his consciousness. He established a mind lock against the sentience reading his own mind and returned to his work, determined to check it out later, when he had time.

He worked steadily before the compiled information brought him to a halt.

"Fate Halligan, daughter of Eliza Halligan, died when Fate was eight years old. Father, unknown. Eliza, daughter of Verna Halligan, father unknown." Caden

~ ☾ ~

ran through the available facts and genealogy he'd
spent the last few hours digging up. As far as he could
trace, all the available information found Fate
Halligan's family tree sadly lacking in testosterone. No
fathers listed, no male children. That, in and of itself,
might not have been anything more than a weird trivia
fact. What the women did for a living added an element
that set off his alarms.

All of the women he could find had been associated
with death in some way. Fate's mother worked as a
nurse on an oncology unit until her death. Another
record revealed a nineteenth century healer and a
notation of yet another revered by villagers for her
abilities to call spirits. Fate's position as a social worker
in a hospice carried on a family tradition.

Separately, the information didn't amount to much.
Combined with the psychic connection Caden felt to
Fate however, the evidence created more of a mystery.

***

Fate leaned back as the waiter set the plate in front of
her. "Chef salad, no turkey, no ham. Heavy on the
cheese. Anything else?"

The obviously bored man turned away from their
sidewalk table even as she shook her head. Fate smiled
at the older woman sitting across from her at the
sidewalk table. Janette fiddled with the burger in front
of her, rearranging the onion and tomato on her bun.
Middle aged, somewhat overweight, with curly hair cut
in a short bob, Janette's blue eyes sparkled with
something Fate couldn't identify but envied.

"I think you need to find another favorite restaurant,
Fate. This one seems to be getting tired of you."

Fate nodded, "I know. It's just so convenient to work
and Refuge. It saves time."

"And the food is okay, but you need to learn to
appreciate life more." Janette pushed the sleeves of her

peasant blouse up and picked up her burger, then took a large bite from it.

"I do appreciate my life. I love my job, I have friends-"

"All of which is connected with your gift and your calling. Don't get me wrong. I love the fact that you're so dedicated. As your Latent, it's going to make my life easier. But I look at you and think, that girl is too pretty and too young to be acting as old as I am."

"I think it'd be nice to be like you." Fate looked at the woman who'd become her virtual shadow. Plump, middle aged, with artfully streaked hair styled in a bob, Janette didn't look like a woman who devoted her life to meditation and sacrifice.

"Overweight and over the hill? Nah. You're almost half my age and my social life is way more interesting than yours right now. I've got a date this weekend. Can you say the same?" Janette bit into her burger with the same delight she seemed to bring to every aspect of life.

Fate shook her head. "I don't see the point. We've taken a vow of noninvolvement." How innocuous that sounded. No falling in love, no children other than as a result of liaisons approved of by the Society.

Janette laughed. "Honey, the point is fun. Having some fun with friends, both female and male. Taking a vacation. You've worked for ten years on your gift. Take a break."

"I don't want a break. I like to work." Fate speared lettuce and vegetables took a bite, and ignored the urge to snatch a fry from her friend's plate.

Janette took life in the Society seriously when she worked and but embraced it when off duty. She lived, played and dated with a verve Fate never possessed and couldn't imagine learning.

Though older, Janette would look to Fate for psychic guidance, a daunting fact. Fate's training and innate talent gave her skills in hearing all souls that were on the

~ ☾ ~

precipice of forever, while Janette only received
communication from her assigned Maiden. A latent
could read her maiden's inner voice only through the
maiden's effort to connect, not her own. Janette's job
would be to protect Fate as she worked with the dying
soul.

"So, we talk work. Are you ready for the assignments,
Maiden?"

"I guess so," Fate murmured and picked at her salad,
suddenly without an appetite. After all the training, she
faced the daunting task of proving she could handle the
job of helping souls to eternity. "You have my cell
number, right?"

"Yeah, and you have mine?"

In years past, Latents and Maidens lived in the same
house. Even now, some Refuges forced women to live in
the same neighborhood or apartment building. But, in
Kingston, the Maidens and Latents were given a choice.
They could live in different neighborhoods, within a
certain distance. According to Selene, this increased the
team's communication abilities while maintaining a
personal sense of autonomy.

For Fate, however, it meant ensuring an open channel
of communication between herself and Janette at all
times. Whether through phone, in person, or through
psychic communication, it increased her vulnerability to
another person in a way she hadn't been in her past.
And Janette picked up on it.

"You're uncomfortable with the whole symbiosis
thing, aren't you?"

"I suppose I am. I haven't encountered the level of
communication we need to have in the past."

"And you're afraid it'll be too much info?"

Fate nodded. "I guess I'm more private than I
thought."

Janette laughed. "I can't believe you have privacy

~ ☾ ~

issues anymore. I know what your training is, honey. You've spent how many years with a Guide inside your head? If you have any issues now, I can give you some points on how to avoid superiors' mind delving."

Fate sensed more to the older woman than the easy banter. "Did you start in Maiden training?"

Some Latents did, only to learn later on that they didn't have the level of power to accompany souls to the portal.

"Yeah, I trained about five years before I was reassigned."

"And you've been paired with other Maidens, before me, I mean."

"For fourteen years." Janette's pleasant expression soured. "She chose to commit."

Fate's breath caught at the statement. "She committed to a man?"

Janette nodded, "And married, I think. I cut mind link with her when she admitted to commitment. It didn't serve the Society to keep the link, and quite frankly, what I picked up was kind of disturbing."

"Love?" That couldn't be so bad, could it?

"It wasn't the kind of love we're taught, Fate." Janette leaned forward and lowered her voice as a couple passed their table. "The Society teaches us to love all mankind, to revere the souls of man. The love I sensed in my assigned Maiden was something stronger, infinitely more intense. And the link she shared with her man," Janette shuddered, "went way deeper than anything I've seen or experienced with the Maidens."

But how did that feel? To have a deeper connection than she experienced with her guide, her Latent, her Society, her souls? Fate didn't think any link could be deeper. Come to think of it, a more involved connection would be scary.

"And you still want to date? I think I'll steer clear of

~ ☾ ~

it, thanks." Fate turned her attention to the salad, almost in defense of her argument. "Doesn't seem worth the trouble to me."

"Your loss, hon." Fate chatted with Janette for the remainder of her dinner, trying to find some level of comfort with the woman she'd essentially share a brain with for the remainder of her life. While Selene matched Latent and Maiden, making the shift to partners depended on their efforts.

Janette cajoled her into ordering a dessert and Fate dove into her double chocolate cake with pleasure. The calorie-laden fork stopped halfway to her mouth when a sense of foreboding stopped her.

Someone, watched her in the shadows.

The sure knowledge ran under her skin, in her bones. Selene warned her new skills would arise, but she'd not anticipated this advance. The awareness of evil, coupled with hot intensity to harm her engulfed her in a nightmarish wave, tainting her.

She lifted her water glass and surveyed the crowd in a checking-out-the-guys sort of way. Nothing seemed out of place, psychically, so she extended her range.

Across the street a man lounged on a bench, either waiting for a bus or taking a nap, she couldn't tell. Another man stood in front of a newspaper machine with his back to her.

There.

The taint of evil and something else, something foreign. A strong pull that she'd never experienced. Not until she'd met Caden Greene.

***

God, she stirred him. The way she moved, ate and breathed. Everything about her called to him at a visceral level. That couldn't happen. Not to a Soldier. *Who is she? And why does she pull me so?*

Caden leaned against the doorway of the tobacco

~ ☾ ~

shop, not bothering to drift into the shadows. She sensed his presence. He knew it in his bones. She'd confront him.

Several minutes later, her friend left and Fate went into the cafe. Caden waited for her to exit the front door, but a niggling awareness that he didn't try to second-guess told him she'd not do the expected. With a last glance around he crossed the street and headed toward the alley that ran alongside the cafe.

A typical alley, smelly, piled with boxes destined either for trash or a recycling facility, it offered plenty of shadowed corners. Prime territory for anyone seeking a lone woman, fragile and frail. He growled as he picked up a presence. Obsidian Guard. Opening his senses more, he attempted to pinpoint the Guard's location and melted into the shadows. Now, to keep Fate Halligan from getting herself killed, again.

Sure enough, the rear door of the cafe inched open and she stepped out. Her slender figure shone bright against the dankness of the alley. She didn't look, didn't scan her surroundings and Caden cursed at her naiveté. The woman had a lot to learn, and he was just the man to teach her.

***

Fate paced down the short alley, her full attention on catching Caden before he blended into the crowd. He hadn't bothered to hide his presence on the street corner, instead almost challenging her to confront him. Well, she would, but on her own terms. *Time to show him I can could take care of myself.*

A hard hit into her side forced her into a pile of empty cardboard boxes. Fate grunted at the impact of cement, sharp box edges and the hard male body on top of her.

"What the hell are you doing?" His rough voice, laced with irritation with an undertone of another emotion startled her.

~ ☾ ~

"I was looking for you, that's what. Get off me." Fate swatted ineffectively at his shoulders, trying to make Caden move faster.

She starred into his dark coffee brown eyes. The hard body pressed her into the boxes beneath them, his face inches away from hers. His arms braced on the ground beside her shoulders.

"You like taking chances, don't you lady?" He growled and shifted against her.

"I take a short cut through this alley all the time."

"That's not what I'm talking about."

He moved again then heaved off her. He stood and held out his hand. Fate grasped it. A twinge of awareness and more ran from her palm up her arm. Something more than simple psychic discernment ran through her. When he pulled her to a stand, she yanked her hand away, anxious to rid herself of the tingling awareness between them.

It didn't work.

"You put yourself in danger." He loomed over her, dark and incredibly sexy. "Never do that again."

"So you say."

"That's reality. Someone is out to kill you. You need to grow up and face it."

Fate tried to slink around Caden, but he grabbed her arm with a firm hand. She wheeled around, "What?"

"Hush," he snarled, his voice a sibilant whisper. "Someone is out there."

"Of course someone is out there, it's a big city," she snapped, her voice equally low.

"This one's different, has a different feel." His arm snaked around her waist and pulled her against him. He inched them back until her back hit the wall of a building beside a dumpster and he ranged next to her, his hand on her waist, restraining her.

His strong essence, might be a bit overbearing, but

~ ☾ ~

not evil. *Whoa. Who would have thought he'd be attracted to me.* Sexual attraction turned out to be an energy she'd have to confront, as well.

A dark shadow passed by her, insubstantial yet full of hateful intent.

"Stay here," Caden hissed, and released her and darted further into the alley. The absence of his warm hand on her waist almost painful. Thuds and a few crashes, then silence. Fate took a breath and stepped forward.

"I thought I told you not to move." He pounced on her again, pressing her back against the wall, a predator. Fate looked at him. She glanced up and down his body. A smudge of dirt stained his dark tan shirt, but no blood.

"What happened?"

"A Guard is what happened," he muttered. After glancing behind them into the alley, he cupped her elbow with his hand and led her toward the sunlit street.

"Is he?"

"Yeah, he's dead. Just like you would have been, if I hadn't been here." His hand moved from her elbow to her waist. Numb with the knowledge that she'd been targeted. Again. Fate walked a few feet without resistance, her mind on the man whose body lay behind them.

"What about the body?"

Caden kept his hand on her and urged her to keep walking. "It'll probably disappear within an hour or so. If not, it'll be recorded as a random attack in the street. Not unusual for this area."

Fate agreed reluctantly. Too many people were senselessly killed. Too bad they were using it in their favor. "And evidence?"

"There's not any. The only prints that will be picked up on a weapon are the Guard's." Caden continued on, pulling Fate along with him.

~ ☾ ~

Deep inside, a sense of belonging, of energy rose inside her at his touch, his presence. Unfamiliar, not totally welcome, it grew to the point of discomfort. Fate stared ahead, her gaze unseeing aware of everything in front of her.

She yanked away from his hold and exited the alley at a fast walk, then veered left, toward her car. The entire way he hovered.

He stomped behind her the entire way. By the time she got to her car, his breath misted on her neck. Too close, damn it. She wheeled around. "Look, thanks for all that in the alley, but I can take care of myself."

"Didn't look like it." He cornered her again, forcing her back against the car door.

"I went into the alley to get away from you." She bit out the admission, flushing at the knowing smile he wore.

"So you knew I was around."

"Yes, and stop it."

"No."

She stepped up toward him and poked a finger in his chest. "I can handle myself, back off."

"Or what? You'll poke me to death?" He grabbed her finger and squeezed. Fate ignored the spark of awareness just from the feel of his rough hand closed around her index finger.

"I don't need you around, Greene."

"Caden," he murmured, surrounding her with his energy. Another push at her psyche jerked her from the sensual fog he'd managed to weave around her. *Is someone trying to get past my wall? Who is trying to invade my mind?*

She searched for the calm that she'd always achieved in her life. "All right. Caden. Look, I appreciate your help back there, but I don't need a bodyguard. If I promise to be careful and avoid alleys will you let it go?"

~ ☾ ~

"No." He advanced to the point he'd flattened her against the car door. The heat from his body overwhelmed the warmth of the sun-heated car at her back. His arousal evident in his expression, he eyed her lips as he continued, "The danger hasn't passed, not by a long shot. And as long as you're in danger, I'm sticking close. Get used to it."

"Close is one thing, suffocating me is another entirely." She pressed her hand on his chest and gave him a light shove.

If he'd wanted to resist, he wouldn't move. However, he backed away, a few inches anyway. It gave her enough room to breathe something other than his scent, an aroma that did things to her libido she hadn't counted on. "Where are you going?"

Fate arched her brow at the imperious tone. "It's none of your business."

"I'm making it my business. Where?"

"To visit a friend." Everything about the whole situation, the attack followed by the psychic push, even the Soldier's continued presence, all of it demanded consultation with her Guide. Fate gasped in outrage when Caden snatched her backpack from her hands and started to unzip a side pocket. "What the hell do you think you're doing?"

"Getting your keys." He held them aloft in demonstration then reached around her to unlock the passenger door. "Get in."

Fate glanced in the car at the console separating her passenger and driver sides. No way she'd climb over the thing with him watching. She flipped the unlock button on the passenger side door and inched around him to the other side of the car. When he stopped her again she glared. "Let me go."

"If you don't tell me where you're going, I'm driving you."

~ ☾ ~

"You're such a hot shot PI, follow me." She yanked the keys from his hand, dropped into the passenger seat and scrambled over the console. Let him see her butt in the air, she didn't care. For once since she'd met the man she didn't feel intimidated, frightened or totally attracted to him. He just pissed her off.

***

Caden grinned as he sprinted to his truck. She might be little and a bit too fragile for his tastes, but Fate Halligan owned attitude to spare. She squealed out of her parking space as he opened his door and he muttered a curse at the traffic before he shot out into the fray. A few minutes of maneuvering in and out of traffic and he pulled in behind her. Just for the hell of it, he got on her bumper and stayed there until she turned into the driveway of a house nestled in the hills outside of town. A low, one-story structure, the building looked small in the front. As he sprinted up the small rise of steps to the entrance and gained on Fate, Caden realized the house stretched out in back. What it lacked in height, it more than made up for in depth. The entire structure, a blend of eastern and modern architecture, could house at least a dozen people and not be crowded. Fate glanced at him over her shoulder and lowered the hand that held a key.

"Lived here long?" He inched a little closer, just to irritate her further, as if he needed to. He could feel the tension rise in her, almost like a heated blanket enveloped her. Not anger or hate, but tension of a kind he encountered with lovers.

"Not your business." She bit out, her face turned toward the dark red door.

"Making it my business. How am I supposed to protect you if I don't know where you live? And she didn't live here, he knew. Her address matched an apartment in an old house in the university district,

~ ☾ ~

modest, artsy, but not on the scale of this sprawling residence. From his work he knew a house in this neighborhood went for a pretty penny.

"I don't, okay?" She sighed and turned to face him. "I'm visiting a close friend. A little privacy'd help, you know."

He grinned, enjoying her discomfiture. She wasn't leery of him anymore, at least. "I'll sit like a good boy in the corner."

She chuckled, "Like you're unnoticeable. You aren't going inside with me, big boy. "As she finished her sentence, he crooked a grin at her flirtatious tone. The look on her face as the words exited her mouth showed she'd realized her comments were more than a comeback, and the blush clinched it.

He quelled his retort when the door opened behind Fate. A tall, robust woman with elegant but friendly features stood in the doorway, eyeing them. "Fate? Are you coming in?"

"My apologies, Selene. I was just saying—"

"That she needed to apologize for bringing an extra person to visit." Caden reached around Fate and extended a hand.

Selene held a knowing expression, slightly suspicious, as if she could guess the true nature of their conversation. She opened the door wider and stepped to the side, indicating they should enter. "Fate knows her friends are welcome, Mr.—"

"His name is Caden Greene. I told you about him earlier in the week, remember?" Fate grimaced at Caden.

Selene took Caden's hand in both of hers and squeezed lightly. "I do indeed. Thank you for helping Fate, Mr. Greene. We would have missed her."

"Missed her? That's a strange way of saying it, but you're welcome. Are you and Fate good friends?" Caden

~ ☾ ~

urged Fate into the house.

Selene led the way to a living area, where several sofas and easy chairs were spread out in the spacious room. The psychic energy alone resonated at a medium level, higher than any "normal" human dwelling possessed.

Fate Halligan and her "friend" were Death Maidens, for sure. The trick for him would be to have them admit it and go on from there. It might complicate the mission yeah, but he didn't see the point in sharing the information with Donan, not yet.

"I was a friend of her mother. Now, we're close friends, I think." Selene sank into an easy chair and Fate sat on a sofa parallel to it.

Caden took a seat beside her, getting another look from the older woman. If the Death Maiden community was cloistered how did he get admitted?

"Then you'll want to know what happened earlier today." He leaned back into the cushions of the sofa and gave Fate a pointed look. "Do you want to give her the news or should I?"

Fate's mouth tightened in irritation. "I sort of got attacked again today."

"Sort of?" He snorted and Fate shot him a frown.

"He didn't touch me."

"Because I stopped him before he had the chance."

"Am I telling this or you?"

Caden waved a hand at her, "Go ahead. Tell her about the 'sort of' knife that he used."

Selene's serene expression disappeared, replaced by concern and a little fear. "Another knife attack? What did it look like? I mean the man? Did you see him clearly?"

"No. Yes. Oh, I don't know. He looked like the other man, I guess. Taller than me, heavier than me, meaner than me." Fate didn't meet her friend's gaze.

~ ☾ ~

"And the knife looked to be the same sort of ceremonial knife the other assailant used. A Soul Taker blade." Caden finished with narrowed eyes. There. Now he'd affirmed his suspicions. Fate and the Death Maidens needed to let him in. If they didn't voluntarily, he'd find a way to remain in the picture. But he would damn sure fulfill his mission, to protect Fate Halligan.

Fate paled at the mention of the Soul Taker. Caden suspected she knew of them, but to have him, a virtual stranger, affirm her suspicions would bring the whole matter to the surface, make her acknowledge it.

"Soul Taker?" Selene kept her tone completely neutral.

Caden snorted, "Don't try to hide it. You're a Death Maiden and if you don't know the Guard you need to."

"We do know of the Obsidian Guard, Mr. Greene. The question is, how do you? And what do you know of us?" Selene's voice remained quiet, calm.

Caden recognized the authority in her tone, similar to that of Donan. She appeared young and vital. But the illusion merely disguised an older, more powerful psychic range.

"The second question first. I recognized the psychic resonance in the house as soon as I entered. No house of a normal human would have this much power in it. I'd guess there's what, a dozen women in here right now?" He nodded at the startled look Fate shot his way. "I can pick up on separate power sources when I concentrate, and there's at least that many. Maybe more, if they have the power to mask. And you," he studied Selene a minute before continuing, "have the most power of all. Right now."

"You're a Soldier?" She scrutinized him on her own before nodding. "That's how you knew Fate was in trouble that first time, wasn't it? You didn't 'just happen to be passing."

~ ☾ ~

"No, I got a read on the Guard. I followed his signature and when I got to the coffee house I found Fate and her friend."

"And today?" Fate inserted, leaning forward, her elbows resting on her knees.

"Today, I followed you," he replied.

"I saw you across the street at the cafe, but not before. How did you know where I went?"

"I'm a hot shot PI, remember?" He grinned.

***

Fate felt like hitting him, or kissing him, she couldn't decide. One would be rude, after he'd saved her life, twice. The other option wasn't available to her. Caden, a Soldier, wouldn't accept distance, at least from her recent experience.

"The answer to your first question," he returned his gaze to Fate's mentor, "My mission is to protect against the Guard and their like. I'm trained to pick up their psychic signature, no matter how difficult or faint it is. Now, I have a question for you two. Why is the Guard singling out Fate? And why the hell aren't you protecting her more?"

Selene stood, her face stony. "I am protecting her."

"Not from where I'm sitting, you're not." Caden didn't stand, didn't confront Selene. When Fate went to stand beside her mentor he lifted a dark brow. "Don't worry, I'm not about to ruffle your feathers. I don't want to disturb the Guide for the Society."

Fate went cold. How good were his skills? If he could pick up Selene's status as Guide for the whole sect here, what else did he sense?

"You are talented, Mr. Greene. And I don't know why Fate has been targeted, yet. But I will find the answer." Selene's authoritative voice rang through the room.

"Fine. But until you find out why and another way to protect her, get used to seeing me around."

~ ☾ ~

"Why such an interest in our Fate?"

"It's my job." Fate tried to pick up on Caden's emotion behind his comment but only saw resolve.

"Is it? Or is it more?" Selene turned and walked toward a bar at the end of the room. A Latent entered, her tread silent and sure. She carried a tray with a teakettle and cups on it, along with a beer. The ale surprised Fate, as Selene frowned on alcohol in the Refuge, said it dulled the psychic senses. Apparently, she'd anticipated Caden's arrival.

"I have an interest in preventing the Guard from taking a soul that isn't ready to pass on, that's all." Caden stood and approached Fate. She didn't move, though the energy that surrounded him pulsed around her like a static storm. When he stopped beside her, she glanced up at him.

The Guide didn't respond for a minute, instead focusing on preparation of tea. She brought two cups to a low table and then sank onto the sofa.

"You are aware of the vows the Maidens take, aren't you, Mr. Greene?" Selene's direct glance prompted Fate to sit beside her.

"No." His expression didn't give any other indication that he withheld info.

Fate studied him. Selene didn't treat the tall, dark man as if he were a threat. More an oddity, considering their conversation earlier.

"I suggest you consult with Mentor Donan before agreeing to protect my charge," Selene's smooth voice held firm directive.

Caden gave a now familiar expression of raised brow and disdain before he replied. "I doubt that anything Donan can say will change the fact that your charge is in danger. If she won't take her safety seriously, then I will."

"Return after your discussion with Mentor Donan.

~ ☾ ~

Only then will I accept your offer of protection on behalf of Fate." Selene sipped her tea in repose.

"Fate will not be left unprotected, no matter the outcome."

His abrupt nod and departure thwarted Fate's indignant reply. She turned to Selene in a rage. "I won't be 'protected' by him. I won't. After all, you said steer clear of him."

Selene walked to the window and assumed her classic contemplation pose of back straight and hands folded at her waist. "If what I suspect comes to pass, I'm afraid we won't have much choice."

~ ☾ ~

Chapter Four

Caden strode into the Soldiers' Headquarters, intent on finding his mentor and getting a straight answer. Caden wasn't interested in Donan's tendency to wrap replies in riddles and smoke. He would climb into the mentor's very psyche to get direct answers this time. He forced himself to stop and center before entering the psi training room. Anyone entering with a cloud or conflict in their consciousness invited everyone present to "help" sort out problems.

Caden learned a long time ago to avoid such interference and became adept at emptying his outer psyche of discord. Now, for the first time since his raw recruit days he experienced difficulty putting that discord—Fate Halligan and her predicament—out of his mind.

Only two trainees were present, nowhere near his level of expertise in psi communication. Caden cut a straight line through the room, avoiding the compulsory contemplation routine, to enter the inner sanctum of his mentor and former guardian.

Donan sat in a comfortable chair, his white hair pulled back in a ponytail, signaling his intent to engage in physical instruction as well as psi training. When engaged in contemplation alone, his waist length hair hung free. Caden suspected vanity and a desire to intimidate trainees as well as tradition played a part.

"Mentor Donan." The formality of his address indicated his stress level as well as the importance of his mission. Caden responded verbally to his mentor but

~ ☾ ~

preferred telepathic communication. He just didn't want to share secrets with others.

"Soldier Caden. Sit." Donan accepted and returned Caden's formal address then indicated a chair at a right angle to his. As he lowered himself into the shorter chair, he noticed the seat pad seemed thin. Again, his mentor used as much human psychology as psi powers.

He obeyed, opening his mind to his mentor. *"I need your advice, and some answers."*

"No smoke and mirrors?" Donan's inner voice held amusement.

Caden used the image of fog and reflections to label his mentor as a teenager when anger seemed his predominant emotion. Now, with Fate, he figured the same label applied.

"I serve the Soldiers' mission. I serve to protect the innocent soul from evil thieves. I serve the innocent soul so it may continue its journey." Caden purposefully uttered the Soldier's Creed. He wasn't in the mood to joke and keep it light. Donan repeatedly reminded him he needed to get a life outside of work, both his cover and real work, the psi work. But for Caden, a timeline inched shorter each day, to something he'd yet to envision. Now, the end seemed closer, to what goal he wasn't sure, but Fate Halligan played an important role.

"I serve as well. Soldier Caden, tell me."

Caden briefly outlined the second attack on Fate the previous day and his involvement. He didn't elaborate on the tenuous link he'd sensed. It might be a psychic blip on his screen, nothing more. He ended his description verbally. "And I found some information about the woman, the target."

Donan kept silent, both audibly and internally. For the first time since he'd been a fledgling Soldier, Caden couldn't pick up on any of his mentor's thoughts or communications.

~ ☾ ~

He waited impatiently for endless minutes before Donan's inner voice sounded in his head. "Who is Fate Halligan?"

"She's a Death Maiden. I met her Guide this evening. Selene."

Donan stared at Caden, for once not bothering to hide his intensity or his ambivalence. "If she's a student of Selene, that means she's important. Only the most talented Maidens are taught by the Guide of the Society de la Morte."

"I got that Selene is experienced."

"Yes, ancient, and powerful. The most powerful Maiden alive."

Caden nodded. He leaned forward. For the next question he needed to be eye to eye. "Is she as old as you?"

Donan added another crease to his lined face with a slight smile. "Not quite. I've been around a little longer than her."

"But she's still a contemporary of yours." Which meant she would be a hell of a lot smarter than any other human walking around right now, including him. While he accepted that he'd grow old at a slower rate than other humans, it still jarred his sensibilities that Donan could be hundreds of years old and still vital.

"She's my contemporary. And yes, very intelligent." Donan turned to his personal contemplation corner, a table with a small figure of a sun resting on it. "The thing is, she's as rational as she is smart."

Thank God for that. If the woman possessed a vendetta against anyone they were toast. "And Fate?"

"As I said, she must be powerful for Selene to take her on as a pupil. What did you find out about her in your inquiries?"

Caden thought only of the research session, rather than trying to put forth the facts in a linear manner.

~ ☾ ~

Donan's exquisite ability to lift out the unimportant and filter the trash allowed him to do so in record time. "So, there isn't much about her family's history on record?"

"No, I spent a couple hours in the DMV data base as well as Social Security and other government records. Orphaned early on, but there's no mention of a father in the picture. Her mother's name was Eliza Halligan."

"Eliza Halligan. I don't remember..." Donan's thought trailed off and Caden lost his mind link.

Again, he waited, trying to relax in the spare chair. Donan stood, his back to Caden and in contemplative mode. After several minutes, he steepled his fingers and stared at Caden over them. "You offered to protect her."

"Yeah. Her soul wasn't ready—"

"No, it wasn't. You got an agreement from Fate and Selene?"

"Sort of. Selene told me to check with you about the Maidens' training."

Donan quirked another smile. "It is something we've neglected to tell you, isn't it?"

Caden frowned at the ever-present grin in Donan's voice. "What is?"

"It shouldn't make a huge difference in your mission. Like the Soldiers, Death Maidens take vows to serve the souls. The women journey with troubled or difficult souls to the portal of eternity. It's a job that can get dangerous at times, especially for the most powerful of the women."

Caden pictured Fate's fragile frame and tried to imagine her forcing a recalcitrant or worse, violent, soul to the portal. He suppressed an urge to return to her side, to convince her she wasn't strong enough, wasn't ready. But then, he didn't know that, did he?

"I remember that from the studies on Soldier history. What else?"

~ ☾ ~

"Maidens are the mirror reflection of us, Caden. They share many of the same abilities we have, psi ability, longevity, and quick healing among them. And they take very similar vows to ours. When Fate took her oaths, she pledged to serve the souls, above and beyond all personal interest." Donan paused. "Including finding a mate."

Everything in Caden stilled. He didn't need anyone to tell him. *So, Selene picked up on my attraction for Fate and she'd declared her off limits. Big deal.*

"You have the choice, Caden. If you choose to protect Fate, you realize nothing can come of the relationship," Donan quietly affirmed.

"I don't go beyond sex. Never have." He'd never lied to any woman to get her in his bed. All of his past, casual bedmates understood his need for no commitment, if not the reasons.

"I understand that you've been careful in all accounts. But in this case, you need to refrain from any relationship, other than professional."

Caden stared at his mentor. Donan didn't warn his Soldiers off women, never gave them personal advice, for that matter.

He'd never been singled out by Donan, but likewise he'd never been ignored. He'd gone his own way, largely independent of guidance from his Mentor, and didn't like the up close and personal advice now. He remained silent and waited. Donan narrowed his gaze and sighed.

"The histories of the Soldiers and Maidens have been intertwined in the past, to the point that we were of one mind, one mission. At that point neither required the vow of noninvolvement." His gaze turned inward at that point and Caden suspected he saw the past, relived it. "Then a soldier and maiden chose each other over the souls of man and the schism divided us and reinforced over the years. We have a connection, I suspect, still. But

~ ☾ ~

that very connection can mean the ruination of both groups. So, you can't do more than protect her, Caden."

"I understand my mission." Keeping his job professional never presented a problem. It wouldn't be now.

***

"Fate Halligan, line three." The message sounded over the intercom as Fate finished the sentence in her proposal for another social worker position at the hospice. Absently, she reached out and plucked the telephone from its cradle and tucked it into the space between her shoulder and neck. "Fate Halligan."

"Your soul." The voice whispered, sibilant and evil, sending a shiver down her spine. She straightened and glanced over her cubicle around the large office serving the various hospice employees. Normally she craved solitude in the office, but now, with no one else in the room, she felt vulnerable in a whole new way.

"Who is this?"

"The darkness will win. Your soul will be mine."

A click sounded, indicating the call's end. She dropped the receiver onto its cradle with a shudder, barely resisting the urge to wipe her hands free of the evil she that soaked them. She stared at the blinking cursor on her computer monitor for a long time before bringing herself to the point of saving the document and closing out.

Why did the threat come through a call, rather than the mind link like the other day? And to what purpose, other than to scare her? She pondered whether to leave the building but that would only put her in open spaces and any number of strangers at risk of the same fate Beth suffered. Did she call Janette and have her Latent face danger meant for her? Neither choice seemed to be a viable one.

She pulled her cell phone from her purse along with a

~ ☾ ~

ratty business card. The card she'd convinced herself she'd forgotten to throw away.

Caden Greene, the sensible choice. She could accept his help this once. He could protect her without exposing anyone else to danger.

Once she made it to the Refuge, she could plan with Selene what her next move should be.

It didn't mean she wanted to see him again.

Not at all.

She dialed the number with fingers that shook only slightly. When she mentioned her name to the receptionist, a quick "hold on" followed. As she waited, Fate moved away from the window space that she'd coveted for her desk placement. Suddenly, bright light and an unobstructed view of the street beyond the grounds didn't seem as appealing.

"Fate? What's up?"

Can he feel my tension? She'd caught a touch of something in the air besides the Guard before, but in the rush of things hadn't figured it for another psychic trying to read her emotions. Now, she wasn't so sure. "I just got a phone call. I'm at work and—"

"What did he say?" His brisk tone calmed her nerves in a convoluted way.

"Just that he wanted my soul. I started to call my Latent but I don't want anyone hurt so I called you."

Caden didn't respond immediately but when he did the warmth of his approval seeped through the telephone and into her. "You did the right thing. Don't leave your office until I get there, okay? Ten minutes."

She glanced at the address printed on his business card as she agreed and disconnected. Ten minutes from his office to hers? Way to disregard the traffic laws.

By the time he marched into the office, she'd moved to the receptionist's desk and chatted with the older woman. Fate got a chance to see his impact on women

~ ☾ ~

not linked to a cloistered society when Bella, fiftyish and soon to be a grandmother, blushed like a schoolgirl.

He cast a glance at Fate before winking at Bella. "Think I can take her off your hands for a few hours?" Caden nodded toward Fate as he flashed a smile.

Fate grimaced inwardly at her coworker's surprised look. So she didn't date a lot, so what? She didn't bring her guys by the office to show them off. Okay, she didn't have guys, but if she did she wouldn't flaunt them. Sex without commitment wasn't in her plan. Sex clearly couldn't be that big of a deal anyway. Proof? Her one encounter in college.

She pasted on a smile for Caden, gathered her laptop case and shouldered her backpack. "Bella, I'll be out for the rest of the afternoon, okay? I don't have anything on my calendar."

Bells wordlessly nodded them out before grabbing the silent phone receiver. Probably to spread office gossip that the virgin Fate Halligan finally landed a date.

As she walked alongside Caden toward the exit, Fate whispered, "What was with the smile and flirting?"

"Wait until we're in the truck." Caden opened the glass door and immediately took her laptop case then took hold of her elbow, leading her to the inside of the sidewalk. He paused only when they got to the corner of the office building where he hustled her to his truck. Fate tossed her backpack into the floorboard of the passenger seat and he hoisted her into the seat and shut the door. She buckled up and hunched as low into the leather seat as possible as she waited for him. The ease she'd attained while chatting with Bella about her expectant daughter and casseroles disappeared as Mr. Macho brought back her anxiety, in force.

Caden rushed through the process of pulling out of his haphazard parking space. Fate glared at him. "Buckle your seat belt."

~ ☾ ~

"Rule follower." He muttered as he reached around for the shoulder restraint and clicked it into place.

"I don't like the constant ringing of those alarms." She faced forward, her eyes moving to take in any unusual activity, as if she'd know it if she saw it. "Besides, I don't want another lost soul on my conscience."

"I won't wreck just because I don't have a seat belt on."

"I don't take chances. Case in point, my call to you, my moving away from the window in my office. My going into a more crowded office to wait for you."

"You moved away from your window? Good job, I didn't think you'd have it in you." Caden waved away her huff of annoyance. "I don't mean I think you're stupid. It's just that most people don't think of that, or of moving out of a solitary office into one with more than one person in them. Good thinking." He glanced into the rear view mirror before changing lanes at a reckless speed. "Now, to the question of flirting. I didn't think you wanted everyone to know about the guy trying to kill you. The next best idea is that you were going out for an afternoon quickie."

"They'd believe the killing part before the dating thing."

"You don't date?" He cast her a glance out of the corner of his eye as he wheeled around another curve.

Fate hated the flush that crept across her face. "I don't mix business with pleasure."

"I have a feeling you don't mix it up at all."

Fate let the topic drop *Yeah, like I'm going to go to battle with a god like him. With his experience, he'd humiliate me in no time.*

They drove through the business district before Caden turned off into a residential part of town. The houses here were old, much like the house that held

~ ☾ ~

Fate's apartment, but these were higher-toned homes, more valuable. And much more well kept.

She risked a glance over her shoulder and sighed in relief. "No one's following us."

"Oh, yeah they are. They're just a few miles back."

"How can they keep up with us? Know where we're going?"

Caden's mouth tightened. "Probably because they've put a tracking device on the truck. Damn it!" He squealed onto a side street and into a parking space along the side of the road. Fate dodged him when he leaned over and popped open the glove compartment then extracted an electronic mechanism of some sort. "Stay here." He disappeared out of his door and around the truck.

Fate let that instruction lie for all of a minute before she heaved herself out of the truck. A glance around the vehicle revealed a pair of boots near the rear wheel well. She advanced and found him hunkered down, his head and shoulders under the truck, his rear and legs outside. She crouched beside him. Sure he'd be pissed, but she wasn't willing to stay alone in the truck.

She waited patiently, in her opinion, until he eased out from under the truck, his mechanical device in one hand and another, smaller patch of metal in the other, dirt-covered palm.

"I thought I told you—"

"To stay in the truck, I know. Is that a tracker?"

"Yeah. I should have swept the truck before I left the office." His disgusted tone curbed her own snarky comment as he marched over to a telephone pole then tucked the tracking patch into a crevice in the wood.

"Okay, let's go. We don't have a lot of time." He took hold of her elbow and steered her toward the front of the truck again.

She opened the door and as she climbed inside, said

~ ☾ ~

over her shoulder, "You sure there aren't other devices
on the truck?"

"Yeah, I'm sure." He handed her the square electronic
device and nodded toward the glove compartment.
"Stow that in there, will you?"

"It finds bugs?" She turned the black plastic encased
tool over in her hands. Nothing too flashy, just buttons
and lights that were black now.

***

"Yeah, a pest control tool." *And if I'd kept my mind
on the mission, instead of your pretty little ass, I'd have
remembered to sweep the vehicle before we left your
office.*

Caden made short work of pulling from the parking
slot and getting the hell out of the neighborhood. He'd
broken every rule he'd known in alluding surveillance,
and almost gotten them killed. A few minutes more and
he'd have exposed the Mentor.

In retrospect, the plan of bringing Fate to Donan for a
discussion of her importance might have been rash. If
the Obsidian Guard followed them, not only would the
Guard have Fate, but they'd have a chance to eliminate
the most powerful Soldier of Light alive and Caden
would have gift wrapped them both.

His thoughts scrambled in a rare moment, Caden
drove around, and cast looks into the rear views for any
sign of the Guard. He cast a psychic line and found him,
frustrated at the sight of the tracking patch tucked into
the pole. Caden chuckled, "We've lost them for now." He
could take her to Donan, after some evasive moves, with
a clear conscience.

"But he's angry. No, more than that." Fate's voice,
faint and dreamy, drew his gaze. Her already pale
complexion turned waxy, the few freckles along the
bridge of her nose stood out like they'd been freshly
painted on a canvas.

~ ☾ ~

"You're picking up on them?"

"Yes." Her whisper gave him more information than he wanted.

"You haven't picked up on a Guard before?"

"I think I did just before the attacks, but nothing as clear as this. He's broadcasting pretty loud." She turned haunted eyes toward him, "Do you hear this all the time?"

"Yeah. Along with the voices of the souls that are being attacked." And they were more painful than any evil could begin to be.

"I've grown up with my dying souls. They're like my own head. This, though— " She rubbed her temples as if to dull a pain. "I don't like this at all."

Caden drew on his knowledge of how Donan instructed him to deal with the voices. "Reach inside. Find a place, that peace that you find with your dying souls." He waited silently for a moment then continued, "Don't open up to the voices of the dying. That'll only lead the Guard to them."

She murmured an assent and slouched lower into the passenger seat. Caden drove, one part of his consciousness aware of the Guard struggling to get a whiff of them psychically, another part attending maneuvering traffic. All the while, he listened to Fate breathing. Her pale face shone in the dim cab, her lips slightly parted as she breathed deeply and whispered a chant in a silent tone.

Each breath she took moistened her pink lips, drawing his gaze on them. The thick eyelashes, blonde at the root and darker ends curved against her cheeks. She looked entirely too fragile to handle myriads of dying souls crying out to her each night. *If she's as powerful as Donan suspects, she'll have to deal with more evil than I ever have. How can they make her do that?* He jerked himself out of a stupor. She couldn't influence

~ ☾ ~

him, not with her fragility, her beauty or her essence. Still, even when he wasn't thinking of her, somewhere deep in his spirit, he felt her. He'd been uncomfortable all morning, restless and unable to attend to his work. Only when he'd been talking about her, with her, did he feel totally at ease, yet incomplete.

Another few turns and they'd be back into the neighborhood housing Donan's Refuge. There he might be able to find the answer to his questions, questions he didn't dare ask.

Fate doubled over in the seat.

"Fate? What's wrong?"

"I don't know. I'm sick to my stomach and my head hurts." She cupped her forehead and folded over even more.

Caden reached over and burrowed his fingers into her hair, massaging her head. "Tell me what to do." He tried to keep his voice low and soothing.

"I don't know." She whispered. "I've never felt this before."

"What?"

"Evil beyond evil. Pure hate." She whimpered.

Caden gritted his teeth and forced himself to drive the last few miles to the house. He parked his truck in the covered garage well out of sight of the road and rushed around to Fate's side. He jerked the door open and reached around her back to cup her shoulder. As he lifted her into a sitting position so he could get at the seat belt she felt like dead weight. He quickly unbelted it and shifted his other hand under her knees then lifted her from the seat. As he strode to the rear entrance of the house he eyed her. A little color returned in her face but it could have been from the heat of the truck. Her shallow breaths misted his neck.

He wasn't surprised to see Donan at the door, his creased face frowning. "Quickly, Caden."

~ ☾ ~

Caden edged past his mentor, oddly reluctant to even brush Fate against the older man. He strode to the room he'd spent his formative years in and returned to for protection and contemplation. No woman had rested in the bed he now lowered her on, and no other woman would. Caden sat on the side of the bed and felt of her pulse. Faint, steady.

Her head sagged to the side and the pale blonde hair covered her eyes. He gently swiped a strand away from her nose and cleared his visual field so he could continue to watch her breathe.

"She tapped into the leader's voice." Donan's voice behind him startled Caden. He stayed in his position on the bed but glanced toward his own leader.

"The leader of the Guard?"

"Yes. And I wager the leader isn't aware of Fate's ability. Yet."

"I didn't get any indication—"

"I know. I barely picked up on it." Donan stepped farther into the room and cocked his head to the side, studying Fate. "She is going to be a remarkable Maiden."

"She has that much power?" No Soldier other than Donan demonstrated that power. It would be a formidable weapon and one that the Guard would fight to the death to defeat.

"She has more power than I've witnessed in one so young. Only the eldest of the Maidens, or of the Soldiers, for that matter, acquire the level of power she's demonstrating." Donan stepped closer to the bed and Caden instinctively shifted to increase the distance between his mentor and Fate then reluctantly retreated.

Caden turned back to Fate. "So that's why they're looking for her."

"And why they're wanting to steal her soul. If the Guard's leader obtains Fate's soul and the powers she holds, no power on earth will be able to conquer them."

~ ☾ ~

Caden raised his head and looked at his mentor. "So, we know what our job is. Protect her, keep her alive and try to eliminate the Guard."

Donan nodded, a wry smile on his lips. "Not bad for a day's work, if we accomplish it."

~ ☾ ~

Chapter Five

Fate woke to a throbbing head and a dry mouth. She lay silent, unsure of her surroundings. The bed, too wide to be the one in her apartment boasted a nubby, old-fashioned cover, unlike the cotton quilt top she favored. Most of all, it smelled of—man. A slight citrus scent mingled with a more elemental musk.

Caden.

She jerked up into a sitting position without thinking only to have a pain knife through her head and surveyed the unfamiliar room. She searched her memory, recalling the frantic but controlled flight Caden orchestrated from her office.

The pain.

She didn't want to relive the dull pain that started when she picked up on the guard's frustration and the more knife-sharp pain that jabbed into her brain as she sat trying to calm. Whoever it was invading her mind and taking over her thoughts and emotions scared her witless.

"Miss Halligan."

She whirled, her hands raised in defense. A tall, thin man with a weathered face, wreathed with flowing white hair, stood across the room, next to an open door. His outfit, faded jeans and a polo shirt, seemed odd. He should be dressed in shaman robes or a Zen monk's shawls.

"Where am I?"

"Caden brought you to my home for safekeeping. Are you well?" He remained at the door, as if he knew he

~ ☾ ~

didn't trust him. Hell, she couldn't trust her own thoughts right now.

"You can trust your mind, Fate. The Guard leader didn't invade you. Not your thoughts. You picked up on his emotions, I think. Not the other way around."

"How do you know that? And who are you?" She held her ground physically but allowed her psyche to shrink away. If he could read that much, how much more could he glean from her?

"My name is Donan, I'm Caden's Mentor, his teacher. With the truck only a couple miles away from here and the leakage extremely high, I picked up on the emotion just after you did. And I picked up your thoughts because you were broadcasting right now. Has your guide not taught you to fortify your casting?"

Fate bristled. "Of course she has."

"You were careless." He interrupted. "You can't afford to be so, not anymore. Your training has to end, Fate. Any doubts in your abilities have to be cast aside, in favor of assurance."

"Easier said than done." She muttered, turning and placing her feet on the cool wooden floor. She needed to get home, or at least to the Retreat. No matter what the danger, she must talk to Selene. Find out what the hell happened.

"You're awake."

Caden filled the doorway as he edged by the older man and approached Fate. She cast a grateful smile toward him. A familiar face, at last.

"Yeah. Thanks for taking care of me. I need to get home, now."

"Home? No. You need to stay here until we've taken care of the Guards."

"I need to talk to my Guide. Figure out what to do next." As she stood, she became aware of his closeness, his size next to hers.

~ ☾ ~

Caden easily topped six feet, towering over her five foot five frame. His muscle mass denoted a man who used his body daily, who relied on whipcord strength rather than weight room workouts. His hair hung loose just above his shoulders, dark brown, almost black, shining in the light from the window behind her. His dark eyes were steady on her, assessing her. Fate recalled the conversation with her Latent. Suddenly, the option of sex for sex's sake didn't seem too bad.

"Fate. You can't leave the Refuge right now. Maybe later. I'll call Selene and have her come to you." Donan took a step toward the door.

"She won't come. She wouldn't enter—"

"A Soldier's Refuge? Maybe not in the past. But, now, I think she may bend her rules. She will be welcome." Donan strode from the room, leaving Fate with her savior.

Caden stood with his arms folded across his chest. "Now, are you willing to stay?"

"For a while, at least until I've talked to Selene." She glanced around for her shoes.

"They're under the bed." Caden tilted his head toward the end of the bed. With a huff of impatience, Fate retrieved her shoes and slipped them on.

"What's with the mind reading? Stay out of my head."

"I didn't have to read your mind. Your toes were curling." Caden quirked a grin at her and continued, "Hungry?"

He led her to a large kitchen where another man busied himself preparing a meal. Caden ignored the slightly older man and headed for the sink. He efficiently washed his hands then went to the refrigerator and opening it, peered inside before removing sandwich ingredients and carried them to the large wooden table.

Caden removed six slices of bread from a loaf before

~ ☾ ~

he noticed her hovering near the door. He indicated she should enter with a nod of his head. "Do you want ham or turkey?"

"Turkey." She went to the sink and washed her hands before coming to his side. She pulled a container of mustard toward her and after he nodded, applied a generous amount to both her sandwich and the two he started assembling.

They worked silently for the time it took to assemble the sandwiches. Caden snagged a bag of potato chips and tossed them onto the table before carrying his sandwiches to the table and laying them on the surface. Fate shook her head at the action then went in search of plates and napkins. She retrieved two of each from cabinets and filled each of the plates with sandwiches and a handful of chips. She sank into a chair at the generous table and bit into the sandwich.

Caden examined the depths of the huge refrigerator. "What do you want to drink? We have beer, soda, milk, and juice."

"I'd rather have water." Fate rose and started toward the cabinet again then returned to her chair when Caden waved her away. He served her water from the tap, along with ice in the glass then plopped into his chair across from her with a beer in hand.

Fate knew the topic of her picking up on the Obsidian leader's evil would resurface but she didn't know if she could deal with the whole issue. Her power shouldn't extend to picking up non-Maidens' thoughts, let alone emotions. *Are my powers expanding? And can I handle them?* She kept her attention on getting the sandwich down, her appetite gone and studied Caden. In the background the slight man prepared food in almost a ritualistic manner and tried not to stare at her.

Caden apparently didn't want to talk about the Guard in front of an audience either. Although, when you

~ ☾ ~

thought about it, it didn't make sense that either one of
them would try to keep a secret in a house of mind
readers. Fate chuckled at the thought.

Caden glanced up at her at the sound. "What?"

"Have you ever tried to keep a secret from Donan?"

Caden grinned wryly, "No. Well, yeah, when I was
younger. It doesn't pay, though. He knows everything,
every thought."

"Does he allow you to shield?"

"Yeah. It's out of courtesy, I know. If he really wanted
to know what I thought, every thought, he'd have no
problem delving into it."

"It's nice, you have that much trust in him."

"You don't with your Guide?" He frowned.

"Oh, I do. Selene is more knowledgeable in the area of
psychic ability than I ever thought of being, so if she
wants to know something, she's going to find it out.
She's always taught me to respect psychic privacy, as
well as physical. I've never forced the issue." *Though I
might have to in the future.*

"So why the laughter?"

"Just that we've refrained from talking about things
in company, when we're both in a house chock full of
psychics." She smiled, "It's really funny, if you think
about it."

He stared at her for a long moment before clearing
his throat and shifting in his chair.

"So you're gaining in power?"

Fate shook her head. "I don't know. That's why I need
to talk to Selene. She's my Guide, the one who can
explain all this."

Suddenly, the whole situation closed in on her and
Fate tried to quell a shot of panic. Caden's next words
calmed her a bit. "We'll get her here. I can send one of
my best men to retrieve her. In the mean time, why
don't you talk to Donan?"

~ ☾ ~

Fate shook her head again. "I'd rather wait." She stood and walked to the sink with her plate, intent on dropping the subject. Until she talked to Selene, she didn't want to get too chummy.

"Why don't you write a note or something to let Selene know you're all right? I'll send it with one of my guys." He leaned away from the table, opened a drawer in a cabinet and handed Fate a pad and pen.

"I'm not sure she's going to come."

"She'll come. Include your cell phone number, okay? That way, she can call you in case she doesn't believe we're on the up and up."

Fate smiled, "You've covered all the bases, haven't you?" She jotted down all the information she could think of and then waited.

***

When Selene came to the house Fate stood to the side of the doorway, waiting anxiously for her friend and guide's arrival. Caden stood sentinel behind her and Donan waited in front as host. When Selene approached the threshold of the Refuge he bowed deeply and intoned, "Welcome My Maiden Selene."

The greeting, apparently an ancient one for related clans, intrigued Fate, as well as Selene's flushed face. Selene bowed in equal distance and replied, "My Soldier. Might I enter your abode and rest?"

Donan gestured with an expansive arm, "My house is your refuge, My Maiden. Enter and find peace."

Selene crossed under the arch with her characteristic regal stride. Fate sensed a change in the house's psychic field. Almost as if the house were welcoming the Maiden leader onto its premises. She refrained from rushing into Selene's comforting embrace, unsure of the protocol. Selene, however, seemed to have no compunction about enfolding Fate in a warm hug.

"I sensed your struggle earlier." She leaned back,

~ ☾ ~

releasing Fate and studied her before continuing. "We have much to discuss."

Fate nodded weakly. She didn't know what the hell was going on, but someone had better start explaining. This new power scared the hell out of her.

A sense of warmth invaded her, but it wasn't Selene. She'd never experienced anything this intense. A heat began in her belly, spreading throughout. It carried comfort and a sensation so strong she didn't know if she could stand the feeling without crying out. Her body itched, aching to rub against something—or someone. Her focus narrowed onto the one man in the room she'd choose to stroke. Caden.

When she turned to look at him Fate found his gaze on her. The dark intensity in his eyes threatened to devour her. "It's you." She whispered.

Caden took a step toward her then frowned and halted. "What are you doing?" A growl rolled through the words.

"I'm not doing anything. Get out of my head." She stammered, flustered that they were having this argument in front of both their mentors.

"I'm not in your head, you're in mine."

Donan's voice interrupted the argument. "I think you're experiencing conjoined thoughts."

Fate frowned at him, "What's that?"

Selene's gaze encompassed both Fate and Caden. "The attraction between you is palpable. Fate will remember her vow during this endeavor. I trust you will, as well, Caden?"

Caden broke his gaze with Fate and growled, "I'll damn well do my job, Maiden."

Selene arched a brow. "That wasn't my concern."

"I will keep my vow," he gritted out.

Fate's face flushed and she lowered her gaze from him then glanced at her guide. Selene's expression

~ ☾ ~

returned to the serene, controlled mask. Donan showed them to the room he'd assigned to Fate, and Fate sank onto her knees in obeisance. "I beg your guidance, My Maiden Guide."

"Rise, Fate." Selene sank onto the small standard bed and patted the side. When Fate sat beside her, Selene took her hand, a rare gesture since most psychics refrained from touching other than in times of great emotion. "Now, tell me everything that happened today."

Fate filled her in on the phone call and her subsequent appeal to Caden, followed by the race to his Refuge. When she got to the invasion by the Obsidian Leader, she quelled the shudders accompanying it. Selene remained quiet and placid throughout the description, but Fate sensed her disquiet.

"May I call on your memories?" Selene's request wasn't surprising but Fate took a bracing breath before agreeing. She opened her mind and allowed entrance to her memory of the day.

Fate relived the difficult events that brought her here. By the time Selene finished calling forth the memory of the invasion, Fate trembled and the sensation of fainting returned. A knock on the door gave her time to take a bracing breath before Caden stepped through.

"Are you all right?" He frowned toward Selene before lowering his gaze on Fate.

She nodded and pulled her hand from its clasp with her mentor. "I'm fine."

His dark frown didn't abate but he did back away with a parting remark, "Call me if you need me."

As the door closed Selene came to her feet and faced Fate. "He's attuned to you."

"No, I think he just—"

"His consciousness is connected with yours, Fate. It's a plus as far as your safety is concerned but beware. Your status as Death Maiden rests as much on your vow

~ ☾ ~

of noninvolvement as on your psychic ability. To get emotionally entangled with him would be to jeopardize everything you've trained for."

Fate stared at her guide with her mind on the man outside the door. He did seem to anticipate her every need and she knew his moods. The mere fact that she'd turned to him when trouble found her should tell her she attuned to him as well.

"I hold too much value in my status as a Maiden to risk it, Selene."

"Good, just remember. A face and body like his are tempting, but not for long. Your vocation is for life."

Fate nodded in agreement. Now, if she could convince her own body of that.

"I'll keep my vow, Selene. But what's happening to me, to my power?"

***

The session Selene and Fate engaged in lasted into the wee hours of the morning and yielded no clear results. Selene couldn't predict if Fate would pick up on the Obsidian Leader's thoughts again or not. Fate almost wished for the ability to foresee such a thing, she wasn't ready for more power, not if it carried such a stench of evil.

She answered questions verbally and psychically until she felt as if she'd been interrogated. Finally, Selene called a halt to the session with a yawn and apology.

"I'm sorry I've stayed with the questioning so long. I'd hoped you gained more information about the leader and why he's targeting you."

Fate swiveled her head on her shoulders in an effort to loosen the kinks in her neck. "I couldn't get beyond the hate, the anger. I couldn't tell if the voice came from a male or female. There seemed to be a total lack of sexual orientation to the voice, which I've never read in anyone beyond an infant."

~ ☾ ~

Selene nodded, her gaze taking on a familiar vacant, introspective look. Her guide presented this façade when she ruminated on a problem. Fate leaned back against the wall to rest. *Please let the session be over. If Selene has another idea and wants to question me further, I may fall over.*

Fate roused from a half doze by Selene's voice. "If you get any more hints of consciousness from the leader contact me."

"If you aren't with me—"

"It won't matter, I'll be able to pick up on the thread, no matter where I am."

A thrill of awareness thrummed through Fate. "You mean you can read me from a distance?"

"I can read many people from a distance, not only you, Fate."

Fate stood and faced the woman she'd trusted for years. "Why didn't I know about that before? And have you—"

"I haven't distance-read you before. And you haven't been informed of that part of my power before since you didn't need to know." Selene's face took on a hard mask, and appeared old for the first time. She seemed older than time, and just as powerful.

"You have other powers, then? Powers you keep to yourself?"

"Yes, and so will you, in time."

Fate tamped down the panic that comment elicited. She couldn't handle the odd invasion from an Obsidian Guard, let alone distance-read people's consciousness on her own. Instead, she focused on Selene's revelation. "If you have so much power, why can't you just deal with the Obsidian Guards by yourself? Why can't you read who and where the leader is and eliminate them once and for all?"

"Yeah, why don't you?"

~ ☾ ~

Selene whirled to face Caden. His solid stance in the open doorway made him a formidable figure. Fate's fatigue vanished in an instant. Did her frustration bring him here? Call him to her?

He glanced her way before his dark gaze returned to Selene. "Well? Can you eradicate the leader or the lesser Guards? Or are you willing to put Fate in harm's way to play some sort of game?"

"Caden." Fate scooted to the edge of the bed and stood, ready to defend someone, but she wasn't sure whom. Selene, her guide and long-time friend? Or Caden, the man who'd put himself in danger repeatedly for her and appeared ready to do so again?

"No, Caden. I won't put Fate in danger recklessly. Nor will I force you to defend or protect her." Selene turned toward Fate. "I have a lot of power, Fate. I won't argue that fact. So does Donan. And the Obsidian Guard leader."

"Alone, neither the Soldiers nor the Maidens have enough power to defeat the Guard." Donan entered the room and stood between Caden and Selene. Fate took another step forward and into the swirling, invisible energy the group emitted.

Donan and Selene's gazes met before he continued. "The Guard's leader gains power through stealing souls, just as the army of lesser Guards do. However, the leader picks only the most powerful of souls to steal, destroy and pilfer their powers over eons of time. The Soldiers have tried to stop him for as long, to no avail. We keep the Guards' numbers down and protect as many souls as possible, but we've never been close to catching the leader." His gaze narrowed on Fate. "Now, with your connection to the leader, your psychic eavesdropping, we may have an opportunity. If you're willing to take the chance with us."

Fate cast her eyes around the group. Selene's

~ ☾ ~

expression held worry mixed with hope, Donan's pretty much the same. Only Caden wore a very different expression. He looked murderous. Fate wondered if her panic showed on her own face.

His gaze enveloped her. His anger wasn't directed toward her. Instead he worried for her. He didn't want her to bear a burden he would rather carry. How she knew all of this she didn't take the time to decipher, but knew soul deep.

"You don't have to do this, you know." He ignored Donan and Selene and advanced to stand in front of Fate. The warmth from his strong body heated her through and through.

She looked up at him, and tried to convince him of her resolution. "I know, but if I don't I die for no reason."

"You won't die. I double damn guarantee that."

~ ☾ ~

Chapter Six

Caden fought the urge to return to his room and comfort her. It wasn't his job to hold her, to comfort her. His job, his only job, remained to protect her soul from the attacks of the Obsidian Guard, to keep her alive, enable her to fulfill her destiny in life. A destiny that didn't—and could never—include him.

The light in the exercise room glared bright in the predawn hours. He threw a punch at the bag followed by several kick punch combinations. Even if he didn't get in a full workout, he'd release some of his pent up frustrations. Or at least it might keep him from going to her.

"You need to focus, Caden. Focus on your tasks, not on the Maiden."

Caden stopped the sequence, his breath furious pants, far too rapid for his physical conditioning. He briefly closed his eyes and concentrated on centering and calming his psyche.

He turned and bowed to Donan formally. "Mentor Donan."

His mentor wore the traditional garb of the Soldiers of Light, a lightweight cotton shirt, button-less and open to mid chest, paired with thin trousers. Not an informal bull session, then. Only when he intended to enforce his rules, the ancient laws of the Soldiers, did Donan dress so traditionally.

"Soldier Caden." Donan advanced into the room and came to a stop at the edge of the workout mat. He glanced toward the punching bag and then at Caden.

~ ☾ ~

Caden quelled a frown and curse; his teacher knew him too well. He tended to take his frustrations out on more mundane "human" sports.

"Do you wish to continue your session?" Donan's eyes were blank, no anger or understanding arose from them.

"No, I'm finished." Or at least finished to the point he could control his frustration.

"Then join me in my room." Donan didn't wait for a response, but turned and headed toward his quarters.

By the time Caden arrived, a tray with coffee and the tea Donan preferred rested on the table beside his chair. To Caden's surprise, Fate occupied another chair. Her eyes were tired and wary, like she'd been cornered. Soft fleece and jeans replaced the sweater and slacks of the day before. Apparently, Selene delivered other clothes. If Fate slept at all it hadn't been restful.

He sank into the remaining vacant chair and eyed his mentor. The expected lecture on keeping his distance around Fate didn't seem to be happening. But what did Donan have up his sleeve?

The older man poured tea and coffee into cups without asking preferences, another sign he wasn't acknowledging the human niceties but doing an end run around verbal intercourse. Caden accepted his own black coffee and watched Fate's reaction as Donan added honey to a chai tea mixture he'd poured her before handing it to her. She accepted the cup, sending Donan a glare.

"I would prefer if you asked my preference, rather than reading it," she murmured as she raised the cup to her mouth. Caden hid a smile of approval. It took some balls to face down his teacher in his formal kick-ass mode.

Donan raised his eyebrows in surprise, a first as far as Caden could remember. But then, his mentor wasn't used to being questioned, by anyone.

"I apologize. I don't get many visitors and my

~ ☾ ~

manners are a bit rusty."

She mirrored the raised brow. "I doubt you're rusty in anything, Mentor Donan. Now, shall we get to the point of the discussion, or spend a few more minutes trying to establish psychic superiority?"

Caden didn't try to stop his chuckle, even when Donan shot a furious glance his direction. "Face it, Donan. She has a point." In a silent voice he continued. *"Stop the pissing contest. She chose not to play."*

"And besides, I think I won." Fate finished his thought. Damn it, her power. He eyed her and found her staring at him in return, her expression full of wonder, fear and a little heat. He'd expected the first two emotions, but the last one threw him.

"That is what I wanted to discuss, Ms. Halligan."

"You might as well call me Fate. I have a feeling we're going to be having several of these conversations. And if you insist on crawling around in my head I think it justifies being on a first name basis."

"Very well. Now, to the matter at hand. The Obsidian Guard—"

"Where is Selene? Isn't she going to sit in on this?" Caden interrupted.

"She returned to the Retreat. There are other matters to attend to besides me." Fate sat straight and tall, her posture almost brittle. Caden knew intellectually that she might be right. Selene may have other charges and responsibilities but no one held more importance than Fate.

Again she turned her gaze toward him, a question in her eyes. "Why do you think I'm so important? I don't have any extraordinary powers. Selene is the one the Guard wants, has wanted for years. *Her* soul is the one that's valuable."

"Obviously we don't know the reason they want you, Fate, but the fact remains they do want your soul, your

~ ☾ ~

powers. If we fail in protecting you, you die and your powers fall to the Guard." Donan left out more than he answered.

"So, I stay here until someone is caught? I don't think so." She shook her head emphatically, her straight blonde hair caressing her cheeks as she settled her gaze back on Donan.

"You stay here until I say it's safe to leave." Caden cut in, disregarding his mentor's seniority.

"I have a job, a career, a calling."

"It'll wait."

"No it won't. Besides, I won't wait. I refuse to sit on my thumbs while someone else takes responsibility for my safety. I have some skills in self defense—"

"If what I saw is your expertise then you're screwed, lady. You're not going to be out of my sight until we finish this. Get used to it."

They glared at each other for a time and Caden quelled the urge to take hold of her, to shake some sense into her. He knew, beyond a shadow of a doubt, if he touched her now, she'd be in more danger of being under him and involved in a very physical way than in danger from any Guard. His pulse quickened, his palms itched to take hold of her.

"I need to go home. I have to work tomorrow and I need rest, more clothes. I need to water my plants." She finished in a near shout.

"You know you can't stay at your apartment—" Donan began.

"The hell you are!" Caden's more vehement response drowned him out.

Fate's frown deepened. "What do you suggest then, I bunk with you two until the Guard decides to give up? I don't know much about them but I'm pretty sure that's not in their rule book."

"You'll stay here." Caden gritted out.

~ ☾ ~

"And how am I supposed to get to work? Not to mention fulfill my obligations to the Society? I *may* be able to get off from work, if they think the patients may be in danger." She halted and Caden could see the decision in her eyes as she realized the patients would in fact be at risk. She continued, "But I can no more ignore the Maiden's call than you can your vocation." She took in both Caden and his teacher in her gaze this time. She might as well share the wealth among them though Donan reacted with silence, while Caden fumed. His mind raced with furious notions of what he'd like to do to the Guards that threatened her.

"What do you suggest, in lieu of staying here?" Donan didn't glance toward Caden though Caden knew he picked up psychic overflow from them.

"I want to go home, to my apartment. It's pretty secure. I made sure the owner installed strong locks installed when I moved in."

""Where is your apartment?" Caden growled as he picked up on her concern about the neighborhood.

She started to rattle off an excuse when she realized she hadn't voiced the concern about the neighborhood, rather thought it. "Damn it, get out of my head!"

"Back at ya, babe." He drawled and he watched as a flush rose in her cheeks.

She folded her upper body onto her legs and groaned. "What's going on? This is crazy."

"Obviously your powers are expanding, growing." Donan's voice lost its severity and almost approached sensitivity. Caden smiled, another man falling under her spell, huh.

"So why is *he* the one I can read? Other than the leader of the Guards." She ignored the huff from Caden. "The only time I'm supposed to be able to read another person is when they're getting ready to die." She jackknifed upright, frantic. "Is he—?"

~ ☾ ~

Caden shot out of his chair when she abruptly changed positions and hovered over her. He dropped into a crouch and laid a hand on her back.

"No, Caden is fine. Obviously." Donan finished his reply on a dry note as he eyed them.

Fate shivered under his touch and Caden tried to dial down the sexual attraction emanating from him. He couldn't do much about hers toward him. Didn't want to. As he continued to touch her, he welcomed the heat of her attraction as it seeped into his skin.

"I'm right here, and I'll be beside you until this is over, I promise." His hand didn't move from the middle of her back but his body reacted as if he'd touched her breast. He breathed in, taking her scent into his body.

"I want to go home, Caden. Take me home." She kept her voice low.

"I will."

***

Caden focused on his driving, his outward attention totally on the road ahead. His inner focus, however, split. He monitored for evidence of the Guard, constantly on alert for any threat to Fate. At the same time, he followed Donan's mental tirade. When he'd ushered Fate from his mentor's room, he'd been sure Donan would find a way to prevent them from continuing the journey to her building. But other than nagging like a concerned parent, his mentor hadn't blocked their leaving.

Soldiers enjoyed gifts of clairvoyance, precognition and telepathy. He'd long suspected that Donan possessed more powers. Powers that could be called upon in emergencies. Thank God this didn't seem to be one of those occasions.

He technically acknowledged Donan's rants about not being objective and following his little head rather than his brain, but he didn't always listen. The other part of

~ ☾ ~

his consciousness tuned in to Fate. She sat silently beside him in his truck, barely breathing, yet he didn't pick up on more fear from her. Rather she emitted anticipation and a little healthy wariness at the situation. More than once he caught her scanning the area, her eyes moving from one side view mirror to another. Still he took pride in his ability to protect her, even if even if she accused him of having a he-man syndrome.

"I do feel safe with you, you know." She turned her gaze toward him, blue eyes strangely peaceful after their arguments.

"So, does this mean you're ready to stay at my house?"

"With you and Donan? Not likely." She scoffed.

"What's wrong with me and Donan? The house is big enough for privacy." But it wouldn't be the one he'd use, assuming she agreed to stay with him.

"I don't think this city is big enough to provide me with the privacy I'd need from your mentor. I might be able to figure out a way to block you, but I have a feeling he's like Selene. She can ram through any block I put up. Always has."

"Yeah, that's Donan." Caden sent a sharp look at her. "What do you mean you'll find a way to block me? Why would you need to?"

She laughed. "Okay, you want unlimited access to my thoughts?" At his decisive nod, she tilted her head and eyed him. "Then fair's fair. I get free rein inside your head."

"So you're finding a block, huh? Good deal." He grinned at her cute laugh.

"I didn't think you wanted to open up your brain any more than I did." She slouched into the seat more, obviously relaxing a bit. Funny how everything about her reflected on him, her mood, her thoughts, her very

~ ☾ ~

tension. And no, he didn't want her to have free roaming privileges in his head. Her very naïve little body would flush from head to toe at the thoughts running through his mind since he'd met her.

Not only did her body enthrall him, but so did her mind. She argued with him with as much passion as she used in her job and when she'd faced off with Donan about his mind delve. That only made her more attractive than ever.

"You held your own with Donan."

"I did, didn't I?" She grinned.

"And to think I thought you were just a little mousey thing that wouldn't stand up for yourself."

"Mousey? Me? Why would you think that?" She stared at him as if he'd spouted off in a foreign language.

He shrugged, "You look like a stiff breeze could topple you over." He held up a hand to stay her retort, "No offense, you're just kinda skinny, you know? And when you were at the hospital you were kind of quiet and let stuff just happen around you."

"I'd just been attacked and wounded with a knife!" She shot up from her relaxed posture, her back straight and stiff. "Besides, I wasn't a pushover there, I just let the people do their job. And when the guy attacked me in the alley, I wasn't a fading flower then either."

"No, just a pain in the ass."

"I'm glad you think this is funny."

"I'm not grinning because it's funny. I'm grinning because I when I'm wrong, I'm wrong, big time. You're not a fading anything, but a little tiger, aren't you?"

She looked at him before slouching back into her earlier position. "I think I'm both. I'm more than just someone who listens to people who need to talk, you know? I excel at cutting through red tape with insurance companies about home hospice care. I can talk a recalcitrant bill collector into giving a grieving family

~ ☾ ~

some time faster than you can dial a phone. And I can meditate with the best of the Maidens. I just don't have a lot of experience with kicking ass and taking names. Or at least not until lately."

"You're doing fine. And hopefully, you'll be able to go back to whipping insurance companies and bill collectors' asses soon." Caden flicked on the turn signal and changed lanes as he neared the exit to her apartment. "What about your Maiden job? Is there any physical training involved?" God he hoped so, she needed it right now, even if he didn't like the thought of her getting close enough to an assailant to engage in hand to hand combat.

"Some, but I'm beginning to suspect not enough."

***

They finished the drive to her house in a companionable silence. She caught herself glancing over at Caden as he handled the traffic. It wouldn't do for him to get the idea she liked him or something. Her attraction had to be pretty self-evident by the flushes and stammering she engaged in on a regular basis. That and the fact that he regularly crawled around in her head.

Fate turned her head away and her attention inward. How did she end up here?

She'd been prepared to complete the Death Maiden's task of calling souls and accompanying them to the portal of eternity. But all this, this cloak and dagger stuff, she'd not bargained for. Even more than Selene, in her wisdom, anticipated. Now she faced the real possibility of having to lean on a Soldier of Light, a member of the very order that severed with the Maidens eons ago, for protection. *And I'm thinking of taking martial arts lessons!*

Fate shook her head in wonder at the ramifications. Her, a passive student of the Society, thrust into danger

~ ☾ ~

and violence. But the surprise from that didn't even compare with the widening psychic powers she'd encountered. The fact that she could communicate with anyone outside a dying soul or her mentor seemed ludicrous. Sure, she could hear the voices of the dying, a version of clairvoyance considered morbid by some, but present since childhood. Her mother and grandmother before her shared the talent and she'd become comfortable with it. To know the feelings, thoughts and even passions of another living soul was something she'd never expected, or wanted.

The evil she sensed from the Guard tainted her soul. A black shadow that flowed over her to the point that she'd never feel clean again. Until Caden.

His anger, pure like a blue flame in the center of a fire cleansed her. And the passion.

When she opened her mind enough to sense his attraction to her she thought she'd self-combust from excitement, embarrassment and even a little fear.

The dual temptation taunted her. She wanted to open up and share his thoughts, try to control the communication wave that flowed between them and to keep herself closed off at the same time. Even Selene, who she trusted more than life itself, maintained a distance that Fate never felt tempted to breech. The very idea of sharing not only her body with a man, but also her soul, her very essence, both frightened and seduced her.

She allowed herself to sink into the familiar meditative state that called her powers.

Slowly, tentatively, she opened the door in her mind that housed the place where Caden lived.

Where she effectively channeled her thoughts and feelings toward him.

A slight jerk of the steering wheel sent the car toward the shoulder of the two-lane highway and Caden cursed

~ ☾ ~

as he attempted to get the vehicle on the straight and narrow. "Warn a guy next time, will ya?"

Fate smiled, her eyes straight ahead. Instead of answering him verbally, she tried silently. *"Sorry. What should I do, whistle?"*

"God, no. What would that sound like in my head?" He glanced over at her and continued. "You decided not to block me? Why?"

"I'm curious. I haven't been able to communicate with anyone psychically outside of my job. I wanted to know if I could do it."

"So I'm your guinea pig?"

"You're the closest person that isn't trying to kill me."

Caden grinned. "You ramble when you're psychic."

"Smart ass." She muttered.

Caden laughed, then flicked on the car's turn signal at the entrance to her apartment building. "Hold off on the practice for a while, okay? At least on the ribbing and stuff. If you need help, though, whistle loud and long."

Fate sat up straight and clenched her hands together to stop the trembling. Why the sudden fear to go into her own house? She'd not felt any evil around during the drive, experienced no real expectation that she should be afraid. Yet, it persisted.

"Caden?"

"Yeah?" He backed into a parking space, she noticed. So, real people did that, instead of only in the spy novels for quick getaways.

"I can block you, and I assume since you have more widespread telepathic ability, you can block others out. So, is it safe to assume that the Guard can block us from sensing them?"

Caden halted in the act of opening his door and met her gaze with a steady one of his own. "That's why we go in the back, and why I'm going in first."

~ ☾ ~

Chapter Seven

The old building, probably built in the fifties or sixties, equaled good construction but lousy security. He cautiously led the way up a flight of interior stairs to the side of the main floor and halted at an old wooden door. Fate started to edge around him with a key in her hand when he stopped her. "Give me the key and stay behind me."

"I don't sense anything." She turned her face up to him.

"Not now, but there's a residue. Stay where you are."

"So, do we go in at all?"

"You don't have to. We can turn around right now and go to my house."

She looked at the door as if it'd give her the answer, and then shook her head. "No. We go in."

Caden studied the situation. While his instincts picked up on no one in the house at present, it seemed important to Fate that she face her demons. He unlocked and opened her door silently. A few inches were all it took to squeeze into the landing. He made the most of the small landing, folding Fate into the corner of the entryway and blocking her, before shutting the door again behind them. He slipped the key to her and opened up a psychic path. *Lock the door and hold on to the key. We may need it in a hurry.*

He got a faint click in response. He reached behind her and taking her hand, eased it to the belt loops of his jeans. *Hold on. When I move, you move at the same speed. If I go down, follow me, unless I'm hurt. Then run like hell and find Donan.*

~ ☾ ~

She didn't attempt to communicate with him psychically, good girl, but he felt the pull of her hand as she grasped the belt loop in the back of his pants.

The area inside her doorway consisted of a wider landing and another set of stairs. As he climbed the shorter flight, Caden identified the apartment Fate lived in as a converted attic with an exterior entry added. He glanced at the walls on either side of the stairs, solid plaster, probably over the older outside wall of the structure. At the top, the stairs doglegged to the left with a blind spot.

"What's at the top of the stairs? Open or closed?" In his mind he asked the question and provided the options of doorways. Fate flooded him with a picture of half a dozen more steps and an open railing above and to the right. So, if an assailant still waited in the room and blocked them, he could easily pick Caden off at the top of the stairs.

He ignored the urge to wrestle her back into the earlier, suddenly more secure stairwell and continued on. His skill and training enabled him to handle anyone at the top of the stairs.

No one waited at the railing, or in the living room itself. Fate tsked over a couple of broken ceramic pieces and fumed at the mild destruction wrought to her television and CD player by a rage-filled ransacking. But when she turned toward Caden her eyes turned fearful. He shifted from his task of checking windows and other rooms for signs of entry and watched her.

She headed toward a small alcove created out of the room that jutted into the stairwell area. The railing he'd dreaded so much held a rich walnut stain and gleamed with both age and the obvious care she'd put into the small place she called home. In about six feet of space she'd tucked a large armchair and floor lamp. But the overwhelming amount of books caught his attention and

~ ☾ ~

apparently her concern. She ran her hands along the shelves that lined two walls of the space, removing a book here and there and checking it for abuse. She treated the books with more affection than others did their pets.

A part of him wondered at the simplicity of her act and another wanted to have the same measure of devotion directed toward him as she focused on the leather and cloth bound books she caressed. The very idea he envied the books seemed foreign to him, and a little idiotic.

"Everything okay?" He advanced slowly as he asked the question.

"I think so." Her voice trembled with emotion as she turned to him, a book clasped to her chest, and smiled. "I know you probably think I'm silly, but they've been my friends since I realized I was different."

He cocked his head and studied her. "No, I looked for something that wouldn't judge me either. It turned out to be physical training. No one made fun of my differences when I worked out."

Or when I read," she laid the book on the chair and when she straightened with determination in her eyes. "So, were my bedroom and kitchen trashed too?"

"Not as bad, from what I can see. The kitchen utensils are dumped on the floor but we still need to check your bedroom." Caden extended his hand in invitation and let Fate lead the way into the kitchen. She grumbled as she retrieved spoons, spatulas and other metal utensils and dumped them into the sink basin.

"Wish I had a dishwasher right now," she muttered.

He checked the stove to ensure the gas line's integrity then followed Fate into her bedroom. She advanced on her closet and he met her at the slim door.

"Let me." He opened the door and swept his hand through the expanse.

~ ☾ ~

Nothing.

He eyed the room while she checked out her clothes. Feminine but not overly so. She'd decorated the room in soft colors, blues and greens, and added touches of a tannish pink color that he saw so often around women. Her standard, double bed, wouldn't provide enough room for his feet if he stretched out over it, but if he lay diagonally he could fit. She'd just have to sleep on top of him.

Whoa. Where did that thought come from? And when could he implement the plan he'd just formulated to get her into bed? Sure he couldn't emotionally commit, but he sure as hell could scratch the itch for Fate Halligan. Unless he was mistaken, she had a yen for him as well.

"I think I'll be fine." Fate came out of the small closet with an armful of clothes.

"We talked about this, Fate. This place is nice as far as apartments go, but security wise, it sucks. The locks are older than both of us. A third-rate burglar could get through them in seconds. The doors are wooden and solid but that's only a delay, nothing else. You live in a converted attic with no second exit and a stairwell that sent my pucker factor up a few notches on the way in here."

"First off, eww. I don't need a second entrance to the apartment, or a fire escape. I have a fire ladder that I practice with every month. As for the stairwell, I have a key to the bottom door and once I'm in the hallway, I always lock it back before I come up the stairs."

"Really? We got in without unlocking it today. Why do you think that happened??" Before she could answer he continued. "Because someone picked the lock. You wouldn't be safe enough from a human assailant, Fate, let alone someone armed with psychic abilities too. You can't stay here by yourself and that's final."

~ ☾ ~

"Really?" She marched to the sofa that dominated her little living room and tossing a couple of throw pillows to the other end, plopped down and crossed her arms. "You said I'm a tiger? You haven't even begun to see my stripes."

***

Fate grinned into her pillow as she heard Caden flop around on the sofa again. After an hour of haranguing, cajoling and then blustering about scooping her up and carrying her down the stairs, he'd given up and called Donan. Ten minutes into the conversation he'd just glared at her and handed her the phone.

Her anti-intimidation skills were improving. After all, she talked Donan into letting her prove she could stay in the apartment, even with a bear as an escort. Another few days and she'd be able to peacefully live her life, helping dying people.

A thud brought her out of her reverie and Fate sat up in bed.

"Damn narrow couch!" Sounds of Caden gathering his pillow and blanket and rustling them on his makeshift bed drifted into her room.

She tried to hide her giggle by resting her head on her bent knees and wrapping her arms around her knees to muffle the sound.

"Don't laugh, damn it. I'm too long for this thing."

"You're too long for my bed too." She shot back then clapped her hand over her mouth. God, it sounded like she'd encouraged him to sleep with her.

"Is that an invitation?" His low voice carried easily through the apartment.

"No, it's not. I'm just making an observation."

"And I'm making pretzels out of my legs. I need to think of something else." He'd returned to grumbling and rustling, to her relief. Even complaining, he kept an even temper. She sensed clean frustration, though she'd

~ ☾ ~

just added a simmering arousal. Fate straightened her own covers in preparation for lying down then leaned forward so he could hear her clearly.

"The couch cushions are removable. Why don't you put them on the floor and lie on them that way? Your feet will hang over but you'll be a little more comfortable."

"Great, I'll go from a bed of nails to a bed of thorns. More comfortable." A couple grumbles later combined with some movement and he sighed loudly. "I think this'll work. At least if I roll off the thing, I won't have as far to go."

Fate chuckled at his dry tone. "Night, Caden."

"Night, babe."

***

She loved the clear, crisp morning. Fate stretched a kink out of her neck and continued to stare at the blue sky out of her kitchen window as she poured a second cup of coffee, adding a dollop of flavored creamer then sipping. "Ahh. One more cup and I'll be sane."

"Speak for yourself. I don't think my back will recover." Caden grumped and approached the coffee maker with a gleam in his eye. "Is your coffee leaded?"

"Is there any other kind?" Fate grabbed an extra large mug from the cabinet above the coffee maker and thrust it into his hand. "If you need to shower or anything you have ten minutes before I have to leave."

He paused from lifting the now filled cup to his mouth, a frown settling over his features. "Leave? You're not going anywhere."

"I'm going to work. Like millions of other people in the world. Like you can if you'll let yourself."

He leaned against the counter, entirely too close for her comfort, and sipped his coffee. His eyes gleamed over the rim of the cup, studying her. Fate quelled the urge to squirm. She refused to give him the satisfaction.

~ ☾ ~

"What happened to the woman who agreed that the Guard couldn't get to you if you were being watched over by me or my men? What happened to the woman nearly killed the other day, by a Guard no less?"

She turned away and busied herself with going through a dish of apples on her countertop. After choosing one Fate took a healthy bite. It'd take a few minutes to chew and swallow, giving her plenty of time to formulate her answer. However, a glance at Caden's wide grin stamped out any satisfaction in her delaying tactic. She hastily swallowed her bite and snarled, "Stay out of my head, damn it!"

"How can I avoid it when you broadcast so strong?"

"Only to you! I don't have this much trouble with Selene, and she's our matriarch."

Caden reached around her and cupped his hand around her shoulder. He maneuvered her past the counter into her smaller dining area and pulled out a chair for her. As he did Fate received an image of herself in front of the kitchen window. Then a projectile, blurred by speed, or maybe her vision, sped toward her. As a man's hand reached out, Caden's hand, she toppled.

Somehow, she knew it wasn't a true premonitory vision, but what Caden feared would happen. She stared unseeingly for a moment then focused her vision on him as she sank into the chair he held for her. "Why is this happening? How can I read your mind?"

He pulled the second chair from around the table close and sank down on it, his knee brushing against her thigh. Fate sensed tension in him, a mirror tightness to her own. Why did this man have such an impact on her?

"I think we're connected somehow. I don't know what your position is in the Maidens." He raised a hand to stall her when she started to respond, "It's okay. You don't have to divulge the secrets of the Maidenhood." A

~ ☾ ~

grimace passed over his face at the misspoken term. "Damn, you *would* have to have a vow of chastity."

"Not chastity. Just no emotional involvement."

Where did that come from? She'd pretty much just admitted her interest in him on a physical level. Hell, she was interested on a microscopic level right now.

His eyes darkened to a deeper hue. Warmth seeped into her stomach and sank to her groin. She quelled the urge to moan. She drifted toward him, her eyes on his mouth. What would it be like to taste that full lower lip?

"No, not yet. Damn it, Fate. Not until we figure this out."

She cupped his chin and stepped closer. Even as she lifted her head toward him, she realized what her actions were revealing, both to her and him. Gasping, she jerked away from Caden as if burned.

"Problem?"

"No." She watched as he drew in a breath, as if pulling her scent into him. Heat flowed through her.

He took her hand and brought it to his face. "You smell good."

"Thanks." A vision flashed, one of them naked, on her bed.

"You said we couldn't." Her voice held a slight rasp as she forced the words. He nuzzled her hand a moment more. The texture of his lips smooth against her palm. The warmth of his breath intoxicated her. He dropped her hand to his knee, covering his jean clad leg with her hand then rested his on top. The rough denim stretched tight on his knee, encasing his skin. What would it feel like to touch him, minus the clothing?

"I think—" He cleared his throat. "I think we're connected on a level that the others aren't."

"I guess it makes sense, since we both train to communicate psychically."

"Maybe. Maybe because our psi abilities are similar.

~ ☾ ~

Hell, we may have equivalent brain paths or something. Or, maybe it's because I want to get into your pants." He finished on a mutter. Fate chuckled and wiggled her fingers in response to his mention.

"Don't do that."

"What?" She moved her fingers again. He squeezed her hand in retaliation, as if that would stop her. He leaned forward to capture her lips then stopped.

"Why'd you stop?"

"Because if we do this, I might not be able to stop."

She sent a vision of her own, one of her accepting his kisses, and more.

"Fate." He started to withdraw his hand only to halt when she squeezed his knee lightly.

"I'm sorry. Go on. What do you think?"

"I think that, no matter why we have this connection, we need to take advantage of it. Use it to keep you safe."

Fate leaned away, not out of reach but distancing herself anyway. Darker scenes quickly eclipsed the playful ones she'd envisioned.

"If we don't use every tool we have, you might not come out of this, babe."

She nodded and with a gusty sigh slid her hand out from under his. "I wonder what Selene's going to think of this. Of us."

Caden grimaced. "Why don't we keep it between us for now? I know exactly what Donan will say. We're too close, or more to the fact, *I'm* too close to the situation."

"You mean someone else may be assigned to me?"

"Yeah."

She shook her head, "Okay, we'll keep it quiet for the time being. But Selene is powerful, she may pick up on the connection anyway."

"Donan too."

"And I get to work, right?"

Caden shook his head, "Remember, if you work you

~ ☾ ~

put your patients, coworkers, and everyone you come into contact with at risk." At her muted cry, he continued, ruthless. "You know they won't care if they take extra souls while gunning for yours. The only way to get around it is to stay out of the line of fire. I know you fulfill your calling through your job, and I know you want to care for the souls of the dying. But we need to make sure the living are taken care of, too."

"You're right. I get tunnel vision about my job sometimes." She sat for a minute, then rose and walked to the cordless phone mount. A quick moment later Fate breathed a sigh of relief as she managed to get an emergency leave of absence. While she answered questions and dodged issues she watched Caden watch her,

She finally dropped the phone on the counter and propped her elbows on the surface then her chin on her hands. "Great. Now, I'll probably lose my job."

"They didn't believe the sick relative gig?" He advanced on her.

"Nope. I don't think I'm a good liar." She pouted as she stared morosely into the dining area. Caden moved beside her and caged her in with his arms extended, her bottom nestled in against his groin. She felt his erection against her, increasing her tension.

He leaned over her, his mouth brushing the silky blonde hair that covered her ear. "What are we going to do to fill the rest of the day?"

She turned her head slightly, offering the line of her cheek for exploration. He brushed his lips along her skin and turned her toward him. He tilted her up and brought her front flush against his, more even with his hard-on. She squirmed against him, making him groan and bring the other hand up to draw her closer with no room to spare.

"I thought you said we needed to wait."

~ ☾ ~

"I lied."

Fate lifted her hands and found the thick black hair at the nape of his neck. The elastic band he used to keep the shoulder-length strands pulled away from his strong face ended up on the floor with a simple tug and she sank her fingers in the warm, sleek black strands that fell forward. She watched as he lowered his head, his eyes glittering with intent. Her eyes drifted closed as the warmth of his breath drifted across her mouth then everything disappeared. She tasted coffee blended with something sweeter and spicier than she'd ever tasted.

Fate put everything she'd ever hoped for in that kiss, tightening her hold on him. She floated above the ground, yet she felt more grounded than she'd ever been.

His mouth opened over hers and she responded in kind, accepting the firm yet gentle thrust of his tongue with a glide of her own along the underside of his. She felt his shudder before he lifted her against his erection and she sighed into his mouth.

How much time passed before she noticed the phone ringing, she didn't know, or particularly care. He eased his mouth from hers, returning again and again for steadily lighter kisses against her now tender lips. Fate opened her eyes, stared into his until he cursed.

"Damn it. I have to get this. It might be Donan."

He lowered her until her feet touched the floor and lightened his touch so she could step back and put a couple inches' space between them. When Fate tried to step out of his arms, though, he stepped forward, bringing her back in contact with the counter. She eyed him as he reached into his jeans pocket and extracted a cell phone, now silent. He punched a few numbers, waited then greeted his coworker.

"Yeah. I remember. I'll be there in about twenty minutes. Yeah, do that." He flipped the phone closed

~ ☾ ~

then returned it to his pocket. "I gotta go."

"Okay." So much for her liberating thoughts of going for it, as Janette suggested.

"Are you wearing that or do you want to change before we leave?"

"Change? I'm not going with you."

He stepped forward, erasing the slight space between them. Caden took her chin in his hand and stared into her eyes. "Honey, til we stop the Guards' attacks on you, you're going everywhere I go and vice versa. Now that I've got a taste of you, I'm not letting you out of my sight until I get more." A hard kiss punctuated his words and he patted her butt. "Now, do you want to wear your jeans and t shirt or something else? We're going to my office."

"So, it's not safe at my job, but it is yours?"

"It is when I have two Soldiers on staff, as well as a hell of a lot of security measures your place doesn't. Now, clothes?"

~ ☾ ~

Chapter Eight

Fate took Caden's office staff by storm. Everyone, from his taciturn secretary who thought all women that showed up at his office were sluts, to the other security employees, all smiled and followed her around like little dogs. Caden growled an answer in response to his client's question. A business system wasn't the most complicated system to install, but this client, a software designer, wanted the most up to date technology available. So that tied Caden up with him. Fate stayed in the other office with Jake. His best buddy. Ex Special Forces, martial arts expert and ladies man.

Caden heaved a sigh as Zimmerman glanced at his cell phone, which beeped again for the third time in a minute. "I have to go, Mr. Greene, but I'm pleased. When can you start installation?"

"I'll have some men at your office building tomorrow morning. You understand the installation will take several days, right?"

"I don't care. I want the building as tight as possible. I've had too many formulas stolen over the years. I won't take chances with something this valuable." Zimmerman patted the briefcase that remained tucked between his foot and the leg of his chair the entire meeting.

For an instant Caden wondered what could be so important, and then he heard the trill of Fate's laughter. "Yeah, some things are worth any price. I'll show you out."

Zimmerman muttered something, his attention on

~ ☾ ~

the cell phone. Caden mentally shook his head. *No wonder the guy got stiffed, he doesn't know the world revolves when he gets into his computers.*

Caden finally got the client ushered out of the office. The entire way he attuned to Fate's movements in the building. Though she remained in an inner office for security reasons, he felt the pleasant buzz that kept his erection at half-mast. The little minx didn't have a clue of her allure.

But he would show her.

He made himself return to his own office and make a few calls concerning the Zimmerman project, instead of hustling Fate from the office and out of range of Jake's flirtations. The man could be dangerous to females if let loose.

Caden spent a second remonstrating himself at the thought of taking a virginal Maiden as a lover, even for a brief time. Used to scratching his itch if he desired, he'd never encountered such a temptation with a woman like Fate. When Donan learned of the liaison, and he would, fur would fly. Donan rarely warned a Soldier about lovers, but Fate remained off limits. But damn, she'd be worth it. The mild sense of disquiet from earlier in the morning reared its head again. He'd assured Donan, and himself, that he could handle the situation professionally. Yet she'd gotten under his skin in less time than it took to cool down from a workout.

He finally gave himself permission to retrieve her and as he headed back into the bowels of the building, he twisted to stretch a kink in his back. He needed to find another sleeping arrangement. He discarded the notion of the couch, and her bed wouldn't accommodate both of them, unless she slept on top of him. He grinned. A standard double bed could be a good thing, after all.

At his entrance, Fate turned away from Jake and leveled a glare on Caden.

~ ☾ ~

"What?"

"My bed?" she gritted out, her face flaming.

His grin widened and he shot a glance over her shoulder at his friend and coworker. Though Jake wasn't picking up on the psychic connection, he sure got the vibes. His shit-eating grin told Caden he'd figured out that some inner conversation took place.

"You sure you want to have this conversation here, babe?"

"I don't mind." Jake's grin widened then disappeared as Fate turned her frown on him. "What? I didn't say anything."

"You didn't have to." She huffed and marched past Caden toward the hallway, grumbling. Jake chuckled as they heard isolated curse words and the odd "pig" and "men".

"You found a firecracker this time, buddy." Jake crossed his arms and settled back on his heels in satisfaction.

"Yeah. Who knew?" Caden murmured as he watched Fate plop down on a chair in an empty office at the end of the hall. She stayed away from open doorways and public spaces. Good girl.

He realized Jake continued the conversation without him and tried to pick up the stream. "Pass that by me again."

Jake laughed then sobered quickly. "You better scratch, buddy. You need a clear head, from what Donan said."

Caden nearly snapped at his friend until he realized Jake got it right. He was off his game. "I guess I need to—"

"Like I said, scratch that itch. If not with her, some other lady. You aren't on your best game. Do you want me to cover her security?"

"No." Caden stopped the thought before it could be

~ ☾ ~

uttered. He couldn't let anyone else near her, it just wasn't possible. "I'll take care of it."

"Of everything?" Jake pressed.

"Yeah, of everything," Caden growled in return. Having other psychics around could be damned irritating.

He picked up some supplies from storage, retrieved Fate, still ruffled and stiff, and ushered her out of the building and into his truck. He stowed the supplies in the toolbox attached to the bed of the trunk, scanned the area for a presence and climbed in beside her.

She sat with her face turned from him for a good ten minutes before apparently deciding she wanted to finish the argument. "What makes you think I'll let you share my bed?"

"Honey, with the thoughts that have been running through my head and what little I've picked up from you, we're not only going to share the bed, we're going to burn it up."

"Hmmph. I still have a say, you know. I don' t have to follow my libido."

He chuckled at the pout combined with scarlet cheeks she presented as she realized she'd admitted her attraction wasn't a one-time thing. She didn't look him in the eye but stared straight ahead.

He let her stew a few more minutes before quietly continuing the conversation. "Is there a problem with having sex with me?"

Fate sighed. "You won't let this die, will you? Is there someone in my life? No."

"No, I didn't mean that. I know your vows are similar to ours, no emotional involvement. I meant, are you, uh, against sex? With me?"

She arched an eyebrow at the sudden hesitation in his voice. "Insecurity? From the almost superhero Caden Greene? If I had a problem with sex with you, would I be

~ ☾ ~

sending the signals you've obviously picked up?"

He grinned, his clenched jaw relaxing. "I wanted to be sure. It'll actually be better if we have sex, you know."

"It will? This I have to hear."

"We'll be together twenty-four seven for the duration. And if we don't get rid of the tension—"

He stopped when she snorted in an effort to hide her laughter. "You really think that argument will fly with Donan and Selene? We're going to be in such deep stuff when they find out."

His grin widened. He shot a hand out and clasped her knee for a squeeze. Yep, she'd said *when* they found out, not if. She accepted they'd have sex. If the gleam in her eyes told him anything, it told him they'd have a lot of the stuff. .

***

By the time they got to the apartment Caden's hand rested near the top of her thigh and hers covered his, preventing it from traveling any farther north. A truck wasn't her idea of a romantic tryst, she argued and he reluctantly gave in, though he didn't move his hand. The warmth kept her mind on the evening ahead. While her body definitely prepared for the events to come, her mind whirled with the possibilities.

She revisited Selene's warnings about the Soldiers. But wasn't it by Selene's directive that she traveled with Caden now? Selene knew they'd be in close contact for the duration of his protective services. As the truck moved farther away from Caden's office Fate wondered at her newfound emotions. Caden managed to evoke feelings in her she'd never dreamed. And if his own heated glances were any indication, he dealt with his own issues.

The parking spaces near her building were full when they arrived at the apartment. Most of the neighborhood parked anywhere they could find a blank spot and

~ ☾ ~

unfortunately, there were no spaces near the building. Caden circled the block before finding a space near the rear of the building but still a small hike away.

"Don't you have assigned parking or something?" He asked as he opened her door.

Fate followed him to the rear of the truck and watched as he extracted what looked like a sleeping bag and a smaller duffle from the tool chest. "No. The house just has the two apartments, the owner's and mine. He has his car and his wife's, plus one that they keep for their son, I think. They take up the driveway, so I usually try to find a space on the street. Sometimes, I'm lucky. Sometimes, like today, I have to walk."

Caden started toward the building with his hand resting on her lower back. Fate walked quietly beside him, aware of his constant vigilance. He strode alongside her, matching her step, but she noted that he'd put her on the inside of the cracked sidewalk again, preferring to walk on the street side. And his eyes constantly scanned the surroundings. She mentally listed the security errors in the area. Not enough streetlights, too many shrubs, and trees blocking eye level view of the houses' entrances. She hadn't thought of the lack of security any more than any of her friends. Now, every shadow made a potential hiding place.

She sent out feelers in an effort to try to pick up on the surge of evil she'd felt before the other attacks. Nothing came through clearly, but a vague sense of unease washed over her. She shivered and Caden glanced down at her, his hand momentarily pressing into her back before dropping to his side.

"Feel anything?" he muttered.

"Not really, just a fuzzy something. Nothing like before." She heaved a sigh of relief as the rear of the house came into view. They'd have to go around to the front, considering the fenced in yard of the house next door.

~ ☾ ~

Caden's steady pace belied his need to get there too. For once, the sexual tension that seemed to run through his every thought and action with her became subjugated by his need to protect. Did he have more at stake this time or did the Soldier perform with this much intensity all the time? *Does he know more than he's telling me?*

They entered the house without any other problem, though Fate remained tense. Caden's smooth movements covered something, a stiffness that hadn't been there all morning.

She unlocked the apartment door, refusing to turn the key over to him. She did let him enter first. She might be stubborn, but she wasn't foolish. At least with her safety, she mused as she eyed his jean covered rear disappear around the corner and up the small flight of stairs leading to her living room.

"All clear." He came down to greet her and grinned slightly. "I like your ass, too."

"Smart aleck." She adjusted her purse on her shoulder and went past him and into the living room and tossed her bag onto the sofa. "Do you want some coffee?"

After a short moment he followed her into the tiny kitchen and crowded her up against the counter. "I don't want coffee. Or tea. Or a soda. Or beer. I want you."

"But I thought we'd talk or something." She stared at his chest, opting not to look into the eyes that could convince her of anything at that point.

"We can talk anytime." He lowered his head and nuzzled her neck.

Fate tried to tamp down the moan his lips brought forth but ended up sighing audibly instead. "So, no talking?"

"No talking." He tilted her face up with a finger and closed his lips over hers. Though light at first, the

~ ☾ ~

pressure increased as she sighed her satisfaction into his mouth. Then he grabbed her and pulled her into him, making her aware of his arousal. His tongue invaded her mouth with a sure thrust and she answered with a glide of her own along the underside of his. Caden's shudder convinced her of her actions and she closed her mouth on his tongue and gave a pulsing suckle as he began thrusting in a promise of things to come.

She came up for breath only when he reared back and murmured, "I thought you didn't put coffee on."

"I didn't." She went in search of his hot spots and nuzzled into the hollow of his throat.

"Then what's that smell?" His voice lost the husk that kissing her elicited and he stepped away from her.

Fate looked up at him in confusion then sniffed. Something drifted in the air, something burning. She turned and inspected the stove then inspected behind the range itself and refrigerator.

"I'll check the living room, you get the bedroom," Caden headed into the rest of the apartment and Fate scurried to the bedroom. All the while her head spun with the possible shortcomings of an old house's electrical wiring.

A quick inspection, using eyes, nose, and even a hand pausing at the wall of an outlet didn't uncover any suspicious warmth or smoke. Still the smell of burnt paper and a faint stench of scorched plastic remained. Caden stalked into the bedroom where she stood puzzling over the smell and gestured toward her closet. "Get a couple outfits. We're going to go downstairs and check out the rest of the house, just in case."

"I'm sure it's someone burning something in the neighborhood, maybe a trash fire or something." She couldn't bear the thought of her books, her mementos going up in flames.

"Maybe, but just in case, grab something, okay

~ ☾ ~

honey?" He nodded to the closet.

A spurt of warmth went through her at the nickname, but she went to follow his directions. She couldn't think about what she plucked from the closet, just of what remained. She shoved the few items in her hands into a canvas bag and zipped it closed as she hurried from the room and into the main area of the apartment. She eyed the stuffed bookcases that lined her walls. Was it foolish to pray for inanimate objects' safety?

"It'll be okay, honey. Let's go." Caden grabbed her bag and tucked it under his arm, along with his own carry all and the sleeping bag. With his other hand, he gathered her to his side and urged her into the stairwell.

***

The smell became stronger as they descended and Fate reached out a hand to trail against the wall of the stairwell. "It's not hot or even warm. Surely, there's not a fire."

"It may be the wiring." They stepped outside into the dusk of evening.

"Do you know your landlord?" Caden surveyed the area as he led her toward the front of the building.

"Not really. We just exchange pleasantries when I give him my rent check. I've met his wife, but not his son."

"Okay, we'll play it by ear." He ignored the doorbell and opted to open the dented aluminum storm door then bang on the solid door. When Fate raised her hand to press the bell he shook his head. "It might be a short in the wiring, remember? We don't want to trigger any more connections than we have to."

"Oh. Should I have unplugged all the electrical appliances?" She glanced back toward her door.

"Probably. But we don't want to go back in until we check out the bottom floor." Caden's words drifted into the opening door.

~ ☾ ~

A short, plump man in a t-shirt that strained over his paunch squinted at Fate and then Caden. "Ms. Halligan? Is there a problem?"

"Yes, Mr. Webster. We caught a whiff of something burning in my apartment and in the stairwell. There's nothing obvious, but we wanted to check down here."

"I don't think so. Hold on." He turned slightly and yelled, "Mary? Did you put something in the oven?" A faint no returned and he shrugged, "We haven't smelled anything in here."

Caden shifted. "The smell seemed heavier in the stairwell. Is there another room that's adjacent to that area?"

"Yeah, our laundry room, but no one goes in there but me and the wife." Webster glanced over his shoulder again. "Come on in. I'll check it. You didn't call the fire department, did you?"

"Not yet." Caden held the door open for Fate and then followed her and the landlord down the hall toward a closed door.

"Don't. I don't want anything added to my fire insurance payments."

Fate slowed and put a steadying hand on Caden's arm. "He doesn't mean to be inconsiderate."

"No, he just wants to save a buck." He muttered under his breath. "This place is a death trap."

"I love it. It has character."

"Well, the character is smoking right now."

When Webster opened the door, they found their answer. A smoldering bucket of rags lay in the area between the washer and dryer and as Caden approached it, the smolder became a flame. He opened a bottle of fabric softener and dumped the contents over the flame. Though the fire extinguished, the resulting stench wasn't much better than the smell from the original flame.

~ ☾ ~

Fate stood near Caden as he straightened from inspecting the bucket to find a woman slightly taller and heavier than Webster staring over his shoulder. "What happened?"

"Did you bring that bucket in here?" Webster uttered in a thin voice. Fate eyed the couple. The man didn't recognize the bucket.

"No. Have you started smoking again?" His wife glared at him. "If you did this, you clean it up."

"I'm not smoking." He looked at Caden. "We just got home. Haven't been here an hour. I don't know about Mary, but I haven't been in the laundry room in days."

"I washed a load a couple days ago, but not since." His wife just looked confused and a little miffed that she'd have to clean.

"Caden." Fate tried to keep her voice even and calm, but the surge of unease threatened to empty her stomach.

"I know, baby. I'll call Jake." He stood and gestured toward the plastic bucket. "It isn't familiar to either of you?"

The couple shook their heads and Caden gave a single nod of his own. "Then we need to call the police. I think someone broke into your house and deliberately set this."

He made short work of securing the room as Fate stood by. The wife wanted to clean the room and Fate thought he'd have to bodily force her out when her husband actually drew her into his arms and told her no one cared if his undershorts were on top of the dryer, unfolded.

Fate sat on the Webster's sofa, trying to blend into the floral design when the police arrived. A sick feeling washed over her as she realized the slightly odd but perfectly nice couple might have lost their home because of someone's hatred toward her. She turned her key over

~ ☾ ~

to the patrolmen and allowed them to inspect her apartment, content for once to let someone besides Caden take the lead.

Caden managed to take charge of the whole scene. Webster, the police officers, even the Fire Marshal looked to him as the authority. He quietly led them into the laundry room, explained the drenched bucket and then the tale of smelling the smoke before the fire worsened. Apparently, the combination of the plastic bucket, a paper bag crammed into the bucket, along with rags and other items and an opened vent alerted them. The fire smoldering in the plastic sent a strong scent into the air and the vent carried into the stairwell, then into Fate's apartment.

"After the house is aired out the smell should go away. Maybe wash the curtains or some other fabrics. No reason to evacuate." The Fire Department official smiled at Fate and Mrs. Webster, who now perched beside her.

"And the front door?" Caden asked the police detective standing near the outside of the group.

"It looks jimmied, just like you said." The detective, whose name Fate hadn't caught, eyed Caden. "Who did you say you were?"

"I'm Ms. Halligan's boyfriend."

Fate didn't dare meet anyone's eyes, but evidently the detective accepted the statement at face value. He turned to Mr. Webster. "And your insurance on the house, Mr. Webster?"

Webster bristled at the implication that he may have set the fire himself. "I can get the policy out of the lock box, but it's not even close to being enough to cover replacing this house."

"We got the policy when we first bought the house, for as little as we could afford with the mortgage." Mrs. Webster added. "We meant to upgrade as the house

~ ☾ ~

went up in value but didn't. And Fred's right. We depend on Ms. Halligan's rent to help out with expenses. There's no reason we'd burn down the house we live in, not to mention our rental."

The detective jotted notes in his book and asked Mr. Webster for a copy of the insurance form. He asked a cursory question about the son and dismissed him when the couple mentioned he attended a college out of town and hadn't been home for a visit in over three weeks. Fate observed when the police officer's suspicion turned from anyone in the room. She sighed with relief. How could she explain to him that she knew the culprit's identity and it wasn't anyone here? Or anyone that knew her or the Websters? Someone wanted her dead for the sake of her powers, the very thing she couldn't reveal to the policeman.

An hour later she sat in Caden's truck again, heading into the night. He hadn't told her where they were going, but it didn't matter. Until she found the man or men who wanted her dead and eliminated them, her life wouldn't be the same.

***

Caden swore again as he swerved into the passing lane of the interstate. *Damn Zimmerman's hide! If he'd take his nose out of the computerized world he lived in once in a while, he'd be aware of the everyday world.*

Zimmerman's account, while not complicated, required his personal attention. After the danger he'd perceived the night before, he'd not been willing to risk more exposure for Fate, so he'd called in Jake to watch over her at the cabin while he dealt with the client.

"Way too much time to spend on a cover." He muttered as he moved back into the right lane of the freeway and put his turn signal on. He glanced into the rear view mirror. No evidence of any one following him, no psychic warnings. Hopefully, the Guard hadn't

~ ☾ ~

picked up on the fact Fate rested under his wing now. But how long did he have before they found out and started their attacks again?

He'd sweat bullets all the way to his country cabin last night. The one place he could go to for peace and quiet. He'd chosen the most secure, peaceful place he'd ever known and the one place he could bring Fate and know she'd be okay. By the time they arrived, she'd fallen asleep, her face pale with fatigue. She hadn't stirred when he carried her in and put her in the spare bedroom. He, on the other hand, laid awake in his bed, all too aware of her presence in the other room.

The cabin, isolated in the woods and a perfect hiding place, would be difficult enough to find on a country lane that he believed it safe enough for her.

Dusk fell as he pulled the truck behind the snug cabin. A light shone in the main room and a faint whiff of wood smoke hinted at the presence of a fire in the large hearth. As he climbed the steps, he readied himself to comfort Fate. She must have been frightened of being up here without him. Her laughter caught him as he walked into the living room. A golden light surrounded her as she leaned toward Jake and patted him on the arm. Her perch on a pillow in front of the fireplace fit her. The light from the fire made her hair glisten with golden glints. Jake put his hand on top of the one resting on his arm.

Caden stepped forward. "Having fun?"

She popped up and almost ran to him. "This place is wonderful! Did you know I saw a deer in the back yard? She's beautiful, and her eyes—"

"I get it, honey. So, you haven't been afraid?" He glanced down at her uplifted face, aching. He shouldn't have emotions toward her beyond the obvious desire to protect her.

"Jake's here. I figured you wouldn't have left if I

~ ☾ ~

wasn't safe. I'm right, too, aren't' I?" She smiled and, taking his hand, pulled him into the circle of light she'd created in the large open room. He eyed his best friend, slouched on the floor, his back resting on a propped pillow and his legs crossed at the ankles in front of him.

Jake stood from his slouch and plucked his denim jacket from its drape on the chair. As he headed for the outer door he tossed over his shoulder, "I checked everything out every hour. No signs of disturbance, no ripples, nothing. I think you're in the clear, so far."

"Thanks, Jake. I'll call in tomorrow morning but otherwise, I'm not available."

Jake grinned. "Gotcha. If Zimmerman cries wolf again, I'll sic Brenda on him. I'll give the exterior one more sweep before I head out. Call if you need anything."

Caden released Fate's hand reluctantly to lock the door. With Jake outside doing his thing and the house as secure as he could get it, his attention turned to Fate. He meant to take advantage of the extra time he'd been granted. He turned toward the fireplace only to find her cushion empty.

"Do you want some coffee? Or I found some cocoa mix in the cabinets."

Caden turned toward the kitchen area. Fate held up a box of hot chocolate packets in demonstration, making him smile. "You always cook when you get nervous?"

"No, only with you, apparently." She lowered the box with a huff then headed back to the nest she'd created. As she plopped down on the cushion she frowned up at him. "You know, it's pretty frustrating when I can't put on airs with you."

"What'd I do now?" He tossed another cushion from the nearby sofa onto the one Jake abandoned and lowered himself beside her.

"Only read my mind every ten minutes. Stop it now or

~ ☾ ~

I'm going mind diving, too."

"Honey, I didn't read your mind that time. You were broadcasting in an entirely different way."

"Huh?"

God, a confused woman shouldn't look so adorable.

"You blush, you fidget," he reached out and stilled her hand as it fiddled with the corner of the cushion as she lounged. "You have a look," his hand drifted up her arm to her face and cupped her cheek, "like you want me to do this," he nipped at her lips, "but afraid I'll do it at the same time."

He used as much control as he could ever remember when he kissed her. He wanted to devour her, to sink into her in so many ways. He'd really scare her off if he did exactly what he wanted to do to her.

She answered his kiss as she'd responded before, with a shy but sure stroke of her tongue followed by slight suction that almost did him in. Caden shifted closer, his erection in search of the softness of her lower body. He reached out and pulled her onto him, finally cradling his erection against her groin.

A sigh followed by a slight groan signaled her acceptance, her participation. He allowed himself the luxury of tasting her skin along her jaw and down the curve of her neck. The urge to mark her, to tell everyone she was his overwhelmed him. He nipped the curve leading from her neck to her shoulder hard enough to elicit a gasp. In apology, he laved the area with his tongue, repeating the process until she arched into him.

"Caden." His name contained her breathless plea and he answered it as his hand moved to the waistband of her sweater. As he delved underneath, he reminded himself to go slow, but when he felt the silken texture of her skin he couldn't do it. His hand found the clasp of her bra and finessed it open then followed the trail of cotton to the sweet curve of her breast. Answering the

~ ☾ ~

overwhelming need to feel more of her, all of her, he lay back on the cushions and pulled Fate on top of him.

She lay over him and it both flattened and plumped her breasts, filling his hand with the softest skin he could remember. As he explored her Caden found her mouth again, thrusting into the warm depths in a blatant imitation of his desire.

***

Fate didn't answer this time. She couldn't. The hand on her breast wasn't intrusive, far from it. She wanted to wrap her hand around his and push. Push his fingers down to her nipple and hold him against her until the ache disappeared. She wriggled, trying to find a better fit for his erection. If only her clothes would disappear.

"Stop." He gritted between his teeth as his head reared away from her mouth. .

She froze. He didn't want her?

"Oh, baby. You have no idea what you're doing, do you?" With ease that spoke of too much practice, he flipped them until she laid on the cushions with his body resting on hers. He thrust his hips in a single pulse, assuring her without words he did want her.

"I don't have a lot of—"

"Experience? Yeah, if you did, I'd explode. Lay still, let me do the work." He murmured against her lips before enveloping them again. She shivered at the thrill of having his tongue in her mouth again and held onto him with all her might.

His hand moved from her breast, creating a protest in the back of her throat. He lifted his mouth from hers long enough to comfort her with wordless murmurs as he unfastened her jeans and eased down the zipper. As he slipped his hand into her panties, he came back to her mouth again and again in small, quick, hot kisses.

When he parted her she caught her breath at the heat of his hand against her moist center. Her eyes drifted

~ ☾ ~

closed at the sensation. Then he moved his fingers. He'd found the one point on her body that needed the most touch and he created a firestorm in her with a glide of his hand.

She clutched at him as feelings she wasn't ready for took over, flinging her spirit about the world. She needed an anchor. Her eyes snapped open, darted about in search of something to hold on to. She found it in his gaze.

His eyes, dark and gleaming, watched as she flew apart at his caresses. Fate cried out and raised her head in search of him. He answered with a sharp, full kiss, thrusting in time with his hand's movements, intensifying her crashing orgasm.

Fate broke the kiss from necessity, to breathe. But she buried her face in the curve of his neck and absorbed Caden's scent. Her heart began to calm and her breath to regulate as she held on to him.

Finally, he eased her away from him. In any other situation, she'd be terrified of the gleam in his eyes; he looked feral. She loosened her hold on him enough to reach for his belt, sure she could tame this beast.

Caden's animalistic grunt as she started to free his erection from his pants gave an indication of his arousal but he kept his senses about him long enough to ask, "Are you on the pill?"

Fate's hand stilled, "No."

There'd never been the need.

"Honey, there's a need now." He rolled from her, his hand draped over his eyes an indication of his tight hold on himself, as well as the other hand, fisted at his side.

"I'm sorry. I never—" she began.

"Never mind. I should have bought some condoms."

She smiled when the picture of him speeding down the highway flashed before her consciousness. He'd been in too big a hurry to see her to think of condoms. A

~ ☾ ~

flush of warmth spread through her. "You don't keep any here?"

He shifted the arm covering his eyes and looked at her. "I don't stay here all the time. Anything I leave here would be too old."

He drew his arm down and started to lever himself into a sitting position. Fate's hand stopped him. "That doesn't mean we can't do more, you know."

He smiled at her. "I know, but right now, if you touch me I'm going to go off like a bottle rocket."

"You underestimate yourself and me." She laughed.

He shook his head, and then continued. "I'll run out tomorrow morning and pick something up. Until then, lady, stay away from me."

Fate quelled a groan and instead giggled as he stood and stalked into the kitchen to start coffee. In comparison to the one awkward event in college, Caden's foreplay alone left her breathless and ready for more, soon.

~ ☾ ~

Chapter Nine

Fate sat on the floor, her knees drawn up and arms crossed over them. After over an hour of work, Caden still didn't look tired. A series of push-ups, followed by chin ups at a bar outside on the back porch, and then a sprint around the back yard apparently constituted only a warm up. He went through a series of movements similar to her physical conditioning for the Maidens, combined with more complex, martial arts moves.

"Do you do this every day?"

"If I can."

He didn't even have to catch his breath, darn him.

"For how long?"

"Three hours or so, if I can fit it in one session. If not, I get what I can in." He shrugged.

It paid off. He'd taken off his t-shirt when he started the last portion of his workout and a faint gleam of sweat covered his torso now. He had incredibly wide shoulders, firm pectorals and a six pack that all the athletes touted but on him, it equaled sex personified. Or it could be her mood, after her eye opening experience the night before.

Who would have guessed an orgasm could be that great? She'd never missed sex, the one experience in college being underwhelming, at best. Besides, since she knew she couldn't have a relationship it didn't seem important.

Now, she wanted it, and badly. If he didn't say something about getting the condoms, she'd tackle him for his car keys.

~ ☾ ~

Fate sighed against her knees and settled in for more entertainment.

A buzz interrupted Caden's movements and he walked to the towel he'd tossed onto the floor before starting his workout. Out of its depths he withdrew a cell phone and flipped it open. After a brief, "Greene", he went silent.

"Damn it, Donan. Isn't there anyone else?"

Fate let her amazement at his tone sift through her sexual daze. He talked to his mentor like that? She'd never been cross with Selene, at least verbally.

"Yeah, I'll be there. Listen, I need to make one call, then I'm on my way."

Caden closed the phone with a snap and turned to Fate. "I gotta go."

"I heard."

"I'll call Jake. He can be out here in forty minutes."

"I'll be okay by myself, you know." She really did feel safe here. There were no indications of danger anywhere, no shadows.

"Probably, but if something did happen, you'd also be here by yourself. Humor me, okay?" He crouched down in front of her and cupped her knee with his warm hand.

"Okay. Is it the Guard?"

He shook his head, "No indication. I'll find out when I get there. I don't know how long I'll be."

She nodded, and then stared at him. "Be careful."

He squeezed her knee and stood, then offered his hand to help her up. "Always. I have some things to bring home to you."

Caden cursed again, his attention focused on getting the drug dealer who'd decided to kill everyone who'd "done him" under control. As he pushed the elderly woman the punk targeted out of the line of fire he grunted an apology.

~ ☾ ~

What was the deal with this? Donan could have handled this with a trainee, for God's sake. A few evasive tactics until the cops arrived and nothing to it, drug punk up for another ten years for attempted murder. The fact that the old woman's soul needed protection warranted a Soldier's involvement, but not necessarily his.

He relaxed when the squad cars rolled in place. A quick scan of the area assured him the punk feared being sent up for life too much that he'd cave. Caden stayed for a couple more minutes then gently patted the old woman on the shoulder and let her know someone would take care of her.

He sprinted around the corner and headed toward his truck. He always managed to keep a low profile in his cases, both by using military tactics and occasionally some mild psychic suggestions to the witnesses and cops. The only drawback, the need to park at the back of the beyond to keep his license tag from being picked up.

He called Donan from the expressway on his way back to Fate. His mentor didn't bother saying hello, he just congratulated him on a job well done.

"Yeah, but I wasn't needed, Donan, and you know it."

"Maybe I required you for another task, a hidden one."

"Damn it, don't start spouting all that wax on-wax off crap."

Donan chuckled. "I'll watch it. You're going back to Fate?"

"Yeah." After he made one quick drugstore stop.

"Is she well?"

"She's fine, and well hidden. Any sign of movement?"

"Not yet, but there's a disturbance in the air. They're looking."

Caden took a different exit this time. He'd make his pit stop and then travel more country roads, choosing a

~ ☾ ~

different route to the cabin. That way, if anyone tried to pick up on his actions or his memory, he'd have more than one choice for them to make.

"I wondered how long it'd take for them to figure she'd been stashed."

A silence followed before Donan replied. "Take care Caden. You have a lot at stake."

"I'll protect her, you know that."

"I know you'll do your job, but at what cost?"

Donan disconnected after his last vague comment. Caden glanced at the cell phone as if it could issue some answers then flicked it closed. He knew his job. Protect Fate's soul at all costs. And in the meantime, he could cure himself of this obsession with her body.

***

Fate bent over and stretched her arms toward the ground, slowly curving her spine and resting her palms on the floor. She tried to concentrate on her position, head down and back stretching. She'd almost gotten the kinks out of her spine and achieved some level of relaxation when she heard a car door slam.

She jack-knifed her body into a standing position and winced at the twinge that resulted in her side. She padded in her bare feet toward the window at the end of the room and smiled as she watched Jake meet Caden at his truck. She'd sent the other Soldier outside on the pretext that she saw movement in the field, when in reality he'd been driving her nuts with his pacing the floor in boredom. A brief chat and Jake walked to his own truck and sped off, then Caden retrieved a small bag from the seat.

A pang of something hit her stomach. Fear? No. Anxiety? Yes. Was she ready for this?

Any other woman her age could have been married and possibly borne a child by now. But, for Fate, her path went a different direction. Now, a physical

~ ☾ ~

relationship presented itself. No, not relationship. A physical release. There could be nothing more.

Caden didn't enter the house at first. Rather, he circled the exterior of the house in ever widening circles until he came to the edge of the yard and the woods. Fate watched as he came into and went out of the range of the window, his patrol checking for footprints or other evidence of intruders. She put out psychic feelers. Nothing. Again. A pang of irritation went through her. As much as she loved the cabin and the idea of staying with Caden, when would the interruption of her life end?

She greeted him at the door. "Was it the Guard? Did you pick up anything about them out there? Are we going to stay holed up here or are we going to go out there after them?"

She would have continued asking questions if he hadn't put his hand over her mouth. She glared over his hand and tried to pull it down to no avail.

Caden looked her over before tossing the small drug store package on the kitchen counter and removing his jacket.

"It wasn't the Guard, just a routine job. Why all the questions?"

"I'm going nuts here. I'm done with all the waiting."

"You don't like the cabin?"

"I love the cabin, and any other time, I'd be happy to take a break from work and relax. But knowing I can't move without someone looking over my shoulder is just too much, Caden. We need to *do* something."

He strode to the fireplace and crouched down to stir it with a poker then added another log, stalling. After he rose and dusted his hands he glanced at her. "What do you suggest? Put out psychic feelers and announce where you are? I can't do that. I won't do that."

Fate pushed a hand through her hair before

~ ☾ ~

approaching him and dropping onto the sofa in front of the fire. "I don't know. I'm afraid of facing them, but I'm almost as afraid of having to hide for the rest of my life."

He joined her at the couch. He bent at the waist and propped his elbows on his knees then stared at his hands for a minute. Then he looked back at her. "We need to talk to Donan and Selene. Get them together. Maybe they know what's going on."

"You realize the only time they've been in the same room is when I stayed at your Refuge, right? With all the trouble between the Soldiers and Maidens, it would take a disaster for them to meet."

Caden shrugged, then continued in a hard voice. "Well, this time they need to meet to avoid the disaster. It's time to get over the historical crap."

His head panged in the next instant and Donan's voice drifted across his consciousness. *"Take care not to step beyond your boundaries, Soldier."*

Caden shook his head and answered his Mentor. *"I can't disregard the fact that the Guard are targeting a Maiden, and neither can you, Mentor. We need a plan beyond hiding her out. You know this, as must Selene."*

Donan's voice reflected a wry note as he continued. *"And we must meet, I agree. I will be at the cabin tomorrow afternoon. I trust your Maiden will contact her Guide?"*

Caden agreed and broke contact with Donan. This time, however, he made sure he erected a shield against his Mentor before continuing his conversation with Fate. As he built the wall he could feel Donan's chuckle. Hell, yeah, he wanted armor between them. Especially with his plans for the evening.

"Donan can be here tomorrow afternoon. Will you contact Selene?"

"I just did, or rather she contacted me." Fate grimaced. "She sounded more than angry. I almost felt

~ ☾ ~

like she might be intimidated, or fearful, which doesn't make sense. Anyway, she'll be here, too." She eyed Caden. "She suggested tomorrow afternoon. Think there's some connection there, too?"

So many factors. Connections. Maybe that was the issue, after all. Connections.

***

They ignored the package on the counter for the remainder of the evening. Caden helped Fate prepare supper, a chili that she'd managed to start before he arrived. As he set the table in the dining area, he studied her.

She might look like a fragile fairy or wood nymph but since they'd been thrown together, he'd learned of her strength. A steel core ran under the soft skin and feminine mannerisms she showed the world. As if to emphasize the fact she suddenly turned to him. "Would you teach me some of your combat moves?"

"Huh?"

"Your workout. It looked similar to one I do for the Society, but I'd like to learn more of the defensive moves. Would you teach me?"

"I don't know, Fate."

She'd unearthed a large bowl she called a soup tureen and dumped the chili into it, scoffing at his assurances that the stew wouldn't taste any different in the stoneware bowl than it did coming from its pot. She carried the bowl to the table and set it on a folded dishtowel. As she returned to the counter to retrieve a pitcher of something Caden didn't intend to drink she tossed over her shoulder. "If you don't want to train me, I can ask someone else. Jake is skilled too, isn't he?"

Caden intercepted her on her way to the table and plucked the pitcher out of her hands. He set it on the counter then backed her against it and bracketed her arms with his hands. "If anyone is going to teach you

~ ☾ ~

some moves, it'll be me, and you know it. Don't try to
play the jealousy card with me, babe. It won't work."

She eyed him from under her lashes, "I think it just
did."

And then, to his shock, broke his hold with an upward
thrust of her arms and retrieved the pitcher. As she
rounded him she grinned, "I do learn quickly, you
know."

She did indeed. After a meal of chili, crackers and
surprisingly tasty iced tea, Caden found himself in the
workout room of the cabin, putting her through some
paces. She only needed to be shown a move, didn't rush
to practice it as other novices would, but stared intently
at the slow motion movements he made. Then, after a
moment, she would move in front of the wide mirror
flanking the wall and execute the movement in near
perfection.

Caden showed her a series of defensive movements
designed to break holds and prevent attacks then moved
to offensive maneuvers. When he tried to get her to
imitate a carotid blow she refused. Exasperated, he
threw at her, "What do you expect to do when a Guard
attacks you with a knife, then?"

"I expect to be able to defend myself enough to get
away. I won't take a life, I won't expose a soul."

"You wouldn't be exposing the soul to danger, and
you know it. You'd be freeing a soul, cleansing its evil."
He advanced on her. "Now, do it."

With an expression of pure fury she countered his
strike with one of her own and then went for the carotid
blow. Caden barely blocked it with his hand to prevent
being rendered unconscious from lack of oxygen. He
stepped back, "Better. What brought that on?"

She glared at him. "You think I'm not familiar with
the evil in some men's souls? What do you think the
Maidens do, Caden? Hum pretty little songs while they

~ ☾ ~

accompany souls to white fluffy clouds? Sometimes we have to force a soul to the portal and they don't like it. They don't want to enter the portal when they've lived a lifetime stained with malevolence."

"You've done that?" He couldn't imagine her handling some of the wickedness he'd seen.

She pushed aside strands of hair that escaped her ponytail and sighed. "Not alone. I've only finished training for the next level. Actually, I've only done the puffy cloud jobs so far." The tone in her voice sounded wistful.

"And you *want* to do the job? It sounds foul to me."

"It can be, but if I don't deliver the soul, it remains in our world, disrupting us." She shook her head, "Never mind. Let's continue. What's next?"

He drew himself up and grinned. "Now we put it all together. I advance and you defend."

***

His expression reminded her of a wolf on the prowl, intent and a little frightening, but also exhilarating. Fate took her stance and tried to delve into his mind. His smile told her he'd felt her touch but she couldn't get past the wall he'd erected. A tickle touched her mind and she returned his grin with one of her own.

Two could play at that game.

She'd begun to relax when he surged forward and took her down with hard arms around her waist. Fate landed on the matted floor with a grunt, vaguely surprised she didn't lose her breath. She frowned, disgusted at her lapse in alertness. "I lose, huh?"

Caden's dark gaze gleamed and his hair framed the harsh lines of his face. "Not really. You trust me, I took advantage of it."

"But I let down my defenses,"

"You won't with a Guard. You sense when they're approaching and you'll be ready. Can you determine

~ ☾ ~

direction when you sense them?"

She shook her head, "I've never really tried. I didn't think I'd need to use that kind of skill."

"Maybe we need to try to hone it. We'll go out tomorrow morning and you can practice finding me."

She eyed him. He might be talking about training and honing her psychic skills, but his expression told her a different story. Not to mention the erection prodding her in the belly. She wriggled a bit in response, eliciting a flare in his eyes. Another nudge got her a thrust.

"You think I can enhance my powers?" She wasn't surprised at the husk in her voice. She didn't want to have this conversation, not now.

***

"You don't need to enhance them, just hone them. And yeah, I think we can." His voice trailed off as she licked dry lips. He lowered his head and took her mouth with his, giving her the thing she'd been missing all afternoon. The fiery connection between them became almost combustible at times. How could she have even thought she could control it?

He groaned and pulled back. "Damn it, Donan!"

He pushed away from her and wheeled away from the mirror and her. She slowly came to sitting and crossed her legs as she watched him battle with his superior, a little surprised Selene didn't eavesdrop on her, as well. She could imagine the inner conversation. Finally, Caden turned to her with an apology. "Sorry, babe."

"Not tonight, huh?"

"Not unless we want an audience. He got through the wall and warns me he'll be here all night. Until I can build another barrier, we're out of luck."

"Until?" She smiled.

He advanced and held out a hand to pull her up and gave her a quick kiss. "Until. And Donan be damned."

***

~ ☾ ~

Fate slept the night in fits and starts, interrupted by dreams of attacks and trying to defend herself and Caden. While it could be the result of the training, her constant vigilance and the ever-present thought of the Guard, could it be something more? A warning? She'd never experienced precognitive warnings, but with her powers surging, she wasn't sure she could trust them.

She'd finished her shower and dressed and headed toward the kitchen and coffee when Selene called her inner voice. *"Fate, you have an assignment."*

Fate's surprise brought her to a halt in the hallway. *"An assignment? You've decided to send me out?"*

"We can't continue running scared from the Guard."

Fate resumed walking to the kitchen, a surge of adrenaline running through her system. She might not need the caffeine pick-me-up now, but the rush would abate before she completed her assignment and she'd need the energy then. As she poured a cup of coffee, she continued with her conversation. *"So, we're putting me out there to see if I can draw out a Guard?"*

"No! I'm assigning you a job, just as I'd do in any other situation. You'll have a Latent go with you, as usual, and when you're finished, you'll return to the cabin and ready yourself for your meeting with me. We'll push the meeting back until tomorrow."

"And Donan," Fate inserted and smiled inwardly at the growl she felt from Selene. Something definitely brewed between the two elders. She glanced around the room. No sign of Caden. *"Can you send someone for me, Selene? I didn't bring my car and I don't think Caden is going to be too keen on the idea of me going on an assignment."*

"And you listen to the Soldier?" Selene's voice held almost a sneer.

"You had the idea of protection, remember." Fate shot back.

~ ☾ ~

Selene lessened her venom but agreed to send the Latent to pick up Fate. *"It will be close when you get to the soul's home, so don't delay."*

Fate sipped her coffee and searched for Caden in the house. What would the job hold? It would be her first real stand-alone assignment and she couldn't quell a jab of excitement, blended with some worry. She couldn't let the possibility of a Guard taint the experience, neither for her or the dying soul.

"Where are you?" she muttered and returned to the large open aired living room. As she finished the sentence she got a vision of Caden, his jean covered rear leaning over an opened hood of his truck. She grinned. He didn't realize he'd just broadcasted in response to her. So, her powers weren't the only ones needing some tweaking.

She shrugged into a light jacket and left the house. As she rounded the rear of the structure and neared the garage, he straightened. Wiping his hands on a rag, he eyed the coffee in her hand. "Didn't you bring me one?"

She offered him her mug and tucked her hands into the jacket pockets. "I've got an assignment. I'll be leaving in a few minutes."

His eyes flashed over the rim of the coffee cup before he lowered it. "The hell you are."

She stood her ground. "We've already discussed this. I can't keep hiding from the Guard. I'll have my Latent with me. Besides, if Selene thought I'd be going to be in danger, she wouldn't send me out on assignment."

He tossed the dirty rag he'd been holding to the ground near a trashcan and propped his hand on his hip. "I won't change your mind."

"No."

"Then I need to make sure the house is secure before we go." He thrust the cup back in her hand and rounded the hood of the truck. After he shut the hood, he

~ ☾ ~

returned to her and wrapped his arm around her waist and started toward the house.

"You're going?" No wonder he'd given up so easily.

"I'm going. It's the only way I can be sure you're okay." They entered the rear door and he started checking doors and windows, though she'd not touched any in the cool fall air. "How were you planning to get there without me? You left your car at your apartment."

"I have someone coming to get me."

"Then call her and have her meet you at the assignment, I'm taking you."

"I'll call her." She headed toward the phone in resignation.

Caden finally seemed to be satisfied that he'd secured the house and grounds. He hustled her out of the house and, before shutting the door, clicked a remote he returned to his jacket pocket. Fate sent a questioning glance toward his pocket. "It's a security system." He led her to the truck.

"I thought security systems used keypads. I didn't see one in the house."

"It's not in plain sight. And it's a new system, an experimental one that can be activated remotely."

"Has it been on since I've been there?"

"Yeah. It clears people leaving the house. Only alerts when someone enters." Caden started the ignition and put the truck into gear.

"So, when you or Jake entered?"

"We activated the remote."

"If I'd decided to take a walk?" She bristled at the thought of being a virtual prisoner.

"We would have turned it off." He glanced at her as he left the cabin's drive and entered the gravel road that led to the small county road. "Look, it's just another security measure. No big deal."

"Except that you didn't let me in on the fact that I've

~ ☾ ~

been a virtual prisoner in the house."

"You weren't a prisoner. We'd turn off the system when you left the house, or me for that matter. Just like this morning. I didn't think you'd care one way or the other."

She glared at him. "Well, think again. Next time you think you're going to make a decision about me, check with me first, okay? I'm finished with people manipulating me like I'm a chess piece."

Caden grinned at her. "Honey, the next time I manipulate you, you'll be in complete agreement."

***

The assignment took place at the home of a middle-aged couple. The wife and mother, deep into the rigors of cancer and chemotherapy, ceded her fight with the ravages of the disease. Janette linked with Fate on the way to the assignment and filled her in. Fate steeled herself as she thought of the two teenaged children and husband the vibrant woman would leave behind.

Caden, sensing her battle with her own emotions, didn't push her or try to link with her. Instead, he waited until they were almost at the address she'd given him before he asked about the assignment. After she filled him in, Fate added, "She's been in the hospital with a respiratory infection until last night. She wanted to come home to die."

He glanced at her. "Is it hard? Going into the homes and having the family around?"

She nodded, shoving her chilled hands into her jacket pockets. "I've done plenty of supervised jobs in the hospice and in a hospital setting, a few in the homes. Anytime the family is there, I have to watch what I say aloud, as well as my actions." She grimaced slightly before she continued, "You should know how hard it is to hide your talents from people."

He shrugged. "I'm usually not performing in front of

~ ☾ ~

bereaved family members. Besides, I use enough physical combat moves to mask the psychic moves."

They fell silent as they approached the house, a typical two story brick in a cul-de-sac subdivision. Janette moved from the car she'd parked at the edge of the driveway to greet Fate. Caden parked along the street, the truck facing the exit.

Fate started to open her door when Caden stopped her with a hand on her arm. Impatient to get started, she turned to let him know she'd watch herself when he surprised her. "You're going to give them a gift, you know. She deserves a peaceful death and you're going to help her do that."

She smiled her thanks and opened a portion of her mind to him. He smiled in return, assured she wouldn't be out of reach. As Fate exited the truck and approached Janette, she wondered why she'd thought to open a connection during her assignment. When the Maiden came in contact with the dying, only her Latent or supervisor also shared in the connection. To allow Caden even a sliver of light into her world at that time probably constituted a huge violation of the rules, but she didn't care. He'd put himself out there too many times to stay in the dark now.

"What's our way in?" Fate questioned Janette as she started toward the door.

"Your position with the hospice. You're a counselor and I got permission for you to go in and talk to her before she moves on. The husband is okay with it, but the kids are a little territorial. She has a lot of friends and they've been in and out of the house all day."

Fate nodded, "Nice for the friends and Carol, but not so nice for the family, huh."

"At least that's how the kids are seeing it right now. They'll probably be grateful for it later."

Fate didn't bother ringing the doorbell, but opened

~ ☾ ~

the door and entered, followed by Janette and Caden. The Latent glanced over her shoulder at Caden with a questioning look then toward Fate, but now wasn't the time to answer her questions. Later would have to do.

As she walked down the entrance hall, Fate could see into different rooms, all cluttered with people. Friends, family members, she assumed, as well as a knot of miserable looking teens, the kids' buddies.

While she'd dealt with groups of people in hospice and medical settings and a couple of private homes, this would be the first time she'd have to deal with a mass of people in a crowded home. She sent a plea out to Janette to assist with calming the visitors. The Latent did what she needed to do and any help in that quarter would be appreciated.

Unerringly, she found the bedroom where Carol lay, surrounded by her family and friends. Fate approached the friendly but haggard looking man nearest the bed. "I'm Fate Halligan from Weatherly Hospice."

He turned from watching his wife struggle to breathe and eyed her. "You wanted to be here, but I don't know why."

"I can help ease the way, sometimes. It's hard to explain, but my talking with your wife may give her some peace and, in a way, permission."

"To die?" His expression as he glanced back at his wife held love, pain and more. "I don't want her to go but she's not Carol, you know? She asked her friends not to come to the hospital a couple of days ago. And that's the last thing she'd ever do."

Fate touched his shoulder lightly. She couldn't touch him too much or she'd interfere with his grief, possibly pick up on his thoughts, intense as they were. "I *can* help."

He didn't say anything else, just nodded. Fate advanced to the other side of the bed and readied

~ ☾ ~

herself. She didn't bother looking for Janette or Caden. She knew where they were. The Latent stood quietly talking to a couple of teenagers, the girl's tearstained features so like those of the woman on the bed. Her brother stood at her side, his own face closed and hard, as if he were barely holding himself together.

Caden stood near the door, out of the way but near enough to intervene if danger approached the house. Fate picked up a message, faint and low, that he'd protect all those in the room, if necessary.

She glanced at Carol once more, taking in her features so she could communicate with her on a familiar level. What Fate really *saw* wasn't a physical being, but energy. Unfortunately, most people weren't secure in being a beam of light. When she introduced Carol to the portal, it would be the corporeal being.

Fate placed her hand on the colorful quilt that covered the hospital bed, near Carol's hand. She didn't have to have tangible contact, only proximity. Then she let her mind go into the depths of the woman's consciousness.

Nothing registered at first, though it wasn't surprising. She gently called Carol's name and began her search. As she'd expected, she found the woman standing near the edge of her consciousness, looking into the gloom beyond.

"Carol?"

Carol turned with a quizzical look. *"I'm dying?"*

Fate gave a mental nod and advanced slowly. *"You've fought a long time, now it's time to go."*

Carol glanced back toward the gloom beyond. *"Is that where I'm going?"*

Fate sent a smile to her. *"No, that's where you've been. You said goodbye to your children and husband?"*

Carol nodded, her eyes glistening. *"That's the only thing I worry about, you know? What will they do*

~ ☾ ~

without me? Will they remember me?"

"Yes. You were the laughter and joy in their lives, you'll be remembered and revered as a mother and wife should be. And as a friend." Fate read the woman as if she'd known her for a lifetime. She let her consciousness approach more. *"If you'll let me, I can help you find your way to the portal."*

"The portal? What's on the other side? And what if I don't like it?"

Fate let a trill of laughter blend into the silence. *"You have no worries on that score. What you have been on earth, the love you gave and the people you touched; that's made the journey a joyful one for you."*

Carol glided toward Fate, an expression of relief on her face. *"So, it'll be something besides a void? I always worried that there'd be nothing. Peace maybe, but nothing more."*

Fate couldn't lie to her. Not now. *"I don't know what's on the other side, but I do know that when you step through the portal a sense of joy will greet you and spill over to me on this side."* Then she shared what she'd never shared with anyone before. *"Sometimes, I want to walk into the portal with my charges, just to feel the joy they feel."*

Carol tilted her head. *"Can't you go and then come back?"*

"No. I have to stay on this side. I can only take you to the edge of the portal."

Carol cast one more glance over her shoulder into the gloom then turned toward a faint light in the distance. As she did, the glimmer of light brightened into a golden glow that bathed her face. She smiled and started walking ahead of Fate. As she did, her body began to dissolve until an almost imperceptible mass of energy remained. Fate accompanied her to the portal and stood as the opening appeared.

~ ☾ ~

Before she entered the opening, Carol seemed to turn back to Fate. *"Thank you. I didn't want to leave them but now, it's okay. Tell them I love them. And you're right, the joy is there."*

~ ☾ ~

Chapter Ten

Caden tried to make himself relax as he waited with the rest of the family. Janette now stood near him, her job done. Outwardly, the woman on the bed seemed to struggle to draw each breath. Her husband, silent and still, clutched her hand and a boy stood at his side, his head bowed. A young girl perched on the side of the bed near Fate, her body bent double as she nuzzled the woman's hand as it lay on the quilt.

Fate stood, her head bowed and still, her breath almost nil. She'd virtually disappeared for the friends and family that crowded into the room and Caden suspected it due to the power that emanated from her. He fairly vibrated with that energy.

Her competence wasn't in question. He just didn't know how he could let her go anywhere he couldn't follow.

The woman's breathing became more labored then suddenly quieted and Caden knew when Fate made it through. He'd been in the presence of people dying before, this passing held less struggle. Though the family would grieve and have a hard time adjusting to life without their loved one, they could keep the memory of a silent and peaceful death.

Fate's head lifted and she glided away from the bedside. As she neared him, Caden saw how the assignment drained her. Her skin, already pale, appeared translucent to the point he could see the pulse in her temples and neck. As he watched, dark circles appeared under her eyes. Yet, those blue eyes sparkled

~ ☾ ~

with satisfaction as she met his gaze. He reached out and enfolded her hand in his then led her from the room, ignoring the gasp Janette let escape as she followed.

They left the house, undisturbed by the dozen or so people that milled around quietly. He figured Fate continued to use some sort of masking power on them. He'd allow that until they got to the truck, then she would rest.

As they passed her car, Janette reached out toward Fate. Caden glared at her, and she pulled her hand back. She narrowed her eyes at him then turned her attention on Fate. "Selene instructed me to offer you my house for the night."

Fate turned her head toward the Latent, though Caden got the impression she didn't really see the other woman. "I'm going with Caden."

"But you need protection."

"And she'll get it." Caden interjected.

Janette's frustration came through even without a psychic touch. "She needs to be with her own kind now, to decompress before she sleeps."

Caden didn't bother looking to Fate for confirmation. "I'll take care of her. Tell Selene Fate will contact her when she wakes up."

He didn't wait but bundled Fate into the passenger side of the truck. As he clipped the seat belt around her she cast him a sleepy smile. "I did it."

"You sure did, baby. She had a peaceful death. The family will be grateful."

"There's so much joy, Caden. So much." Her voice trailed off as her eyes drifted shut. She slumped toward the center of the seat and he shut the passenger door then hurried to the other side. As he started the truck, he cursed the bucket seats. With a bench seat in the thing, he'd be able to hold her while she slept.

~ ☾ ~

He used one hand to drive and shift and the other to steady her on the way home. She stirred when he turned onto the gravel road to the cabin and looked around blearily. "Are we home already?"

Caden didn't recognize the spurt of warmth that ran through him at her words but he knew it wasn't something he planned or something that would be welcome in his world. But it felt good to hear her say home. "Almost, baby. Hold on a couple more minutes and you can sleep."

She murmured something and leaned her head against the passenger window.

Ten minutes later he lowered her to the bed in the master bedroom. He removed her jacket and shoes, and glanced at her clothes. The jeans and sweater were fine for day wear, but she'd be uncomfortable in them during the night. Or at least that's what he told himself as he unsnapped her jeans and lowered the zipper.

He tried to ignore the miniscule bikini panties as he peeled the pants off. He tossed them to the floor then turned toward her. She'd turned onto her side, presenting him with her round ass. He stifled a groan at the sight. He couldn't do anything about it tonight, but damn, he wanted to hold those cheeks as he thrust inside her.

He gently returned her to her back and shoved both the cotton blouse and sweater over her head in one sweep. She muttered but turned on her side again. Her matching bra and panties were appealing, but oddly, the blue ankle socks she wore tugged at his heart. She looked utterly feminine in the underwear, but vulnerable in the socks.

He maneuvered her under the covers then wiped the sweat from his forehead. It wasn't the work, but that damned bra, panties and socks did him in. As he left the bedroom to check the house, he adjusted his pants

~ ☾ ~

around his erection and cursed.

So much for the condoms.

***

Fate wasn't aware of waking up in the night, just being fast asleep one moment and the next, she stared into a dark tan sea of skin. She blinked in the predawn dimness, trying to put together the last few hours.

She remembered the assignment and looking up at Caden after she'd finished. Everything afterward became a blur of exhaustion. Now, she studied the sight before her. How did she end up in bed with him?

She stirred, stretching stiff muscles and, slowly, sat up and began to swing her legs over the side of the bed. A brown hand came reached out and wrapped around her wrist. "Come back to bed."

"I need to —."

"Oh. Then come back to bed." He turned over toward her and Fate grimaced at the thought of walking away from him. Even in the dim light of dawn, he would see the weight she didn't like carrying around her thighs. There wasn't anything to do about it. She scurried into the hall and bathroom.

After taking care of her immediate needs, she unearthed a washcloth and scrubbed her face then dried it on a spare hand towel. As she lowered the towel, she frowned. The circles under her eyes were even more noticeable this time and were stark in the naked light of the bathroom. Short of putting on makeup, which she refused to do, nothing could be done about the remnants of the assignment. She retrieved her toothbrush from her makeup bag and scrubbed her teeth then ran a brush through her hair. No way she'd show up with morning breath and bed head.

The trip back to the bedroom took longer, since she needed to adjust the slightly shifted bra and drooping

~ ☾ ~

panties. At the threshold of the room, however, she forgot what she looked like.

Oh my God. No man should look like that in the morning. She forced herself to breathe.

He lay on his side, drowsing. His black lashes lay against his high cheekbones, entirely too long and lush for a man to have. The almost shoulder length hair, mussed in a gorgeous way hers never managed to, framed his face and brought the sharply delineated lines into relief. Shadows dimmed the neatly trimmed mustache and beard but highlighted the lean muscles of the arm draped along the sheet that covered him to his waist. The dark hairs that lightly dusted his pectorals and narrowed into the sheet tempted her to play follow the dotted line.

The sheet moved as he shifted his legs and rolled onto his back. A slight protrusion grew and she became aware of the fact that she watched as he became aroused. She stared a moment at the growing mound then became aware of his stare.

"Come back to bed." His voice, a rough, just woke up quality to it, held something more. A dark, thrilling tone she wanted to hear often. Preferably while he made love to her.

Whoa. Having sex with me. Not love. No love in any way.

"Fate? Baby? You okay?" He rose to lean on one elbow.

She nodded, her face on fire. "I'm fine. I just don't think it's a good thing for me to come to bed right now."

"Why? I thought we were on the same page, here."

She nodded her head, "I know, but I'm still kind of..."

He shot up, alert. "You having some problems from last night?"

"No, I'm fine. A little tired, but it'll wear off in a couple hours. I'm always just a little raw after the

~ ☾ ~

assignments, especially like last night."

He stared a minute longer then nodded. "Okay. What do you want for breakfast?"

"You're okay with no sex?" She watched as he scooted to the edge of the bed and stood. She should turn away and let him dress, she supposed. But what red-blooded woman would turn away from that?

He picked up his jeans and walked to the dresser then extracted a pair of knit boxers. As he advanced toward her, he winked and grinned. "I'm not a slathering idiot that's going to jump your bones in the dark, babe. But if you don't stop watching me like that, I might have to reconsider. Now, what about breakfast?"

She followed his progress until he disappeared into the bathroom and shut the door. Kind of like the horse and barn, she thought as she quickly dressed then went to the kitchen area to start coffee. As she dumped the ground coffee into the maker the thought passed through her mind that they were already into a routine. Or at least a familiarity that she hadn't possessed with a man, ever.

The idea of waking up to Caden every morning didn't seem as strange as it should. Her life, her training, pursued a solitary existence, with only Latents for assistance. In fact, lately Selene hinted that Fate's future might hold more responsibilities in the Society than she'd expected. Now, with the threats surrounding her, she doubted she'd live up to her leader's expectations.

"So, do you always get so wiped out when you do your assignments?" Caden entered the kitchen area in his sock feet. The requisite jeans and shirt covered all the interesting parts, but at the least they emphasized them, rather than hiding him away.

She dragged her eyes from his body and turned to extract eggs and bacon from the refrigerator. After holding up the items and getting a nod, she started breakfast.

~ ☾ ~

"I'm always tired, but last night the fatigue increased on a couple of levels. The physical, which is always there, but also the emotional."

"How? It looked like she was ready."

"She was worried about her family that we dealt with. And the presence of all the friends and family sort of drained me too."

He got a loaf of bread from the refrigerator and started working on toast as she fixed the other items. "If you're that tired, your defenses and protective reactions are going to be low too. That's the prime time for someone to attack."

She nodded. "That's why we have Latents."

"But your Latent didn't do much of anything."

"They don't now. But in the past, they were there to protect the Maiden from a variety of threats, witch hunters, bereaved families, even people who wanted the Maiden's powers." She shrugged. "We knew of the existence of people who meant us harm, but not the names. I guess all of them could have been the Guard, even then."

Caden watched as she divided the now fried eggs and bacon onto two plates, with the heftier serving on one. He plopped a couple pieces of toast on the plates and carried them to the dining table then returned to pour coffee into two mugs. He automatically got the flavored creamer she'd brought with her from the refrigerator and added some to her drink. Then he waited until she sat before seating himself.

"What training does the Latent have?" He dug into his food as she sipped her coffee.

"It starts out pretty much the same as the Maiden's, basic skills in controlling your psychic voice. Then they separate and learn some defensive skills, the power of suggestion, that sort of thing."

"No physical defense training?" Caden's voice held a

~ ☾ ~

mixture of outrage and surprise.

She shook her head, avoiding his eyes. "None of the Maidens use physical violence. It's actually against our code. According to Selene, my Latent mother died in an attack on her Maiden. From what we've experienced, I think it may have been a Guard that killed her." She raised tortured eyes to him. "I know I'm in violation of a lot of rules just by having this conversation and associating with you, but I can't bear the thought that she died that way. That I may follow her."

"And in danger of violating more rules, I'd say." He leaned back, already finished with his food. She smiled and shook her head at him. She'd not taken more than a couple of bites and he looked ready for seconds.

"What you said about the assignments being the prime time for attack? You're right. If an assignment entailed forcing a soul through the portal, I'd be in a near comatose state when I came out. My Latent couldn't handle an attack, she'd probably just be another victim."

She plowed on at his growl. "I want to be trained more. I know we started doing some defensive maneuvers in case I get attacked. But I want to learn how to do some harm to a Guard, if I need to."

He stared at her for a long moment before answering. "It takes years of training to get to that level, Fate."

"I don't want to be an expert, just survive long enough for someone to be able to help me. I never go on assignment without a Latent."

"You won't be without me for a while either."

"But what about afterwards? What happens after we eliminate the Guard? What if an irate family member attacks me? My shields may hold for a while but if I start weakening, I won't be able to shield. I need to be able to defend myself, and be able to eliminate a threat."

"Selene? What does she think about this?"

~ ☾ ~

"She doesn't know, and doesn't need to know until I'm ready to tell her." Fate planted a firm, hopefully resolute expression on her face.

"Are you meeting with her?"

"I told her I needed some recoup time." Fate hid her face in her coffee cup.

"She let you stall her?"

"For now. If she hears about the Latent's weakness in training, she may pull me out of my assignments, not to mention may make me stay at the Retreat."

He stood and plucked her plate from in front of her and, along with his own empty plate, carried them to the kitchen. He then brought the carafe of coffee to the table and refilled the cups.

He handed her the god-awful creamer she used to weaken the jolt of her coffee. "You're right. We'll start training today."

When Fate entered the workout room, she found Jake there, rather than Caden. "Hi."

He turned from his stretches and smiled. "Hi yourself. Ready for a workout?"

She laid the bottle of water and towel she'd carried into the room on the floor near the door and slowly nodded. "Sure. Caden's not here?"

"Nope. Had a meeting with Donan. He asked me to fill in for him." Jake eyed her closer. "You can wait until he gets back."

Fate shook her head and walked further into the room. "No, I'm just a little surprised."

"No more than me when he called. Hey, let's take advantage of it, okay? We'll go over some easy defensive moves and then hit the hot tub." He waggled his eyebrows suggestively.

Fate chuckled. "This cabin is a bare bones

~ ☾ ~

accommodation, and you know it. Besides, I'm the one who wanted a harder workout. So, I'm the boss and you need to impress me."

Jake raised his hands in defeat. "Fine. Just remember the magic word when I get too rough."

"What's that?"

"Uncle." He advanced on her.

Caden drew a steadying breath as he entered the inner domain. In the short few days since he'd been assigned Fate's case, he felt as if he'd lost contact with the Soldiers of Light in more ways than one. He'd practically grown up in the Refuge and now, he felt a stranger.

He stood for a moment inside the entrance and cleared his mind, opening his inner mind to Donan. With one exception. The attraction to Fate, he'd keep to himself.

Donan entered the room from his own private quarters. As always, he requested a tray of drinks to be brought before he sat in the easy chair he called his own. Caden seated himself in the sole remaining chair and waited.

Donan served the coffee the servant brought then sipped at his cup. Caden picked his up but didn't drink.

"How is the Maiden faring?"

"She's getting impatient waiting for the other shoe to drop."

"And you?"

"Pretty much the same. I try to have someone with her when I'm not able to watch her on my own, and I've gone on an assignment with her."

Donan paused in the midst of a sip. "You went on a Maiden journey?"

Caden nodded. "She was exhausted afterwards. It's

~ ☾ ~

the most vulnerable time for her, and other Maidens, I suspect."

Donan nodded absently. "It's been centuries since a Maiden has allowed a Soldier accompany her. We wouldn't have that kind of information. Selene should be made aware of the window of vulnerability."

"So, the Maidens and Soldiers are going to be on speaking terms, now?" Caden couldn't help the sarcastic note in his voice and Donan picked up on it as well, and frowned.

"The rift happened a long time ago and has kept our services apart for eons. Now, I think, we have little choice in the matter. The connection between you and Ms. Halligan is too strong to ignore."

For an instant, Caden suspected Donan read him and caught the physical attraction between him and Fate. Then he realized it his leader referred to the psychic connection. "We've noticed."

"Have you picked up on her thoughts more?"

"Yeah, and her on mine. We've both put up barriers."

"That may be the wrong choice right now. The best defense in this matter may be to enhance the connection between you."

"My question is why the connection?"

Donan placed his cup on the small table that rested between them and Caden did the same with his untouched drink. Donan stood and began to pace, his one sign of disquiet.

"You remember when I told you of the rift between the Soldiers of Light and the Maidens of the Society de la Morte? Well, before that, the two factions worked alongside each other. No, more than that, they worked closely, much like the Latents and Maidens of today, only more as equals. Then, one pairing went beyond the rules of the societies. Souls were lost as a result of the selfishness of both parties." Donan lowered his gaze and

~ ☾ ~

shook his head. "With the severance of the cooperation, both decided separately to avoid emotional entanglements with anyone. We haven't encountered a reason to reconsider the decision."

Caden stood, agitated and started his own circuit of the room. "Damn it, Donan! Fate's mother served as a Latent and died during an attack. Do you realize they've probably been targeted by the Guard for years and we just went our way and let them be mowed down?"

Donan shook his head adamantly. "The Latents are trained."

"In psychic use only. They're sitting ducks, not to mention the Maidens. Our ancestors' decisions to "sever" the connection left the women out to hang in the wind."

Donan, who never reflected anything other than calm control, deflated before Caden. "My god, what did we do?"

"We made mistakes, that's what we did. Now, we have to do something about them. Are you going to contact Selene or do I?"

"I'll talk to her. And I'm afraid it will have to be in person. It's been so long." Donan seemed to gather his wits and reclaimed his seat. "You will begin Fate's training immediately?"

"Yeah. Jake is starting to train her today. I'll ramp it up some." Caden stood, assuming he'd been dismissed then stopped as Donan extended a hand.

"I need to talk to you of another matter."

"Yeah?" Caden wasn't sure his temper would survive another revelation at this point and he felt one coming.

"You know I've spent more time with you, singled you out from the other Soldiers." At Caden's cautious nod, the leader continued, "You have powers you have not tapped, which is another reason I believe you have the connection with Ms. Halligan. You're the sixth generation Soldier in your bloodline."

~ ☾ ~

"So? It'll look good on a wall or in a book, but other than that..."

Donan smiled at Caden's weak joke. "It may explain why you are at the epicenter of the changes we are destined to make. You will be the agent of change for the Soldiers of Light."

Caden considered himself the workhorse of the Soldiers, nothing more. "What if I don't want to be that man?"

"What you want may not be your choice. We all make decisions everyday. Just by being the man you are, you may determine both your destiny and that of your charge. Now, tell me of your plans to train Ms. Halligan."

~ ☾ ~

Chapter Eleven

By the time Fate finished her session with Jake, she believed herself ready to kill someone. Preferably a dark haired, dark eyed hunk of a man who'd left her to deal with a jerk. Jake denigrated every suggestion she made regarding Maidens' modes of defense, and answered every move with, "I'll just have to reteach you everything."

Really, you'd think I've survived so far by sheer luck. And even if Caden believed that, he knew enough not to reveal it.

She waited until Jake borrowed space in one of the guest room showers to make her way out of the house. She glared at the general vicinity of the doorway. If an alarm went off somewhere, so much the better. *Let's see how they handle something out of their plan.* She made her way down the back steps and into the small field that ranged the house.

As she trudged through the knee-high grass, she fumed. Jake not only condescended to her, he'd spent the entire session leering at her. Her actions veered from protection and offensive maneuvers to those particularly chosen to avoid his clinches.

Is that how Caden looks at me? She didn't feel affronted when he gazed at her with sexual promise in those black eyes. Despite the warnings Selene threw her way time and again about the Soldier, warmth infused her lower body, as if readying for him.

She lost track of the time traversing the open area around the house, clearing her head of the anger and

~ ☾ ~

frustration of the training session. Gradually, Fate became aware something else. A dark threat, black and heavy, settled on her consciousness and brought her to a stumbling halt.

She bent as if to pick up a stone in her path and concentrated. *Where is it? Is it Guard or something else? And what could I do about it?*

As she straightened, she focused and took a breath. Behind her, a Guard closed distance, ready to attack. A flash of purpose surrounding a gleaming blade danced across her mind and she forced a steadying breath. In the blurry picture Fate could see someone stalking her. As she stalked two paces ahead, she formulated her plan.

Another step and then a feint to the right, closer to the house. With a sharp turn, she kicked out, instinctively trying one of the Caden's techniques from his training sessions the day before.

A grunt from the black-clad man rushing her told the blow struck home and she saw him go down out of the corner of her eye. Fate didn't take time to see if he still held the knife, she took off in the direction of the house. In her mind, she screamed for the only person she trusted to help her, the only man she'd ever call for, no matter his distance.

Caden sensed the threat to Fate before he pulled onto the gravel road. *They knew where she is.* He sped up, bouncing over ruts and stones in the rough road. With her safe in the cabin he could start the perimeter search. He sent out a call to Jake to secure the house.

As he neared the turnoff to the cabin, he received Jake's news. *"What? What do you mean she's not in the house?"* He shouted in his mind.

"I went to take a shower and she disappeared. Damn

~ ☾ ~

woman." Jake's impatience seeped through the communication.

"Find her, now!" Caden barked aloud, disregarding the protocol of speaking only in his mind or aloud, but not both. If Jake got an echo headache, so be it.

A sharp stab of panic hit Caden as he realized Fate might be out of the house. Why hadn't he heard the remote alarm? What the hell possessed her, being out of the house, anyway?

He skidded into the gravel drive of the cabin when he heard her scream his name in his mind.

God. Where is she?

He jerked open the door to the truck at the same time he grabbed a handgun from under the driver's seat. As he ran toward the house he tried to calm his mind, attempted to pick up on her location.

In the corner of his consciousness where she resided he sensed tall grass and a wooded area in the distance. The rear of the house, then. He sent the message to search the back of the property to Jake and tried to reach out to Fate.

When he opened communication he got blasted with chaos. A jumble of thoughts ran through her mind, with little direction or order. Caden captured images of a rabbit running in zigzags, of a ball bouncing down a hill, of—him standing in the center of a strong wind. *What the hell?*

When he rounded the back of the house his breath caught. Fate ran toward the cabin, her route unclear but her purpose obvious. Caden took the time to admire her plan of confusing her attacker, but cursed that she couldn't get any speed up when she darted right and left. At least she ran toward him.

He sent a plea for her to straighten her route and head straight. Instantly, she darted left again, almost into the path of the Guard closing in on her and came

~ ☾ ~

toward him. Caden sprinted forward to meet her as he palmed his gun.

Jake's voice came from behind him, "to your left."

Caden felt him rush past. Fate landed against his chest in a rush of breath and he allowed himself an instant to clutch her to him before handing her the pistol and thrusting her behind him. "Get to the cabin and lock yourself in."

"I can help," She panted.

Caden didn't look at her, didn't try to push her away, and didn't speak again. He just mentally sent her the command.

"In the cabin, now."

He didn't wait for her response his attention on the Guard.

Jake engaged the Guard, their battle silent and psychic, but that didn't suit Caden. Psychic blows and commands wouldn't handle his rage. He rushed the Guard and removed the blade with a simple twist of the man's wrist. A snap of the bone satisfied him that the blade wouldn't be used for the rest of the fight.

He started battering him, using old-fashioned street brawling techniques he'd learned as a teenager. A red blur took over, sealing every other thought and image out of his mind, his only purpose to eliminate the threat to Fate once and for all.

A soft touch entered his mind. *"Caden, stop. You've done enough. Enough, now."* Fate's voice, her soft, soothing essence seeped through the madness and forced him to slow his blows, then to unclench his fists. Caden became aware of Jake's efforts to force him from the now limp body of the Guard.

He shrugged off his friend, muttering, "I'm fine. I'm okay."

"Damn, man. I haven't seen you go there, ever." Jake's eyes were narrowed as he examined Caden.

~ ☾ ~

"Is he alive?"

Jake felt the Guard's carotid pulse before answering, "Yeah. He'll be out for a while, though."

"Can you get him to the Refuge? Have him detained for questioning?"

"Yeah. You aren't coming?"

"No. I need to talk to Fate." Caden stumbled, his legs felt weak. The adrenaline rush of fear and rage retreated, leaving him limp and exhausted.

Jake nodded. "Uh, go a little easy on her, okay?"

Caden stared. "What do you mean?"

Jake shrugged. "I gave her the treatment. You know, snide, bastard talk, and giving her the eye. Wanted to see how far she could be pushed."

"Did you explain afterwards?" Jake put a lot of trainees through the *treatment*, though the males got the old military demeaning speeches. When Jake put women through their paces he usually recouped by being a softie afterward.

"I got tired and forgot. She puts up a good fight when she's training. Besides, she kinda made me feel like an asshole, treating her that way. Talk to her, okay? Let her know I didn't mean it."

Caden shook his head. His friend never apologized for his actions, even if he did explain them. He'd fallen under her spell, too.

Caden helped load the unconscious Guard into Jake's SUV and then headed into the house. Right now, the next items on his agenda were a shower and his bed, not necessarily in that order.

When he opened the back door to the house any thoughts of resting shot from his brain. Fate stood at the window facing the dirt road and watched Jake trundle down the lane and away from the house. Caden's fatigue left him in a flash as the anxiety and fear he'd experienced before were replaced by anger. "What the

~ ☾ ~

hell did you mean by leaving the house?"

"I was in the backyard!" She wheeled on him and
thrust her little chin forward.

Caden stalked toward her. "Well, the 'back yard'
wasn't safe, was it babe? You almost got yourself killed."

"I handled myself." She huffed and started to walk by
him, only to be brought to a halt by his hand on her arm.

"I saw how you were handling yourself. Another few
jack rabbit turns and you'd have lost too much speed.
He'd have had you. He'd have *had* you." Caden ended
his sentence with a groan and jerked her to him.

Fate wrapped her arms around his middle, absorbing
his warmth. Fine tremors ran through his body and she
hugged hard, trying to calm him. "I'm fine. You got here
in time, Caden."

"Just barely." He muttered and pulled his head back
enough to meet her eyes. "Don't think about getting
away from me again."

***

"I didn't leave you, just the house." She murmured,
her attention on his eyes. They'd darkened to near black.

"Never again. I'm not letting you out of my sight, ever
again." He lowered his head and captured her mouth in
a grinding, forceful kiss. Fate accepted the breach,
taking in his anxiety and frustration and giving back
softness. She put everything she possessed into that kiss,
opening her mouth and her mind to him in that instant.

Caden groaned and deepened the kiss, thrusting his
tongue into her mouth again and again. She answered
by leaning into his body and giving her all to him
physically.

He broke the kiss only to find the curve of her neck
and to spread open-mouthed kisses down to the collar of
her blouse. A rumble began deep in his chest and grew
to a moan as he edged his mouth along the line of her
collarbone, leaving a wake of sensation. Fate tilted her

~ ☾ ~

head back to allow him more room and sighed.

His hand drifted up under her blouse and made a sure route to her breast, covered by thin silk. Fate sucked in a breath as he delved under the material and cupped her breast then thumbed the nipple, bringing it to a stiff point. She wriggled against him, trying to bring her body closer to his. Instead, Caden pushed her away.

She glanced up at him in surprise then understanding when he grabbed the bottom of her blouse and yanked it over her head. She'd only begun to lower her arms when he reached behind her and unclipped her bra in a sure movement.

She didn't cover herself. She wanted him to see her. Instead, she started unbuttoning his cotton shirt. Caden held her gaze as he simplified measures. He held the edges of his shirt and gave a swift jerk. She smiled as buttons went flying and then pushed the shirt off his shoulders. He let it drop off his arms and then bundled her into an embrace that brought her bare breasts into contact with his chest.

The sprinkling of hair that decorated his chest and arrowed into his pants rubbed against her breasts, making them even more sensitive, eliciting a groan of her own. She rubbed against him, trying to get more of the amazing feeling.

Caden stopped her by kissing her again, then picked her up and headed down the hall. "You ready for this?"

"I've been ready since you bought the condoms." She murmured into his neck.

"Condoms. Damn." He turned back toward the living room. She giggled as he cursed under his breath. The package from the drug store hadn't made it from the kitchen. Instead, they'd been stuffed into a drawer in their rush to make her assignment. Caden deposited her on the counter and started pulling drawers out in search of the package.

~ ☾ ~

"It's this one," she pointed to her left and leaned to open the drawer. As she straightened with the bag in her hand she noticed his attention wandered. He eyed her breasts then slowly bent and took the tip of one in his mouth. The moist warmth that enveloped her overwhelmed her and Fate folded her upper body around his head, cradling him to her. "Caden."

He layered kisses on the curve of her breast then took it back in his mouth, gently bit the tip then lathed it with his tongue. She cried out softly. When he raised his head he pulled her to him. She wrapped her arms and legs around his torso and kissed him, holding on to him as he turned toward the hall.

He'd taken only a step away from the counter when his head reared up and away from her lips and he glared at her. "You've got the condoms?"

She gave her the hand that clutched the bag a jiggle, letting it bounce against his shoulder and he nodded then strode down the hallway toward the bedroom. On his way he muttered, "I'm buying enough boxes of the things to have a supply in every room of the house."

She giggled against his neck and delighted in the shudder that ran through him at her glancing kiss on his jaw. "We may need double."

"I'll buy a damn case." He dropped her onto the bed and started undoing his pants. Fate sat on the edge of the mattress, her eyes glued on his hands as they unsnapped then unzipped his jeans. He lowered them, along with his knit boxers and stepped out of them in a smooth motion then took a step toward her.

His erection rose higher as she watched. Fate forced herself to look up into his eyes as he advanced on her.

He bent and kissed her as he pushed her back into a supine position. Fate allowed herself the luxury of running her hands along the line of his arms to his back and then up the indentation of his spine. His hands

~ ☾ ~

dropped to the waistband of her jeans and when she felt
them loosen, she started to help him remove them.

"Uh uh. My turn." He muttered against her lips and
she returned her hands to his arms. She lifted her hips
and he pushed her pants down and off her legs.

Soon, her jeans were gone, along with her panties.
Caden nudged her legs apart with his own and then
settled into the cradle he'd created for himself. She
sighed at the touch of his skin against hers, the feel of
his erection nestled against her groin.

He kissed along the line of her shoulder then lower, to
her breasts. His attention focused solely on her breasts
for a moment. She murmured encouragement as his
hand drifted down to her hip.

Caden couldn't get enough of the taste of her skin, of
her smell. He returned again and again to sample the
silken skin of her breasts as his hands plumped them for
his mouth. He ran his hands along her body. Finally,
after all the false starts, she opened to him and to loving.
He slipped his hand between them and caressed the nest
of hair at the apex of her legs. She gave a short moan at
the touch and he grinned mentally. She hadn't seen
anything yet.

"Baby? The condoms?"

"Condoms?" Her voice, short and breathy heightened
his arousal.

"We need the condoms." He stroked down the line
between her legs and delved into her moist center. She
arched against him, trying to increase pressure and he
obliged, finding the little nubbin of nerves. He gently
rubbed and caressed, sending her into an even higher
arch. "Condoms, baby."

She muttered under her breath, but Caden couldn't
understand her. He needed the condoms, now. The
breathy moans she made, combined with the sight of her
body, gleaming in the dusky room, and her moistness all

~ ☾ ~

combined to tempt him beyond resistance. The urge to slide into her unsheathed and without a barrier between them held him. He'd not felt the compulsion before, but if he didn't find the damn rubbers, he'd explode.

He shifted her a bit and spied the now rumpled and slightly crushed package partially under her shoulder. A simple shake of the bag emptied the contents of two boxes of condoms. Now he faced the prospect of taking his hands off her to don the damn thing.

"Caden," her voice quivered and he felt the first indications of her approaching climax, tiny pulsing contractions as he caressed her. She opened her eyes, searching for him. He smoothed his hand down and gently thrust a finger, then two into her. "Come on, baby. Let me see you."

She cried out then and tightened on him. He stayed with her, gently thrusting and murmuring words he'd not remember later. Only her face, her voice, and the way she came apart in his arms held any sway.

He kissed her before shifting away to don the condom then returned and gathered her in his arms. She stared at him, her face slack with contentment, her eyes sparkling. "I didn't get a chance to touch you."

Caden nibbled his way down her chin and then up to her ear. He laved the delicate tissue. "We're not finished yet. Not by a long shot."

She shivered at the feel of his breath on her skin, her eyes glittering as they met his. He rose above her and came to his knees. Fate's hands fell away from his arms and she rested on the bed.

He stroked the inside of her thighs as he knelt and nudged them further apart. Fate's rapt expression humbled him. He'd wasted his time trying to resist the pull between them. He bent over and kissed her, his erection nudging against her core. When she flinched he drew away from the kiss with a frown, "Are you—"

~ ☾ ~

"No. It's just been a while." She smiled and smoothed the crease between his eyes then curved her hand around his neck and drew him down for another kiss. This one magnified the sensations. The insistent pressure for him to thrust farther inside her, the feel of her hair against his fingers as he caressed the side of her face, the joy her exploration of his mouth brought. Finally, she broke off the kiss and buried her head in his neck. Caden started to rock against her, his movements forcing his erection a bit farther with each tilt.

At last, he stopped advancing and lay with his upper body weight balanced on elbows on either side of her. She panted slightly and he stilled, giving her time to adjust to him.

"Baby? You okay?"

"Mmm. Fate shifted and tightened around him. He dropped his head and shuddered. "God, Fate," Caden whispered into her shoulder before he raised his head and looked at her. Her eyes took his breath away. She gazed at him as if he carried the world and offered it to her as a gift. He wanted to absorb her into his skin. And she looked at him as if she wanted him to. She opened her mind to him and sent a plea for him to move.

He began then, thrusting in short, shallow motions and then longer strokes, slow and deliberate. She kept her consciousness vulnerable to him, and as sensations built in her he adjusted his movements. Then she answered his tilts and thrusts with a lift of her hips. All the time, as aware of his thoughts as he of hers, the words he didn't say, unformed and unuttered, yet blazing through her mind.

Fate answered with her own, both aloud and in her mind. She clasped him to her, her nails biting into his skin. "I—more, move more."

He increased the intensity of his thrusts. The tension between them coalesced and Fate moaned, long and low

~ ☾ ~

then uttered a sharp cry. Caden continued thrusting, fast and uneven, his deliberate cadence forgotten as his release overpowered him. Everything froze, his breath, his body. Only Fate's touch as she held him to her registered. His whole body quivered with a fine tremor. He collapsed onto her with a heavy sigh.

They remained silent, their breathing the only sound in the room. After a bit, Caden stirred on top of Fate then heaved himself to the side and lay on his back, one arm curled over his head. He shifted her with the other hand and she curled into his side. It felt right, cuddling with her.

"You okay?" His voice, slightly scratchy, sounded loud in the quiet room.

"Umm." She nuzzled into his side.

He shifted again and managed to pull covers they'd sprawled on top of over them, then turned into her and pulled her into a firm embrace. Fate lay at his side for a while and he listened as her breathing slowed and evened out and she slept. He eased away from her for the few minutes it took to dispose of the condom, returning to pull her into his arms and hold her.

Eventually, he followed.

***

Fate came awake when he moved from the bed. Now full dark, the moonlight sifted through the opened curtains of the window across the room. She stared into the darkness outside and let her thoughts wander in her half-awake state.

Her forays into adult pleasure in college ended up being awkward and unsatisfying, and she'd written off the whole affair as hype by the artistic community. Now, she agreed the novelists and filmmakers might have something.

She'd struggled to hold onto herself during Caden's gentle assault on her senses. He'd known how to get

~ ℭ ~

under her defenses. If he'd rushed her through the experience, she'd have bolted, and somehow he knew that even before she opened her mind to him. She smiled at memory of the frantic search and retrieval of the missing condoms. In the end he'd practically torn the package open with his teeth.

A warm sensation, totally foreign to the heat of sex, threatened to take over her body. No, she argued. Just *sex*, nothing more. The physical attraction she felt for him came from his proximity. And his killer body. But if she'd not been threatened to the point that they spent every waking hour, and now sleeping hours, together, she wouldn't be attracted to him. Her commitment to Maidens took precedence to all. Maybe if she kept telling herself that, she'd believe it.

Fate sat up and stretched, aware of some muscle soreness. She'd have to take a long shower to combat the stiffness, before she could even think of any type of workout. She shifted from the bed and started looking for clothes. Finally, she located one of Caden's dirty shirts and pulled it on. Having him see her naked in the midst of sex might be okay. Seeing her after sex and a long nap, with bed head, not going to happen.

She edged around the open door and started to sprint to her room in search of more clothes so she could shower when his voice halted her.

"Hey, babe."

She whirled, clutching the ends of the shirt, trying to make it long enough to cover as much of her as possible. Caden leaned against the doorframe leading into the living room area and grinned, his eyes at half-mast. A light shone in another room, down the hall and highlighted his expression, one of satisfied male.

"You sleep okay?"

As he ambled toward her Fate wanted to both run away, sure she couldn't handle such a man, and to leap

~ ☾ ~

on him and kiss him senseless. She settled for standing her ground and answering him with a smile.

"Fine. What time is it?"

"Around nine. Want something to eat?" He reached out to brush a lock of hair from her face. Her face heated and his smile widened. "Why the blush?"

She shrugged. "Got me, I didn't blush earlier when—" She faltered as his eyes heated.

"When I stripped and assaulted you?" His smile dimmed.

She stepped as close to him as she could without trying to meld their skin together. "I was an active participant, you know."

He chuckled, "You were, at that. Now, answer my question. Are you hungry?"

"No, but I do want a shower and something to drink, in that order."

"That we can do. Shower and I'll have something for you when you come out." He slanted a kiss on her lips, short but satisfying, and patted her butt as she turned from him.

She rushed to get clothes and started the shower. When it reached a temperature that she could tolerate without looking like a steamed clam, she jumped inside and in ten minutes washed her hair and emerged clean.

She quickly dried her hair and dressed, then eyed herself. She sighed at the stark image the fluorescent lights cast on her complexion. Caden saw her without makeup more often than with so why worry about what she wore now.

He wasn't in the kitchen when she arrived there, but a fresh pot of coffee brewed and a boxed assortment of tea bags sat on the counter. He'd covered all the bases, so she withdrew a mug from the cabinet and put water in a kettle to boil. As she waited, she wandered the living room, considering and rejecting the idea of a fire and

~ ☾ ~

picking up a magazine then dropping it on the table in front of the sofa.

He appeared a few minutes later, having also indulged in a shower. His hair, slightly damp and gleaming, fell around his shoulders. He'd shaved and trimmed his closely cropped beard and mustache. Fate shivered at the thought of the slight rasp of his beard and mustache on her skin. What would it feel like elsewhere on her body?

He ignored the tea and poured a mug of coffee instead. The whistle of the kettle signaled her water and she returned to the kitchen area. Silently, she prepared her tea, aware of him at her back, then carried it to the sofa and sank down into the soft cushions. He followed her, now without his mug.

He sat and draped his arm across the back of the couch. "Now, tell me what the hell you were doing out of the house today."

"I worked out with your friend," She returned.

"And?"

"What an ass. I got mad and decided to get out of the house, just to get some air. I honestly didn't think." She held up a hand to stop him when he started to speak. "I realize I put myself as well as you and Jake at risk."

His expression turned wry. "You spoiled my lecture, damn it."

She chuckled. "I'm human, Caden. I made a big mistake, but I also learned from it. I'll try to take my anger out in another way, like belting Jake when he is a jerk again."

He nodded and leaned back, letting his arm fall around her shoulders. "He deserved it. He told me about how he treated you. Our recruits typically get it but you didn't sign up for the drill sergeant bit. He apologized, by the way."

She acknowledged the apology. It didn't mean as

~ ☾ ~

much now, in hindsight. She eyed Caden. "What will happen to the Guard?"

"When he regains full consciousness we question him. I checked in after I woke up and he'd not come around for more than a minute or two. He's at the Refuge."

"When you started beating him, I wasn't sure you were going to stop."

Caden stared at his hand as it rested against his thigh. "Neither was I."

Fate followed his gaze. Scrapes and bruises ranged across his hand, evidence of the force he'd used in his blows. She'd been so focused on his lovemaking she hadn't noticed before. She reached over and covered his hand with hers. Caden's fingers twitched then he turned over his hand and meshed their fingers together.

She eyed their hands. He took care to be gentle with her, obviously restraining his strength when he held her. "Why *did* you beat him so?"

He looked at her. "Because he tried to hurt you."

"No more than every other Guard who attacked me. I know they ended up dead, but in a way, this fight became more--."

"Brutal?"

He nodded, his face unreadable now. "I guess so. The other guys, I defended myself as much as fighting them. I don't know why this attack became more. Maybe because after you'd been chased out of your home, they're attacking you at *mine*."

"Yours? I thought it belonged to the Soldiers." She glanced around the room with new eyes. Though sparsely furnished with only the essentials, the room's atmosphere ensured comfort and welcome.

He looked uncomfortable. "I stay at the Refuge or an apartment I have in town most of the time, but it's more crowded than I'd like sometimes. This is *my* refuge,

~ ☾ ~

when I need to get away." He slumped even farther into the cushions of the couch and extended his legs in front of him, a picture of relaxation, except Fate felt the tenseness in his arms, the disquiet in his psyche. Did he feel uneasy confiding in her?

"People leave you alone here?"

"Only Jake and Donan know about it. And like I said, I don't come out here often." He seemed to catch himself in his confidences and grimaced. "Enough about me. Let's talk about sex."

***

Caden mentally congratulated and berated himself for his confidences. He'd not opened up to another person in a long while. He protected a part of his mind from everyone, even Donan, who'd been granted more of him than anyone. Until now. The demands of his Soldier duties pressed hard on him and he needed some respite. And according to Donan, he'd have even less privacy in the future.

He allowed himself the luxury of looking at Fate. Her hair lay smooth and bright against the brown suede couch and his dark tan, and she looked rested. He'd been as careful as he could when they came together, took care not to be too rough, considering he nearly howled from holding back.

She eyed him with some level of distrust. "You want to talk about sex?"

"Yeah. More specifically, sex with me, between us. We kinda broke the rules earlier."

Fate laughed. "We didn't break the rules, we squashed them into the dirt. It's a little late to talk about the rules, now, isn't it?"

He lifted a shoulder in agreement. "Maybe, but I've got plans to smash some rules again later, if it's okay with you."

The hint of pink that stained her cheeks tempted him

~ ☾ ~

to taste her, to sooth the discomfort away. She tilted her head. "You don't feel guilty?"

"About sex with you?" He shook his head. "We're consenting adults, know what we're getting into and took precautions. What do we have to feel guilty about?"

"The fact that you're a Soldier and I'm a Maiden comes to mind. Surely that connection is not something they thought of when they made the rules."

He didn't enlighten her that the connection between the Soldier and Maiden of old served as the catalyst for the prohibition against emotional involvement. Instead, he focused on more interesting matters. "So, you're okay with sex, with me, later?" He leaned forward and started to nibble on her shoulder.

She wriggled until she could insert a hand on his face. She shoved and he allowed her to push him away with a frown. "That's not going to help us think clearly."

He covered her hand with his own and lowered them to his thigh, near his groin. "Thinking is over-rated. Let's take a break from it, tonight."

Her hand tightened on his thigh before loosening. "If you're going to teach me some defensive maneuvers tomorrow I need to call an end to 'not thinking' tonight. Or I won't be able to move."

He mentally kicked himself. She'd not been a virgin, but still far from experienced and sure to be feeling the muscle twinges from earlier. "Only that, babe, is going to get you out of not thinking."

~ ☾ ~

Chapter Twelve

Caden rotated his shoulders as he entered his office building behind Fate. She glanced over her shoulder at him and grinned. "I didn't think I'd given you such a blow that last time."

He grinned, "It wasn't the training, but our workout session afterwards. I think I bent the wrong way." He didn't need a psychic connection to read the emotions in her blush as she recalled the night before and their "workout" session. What started as a defense lesson turned quickly into an exercise both in pleasure and, when he got a call from the security company, frustration.

She spun around and marched into the inner room that she'd taken over the last time she visited the building. Caden heaved a breath and veered off toward his own office. He'd have to speed through the meetings he'd scheduled, or he'd have another restless Maiden on his hands.

He'd dealt with several minor emergencies and meetings when Jake stuck his head in the door. "Is that Fate I see down the hall?"

Caden glanced up from the file he'd been reviewing and grinned, "Yeah. She seen you yet?"

Jake edged in and nudged the door closed. "Nope and I intend to keep it that way."

"I told her what you were doing during the session. She understood."

"Understanding is one thing, being okay with me being on the same planet is another."

~ ☾ ~

Caden's grin widened as he remembered the fierce look on her delicate face as she practiced her moves. She might look fragile but made up for it with a world of effort. "You need something? I'm about to wrap things up, here."

"In a hurry to get back to your hidey hole?" Jake lounged against the wall and smirked.

Caden didn't answer, but eyed his friend. Finally, Jake relented and approached the desk. "I wanted to ask you something about the Soldiers."

When Caden nodded toward the door Jake nudged it closed with his foot then turned, his expression focused and serious. "I've been doing some research about you and our pixie out there."

"Pixie?" Caden's mouth quirked up at the word. "It fits."

"Yeah, anyway. You and she have something of a connection, don't you?"

"Connection?"

"I picked up on something when the Guard attacked at the cabin. Nothing that I could intercept, but something that flowed between you two. Something more than psychic conversation."

A thrill of unease, combined with a sense of inevitability rose in Caden. He waited for Jake to continue. "I decided to do some research. I know we'd done some digging on Fate's family and I thought I'd look some more."

Caden shifted uncomfortably in his seat. "Jake, if you don't spit it out—"

"All right. She's the direct descendant of the original leader of the Society de la Morte and you're a sixth generation Soldier."

Caden shrugged. "So? We both have a history of having strong psychic powers. That probably explains the connection."

~ ☾ ~

"But there's more, a legend. When the Soldier's Sixth Son and the Maiden of Choice come together, their powers will accelerate and multiply. The last stanza of the legend is the most important." Jake leaned against the desk and closed his eyes in concentration. "When powers combine so then a force, a new world will form from the morass."

Caden barked a laugh. "And you think Fate and I are going to form a new world? I'm good, buddy, but not that good."

Jake shook his head, "Man, I know it sounds freaky, but what if it's the real thing? I mean anyone around you two picks up on some weird shit. At least I do, and I'd be willing to bet Donan does too. Why do you think he's watching the progress of this assignment so closely?"

Caden studied his friend. *Maybe—No. Hell no.*

He wasn't some prophet or super Soldier or anything. And Fate, Fate wasn't much more than an acolyte. To say she possessed some fantastic power sounded like a bunch of crap.

So what explained the connection between them? He'd pushed it to the back of his mind for days and yet, even he acknowledged a connection. Not only in the communication end, but also physically. She made him harder than any woman in memory and could send him to laughter or drive him crazy in seconds and seemed to do it often.

He shook his head again. "I don't believe in legends and you shouldn't put much credence in them either. Legends are fairy tales. Nothing more. As to the connection between Fate and me—"

He halted at the knock on the door. At his directive, the door opened and Fate stuck her head in. She smiled, "Did you need me for something?"

Jake, out of her line of sight smothered a chuckle and

~ ☾ ~

Caden ignored his nosy friend. "No, babe, but Jake needed to talk to you."

She stepped into the room and turned her gaze, now narrowed, on Jake. "Yes?"

"I wanted to make sure we were okay." He grinned his stock smile that seemed to work with women.

She ignored the smile and Caden hid a grin at the assessing glance she sent Jake. "I understand the tough man act. But if you ever do it again, be prepared to use some force or lose a body part."

Jake's expression, shock combined with admiration, assured Caden he'd managed to divert the conversation, especially when Jake asked Fate if she wanted to spar that afternoon.

"We're going to be leaving in a few minutes. She won't have time today. If you come out to the house, though, she can show you what she's learned. Right, babe?" He grinned at Fate, flashing images of the other lessons he'd been teaching her earlier in the day to her consciousness.

***

Fate flushed and nodded, trying to get back on track. She kept her eyes fixed on Jake, determined not to look at Caden. He'd sent her images of them entangled on the mat, their clothes in piles next to them. She cleared her thoughts, or tried to and focused on Jake. "If you want to come by the cabin tomorrow, we can spar around nine."

"One would be better." Caden inserted and Fate ground her teeth at his satisfied tone. He sent more images to her of his plans for the morning. She didn't trust herself to fire back some thoughts of her own while trying to carry on a conversation. Instead, she tried to get out of the situation with her dignity intact.

Jake's eyes darted between her and Caden and then he slowly nodded. "I'll see you at one tomorrow." He

~ ☾ ~

cast Caden a look laden with some message, and then excused himself.

"Don't *do* that." She planted her fists on her hips and glared at Caden.

"Do what?" Everything about him shouted satisfied, from his grin, the sparkle in his eyes, to the way he leaned back in his chair and propped his hands behind his head.

"Don't fire off obscene pictures at me when I'm trying to have a conversation."

"So it's okay to fire them off to you when you're not talking to anyone? I can send them when you're reading?" Caden started chuckling as she closed the door and started advancing on him. "Or when you're doing the laundry? How about—ummph."

She shut him up with the simple expedience of kissing him. She placed her hands on his shoulders and explored the seam of his lips before he opened them to her. She nipped his full lower lip and ran her tongue across the inside of his lips before drawing away.

"Come back here." He shifted forward, his hand just short of closing on hers as she stepped away.

"Uh uh." She shook her head. "You need to get your work done. I'm getting bored, looking at magazines. All you have are Track and Field and Field and Stream. Jeez."

He laughed and held up a file. "I have to make a call about this contract, then we're free for the rest of the day."

She returned to the office she'd commandeered and spent the rest of the time on her cell phone with Selene, making sure someone would be available to look after her apartment. Caden's even tread down the hallway alerted her to end the call before he invaded her thoughts again. He leaned against the door jam and smiled as she shoved items into her purse.

~ ☾ ~

"You need to stop for anything or you want to go directly to the cabin?"

She grimaced. "I can't bear the thought of going to the apartment. I called Selene and she said the smoke smell has permeated everything. She's working on having someone come in and clean it for me but I don't want to think of how long it'll take to clean my books, let alone my clothes. And I think I need to steer clear of Selene for a while."

"She give you a hard time?" His hand rested lightly but warm on her back as they headed out of the building. Fate could feel him sending out feelers to pick up on any Guard activity as she did the same and they turned toward his truck as a unit.

"No. I've always been pretty transparent to her in the past. I don't want to have to deal with the issue of my sex life."

He unlocked then opened the passenger door for her then got in on the driver's side. "She doesn't want you to have sex?"

"She doesn't care about the sex. I just know how her mind works. She'll be all concerned about the time we spend together and warn me about getting emotional. I've heard it all before, trust me."

"You've gotten emotionally involved with a man before?" His voice didn't change but Fate picked up on his tension just the same. She didn't look too closely at the pleasure a little jealousy brought.

"I didn't get emotionally involved with anyone. I've heard the lectures with other Maidens. Selene always required that I sit in for some reason. And she lectures *me* about getting too close in my assignments." Not to mention she'd warned her of the Soldiers in particular.

"Like the woman the other day," he nodded and Fate frowned at his understanding.

"I didn't get too involved. Besides, she needed to talk

~ ☾ ~

about her kids—Never mind." She grumbled. "Selene
worries too much about the Maidens. I didn't want to
have to deal with it today."

Caden exited the interstate at a different place than
he'd done in previous trips and she looked at him. "The
Guards know where the cabin is. What's with the evasive
maneuvers?"

He shrugged. "Habit. Besides, I have something I
want to show you."

She perked up. Her life before the attacks, placid and
never changing, didn't offer as much comfort as
sameness. Now, she looked forward to change,
challenges. Influences of life with Caden, she supposed.
"Is it a shooting range? Another training facility?
What?"

He grinned, "It's a surprise." Despite her attempts, he
remained incommunicative until they reached their
destination.

Fate stared at the ramshackle building as Caden
parked. "A fish shack? This is the surprise?"

He shut off the ignition and grinned at her. "I don't
know about you, but I'm tired of our food at the cabin. I
needed a change and I'm hungry. Don't you feel like
indulging?"

She cast a suspicious look at the building. "I guess."

"Hush puppies, fried catfish. Homemade pie." He
leaned close and breathed into her ear. "Ice cold beer."

She laughed and shook her head then shoved her
door open. "I think I've found your weakness. Fried
foods and beer."

They got a table in the corner of the dining room and
Caden made sure she sat against a wall with him on the
outer margin of the table. Fate noted how he glanced
around the room. Business obviously thinned between
lunch and dinner, as there were only a few tables
occupied.

~ ☾ ~

Fate smiled as she glanced at the man with her. He'd made an effort to give her an afternoon free of attacks, without being confined in the cabin or in his offices surrounded by his men. What a sweet thing for him to do.

He picked up the photocopied sheet of paper that served as a menu and caught her eyeing their surroundings with doubt. "Don't let the décor fool you. It's clean and serves the best fish in town."

"And they like having a restaurant that looks like a fishing shack?" She ran a finger along the scarred surface of the table. It came away clean.

"That's what it is. Or at least what used to be here." Caden leaned back as a waitress placed two glasses of iced water and a pitcher of beer in front of them. "The man who opened the shack is a guy who retired and fished every day. He started out frying his catches for friends and as the crowds got bigger, he decided to open a restaurant. This place built up around his old shack. The original one is over there." He pointed to the far corner of the room, where a table sat empty on badly matched flooring and raw lumber walls. "I guarantee, everything on the menu is great."

She nodded and read the menu, her doubt morphing into delight. "They *do* have pie. I think I'll get that to start and follow it with the fish. Not catfish, though. Never liked it."

He grinned and motioned to the waitress, who hovered near the table. After they'd placed their order, he turned the conversation serious. "I want you to try something."

She narrowed her eyes, "I'm not eating anything like rattlesnake."

He chuckled and shook his head, then sobered. "I want you to try to communicate with me. Right now."

"But we've connected before."

~ ☾ ~

"Only in times of stress. I want to see how much control you have over it."

Her eyes widened slightly, then she nodded and lowered her eyes, apparently to study the menu. A few seconds passed. Caden straightened, as if to suggest they find another way.

"No we won't."

Her voice came through loud and clear as she entered his mind and he let out a sigh. *Finally.*

"I couldn't think of anything to say." She countered and he chuckled aloud.

"As if you're usually short on conversation." He sent the message back to her.

"I don't go on and on. I only talk when I have something important to say." She retorted vocally.

"I know, babe. Good job. Now, we can plan a strategy."

She cleared her throat and smiled over his head at the waitress then sighed at the sight of the large slice of coconut cream pie the girl placed in front of her.

"You sure you want that first?" Caden reached for his fork and dug into one side of the pie himself.

She didn't answer but filled her mouth with a bite then closed her eyes. Caden's fork halted on the way to his mouth. He watched as she ate then swallowed.

"I never have room for pie when I eat at a restaurant. This time, I wanted to be able to get dessert before I become too stuffed."

Another bite, another expression of near orgasmic bliss passed her face, followed by a groan.

"Honey, if a slice of pie does that to you, I'm buying the whole damn thing. If you eat the whole thing like that, I'll not be able to walk out of the restaurant without giving everyone an eyeful."

She giggled, covering her mouth with her hand. "Sorry. It's been a long time since I ate homemade pie."

~ ☾ ~

He tilted his head, "Go ahead, but it's a good thing you have to eat your meal. You don't have a jones for hush puppies, do you?"

She laughed and threw a napkin at him. That became the tone of the meal that followed. They exchanged bites of food; she still didn't prefer catfish but acknowledged the restaurant did a fine job with it. He snarled at the thought of smothering the hush puppies in ketchup and they both drained the pitcher of beer before requesting coffee.

Caden leaned back after the waitress cleared the table. He'd brought another blush to Fate's cheeks by ordering a coconut cream pie to go, but she'd also sent a message of what she wanted to do with the pie when they got home.

Damn, he enjoyed her. In bed and out of it, she kept him busy just keeping up with her banter, not to mention her enjoyment of things like pie and books.

He'd leaned forward to pull his wallet from his jeans pocket when he got a trace of dark intent. When he glanced at Fate he found her white, drawn and her eyes haunted. "You feel it, too?"

She nodded, adding, "They're outside, near the parking lot. More than one, but I don't know how many."

He could only pick up a vague feeling of danger. Her enhanced ability to locate the Guards might give them enough time to skirt the restaurant and avoid collateral damage.

"We'll go out the back way." He jerked out some bills and tossed them onto the table and simultaneously took her hand and rose. As he led her through the thankfully near empty café, he tried to formulate a plan. He thought he'd planned for every eventuality but he didn't feel good about this.

~ ☾ ~

They sprinted through the kitchens, startling the cooks and waiters. "Sorry." Caden muttered at the cook he almost bowled over as he skidded to a stop at the rear door. He gathered Fate close to him, trying to quell the urge to hold her, knowing it wasn't the smart or defensive thing to do. "Do you still sense them?"

"They're still near the front parking lot. Maybe they're waiting for us?" She turned her eyes to him and he hoped with all his might that he possessed enough skill to get them out of this one.

"Any ideas of how many there are?"

She shook her head, "Only that there's more than one."

He gave a sharp nod then squeezed her briefly. "Here's what we're going to do. I'm going to send out a call to Jake. He knows where we are. We make a run for the woods along the river. They're straight ahead after you go outside." He pushed her away slightly and held her by the forearms to make sure she understood him. "Don't let *anything* stop you from making those trees. If we can get there, we can stay out of sight long enough to confuse them and take care of them."

Her eyes were bright, almost glassy, but he knew she understood him when she raised a hand and uttered with a slight quiver in her voice. "Will these help?"

He sucked in a breath. She held a couple of sharp knives, each at least six inches long. "Where'd you get those?"

"From the counter as we came through. I think something's on this one." She indicated the larger blade and Caden felt an unfamiliar spurt of humor rise.

He carefully removed the knives from her hand and placed them on a table nearby. "Honey if you carry those without a sheath, you're more likely to stab me or yourself. Use this instead."

He removed his pistol from his calf holster and

~ ☾ ~

handed it to her after thumbing off the safety. "Point and squeeze."

She eyed the pistol with something that approached fury, then nodded and turned toward the door. Caden pulled her to him for one second and kissed her, hard. "Remember. Head for the trees and don't stop for anything."

He edged the door open and glanced outside, hoping their short conversation hadn't given the Guards time to circle the small building. It looked clear and he stepped outside and held a hand out to her.

She cleared the door just as a small explosion erupted near Caden's head and he cursed. "Go!" He started to run, giving her time to start and then veered off to the side. She faltered and he yelled, "Go, damn it. They're behind me!"

Fate ran a few more yards, intent on following his directions, then lurched to a halt. She gulped in a breath and glanced over her shoulder and swallowed a scream.

Three Guards, dressed in their token black, surrounded Caden. He fought, the gleam of a blade in his hand, but they held guns.

She didn't communicate with him, only reacted. As she ran toward them, she screamed, "Stop! He isn't the one you want. Here I am, damn it."

She stopped a few yards away and aimed the pistol at them. They turned as a unit, Caden with them. "Fate, damn it! Do as I told you."

"No. I won't let you sacrifice yourself for me. Move away from him." Her steady voice slightly surprised her. But then, her hand, and her mind remained fixed on the Guard.

The Guard nearest her, the one with the most menacing face of all, uttered an expletive she'd never heard then motioned with his hand. Fate shook her head, "No messages, just move."

~ ☾ ~

He growled. "You can't stop us."

"Fate, back away." Caden's voice became strained but Fate ignored him. The leader planned something.

"Step away from him, now." She squeezed a bit on the trigger, her grip steady. She could kill, would kill for him.

The leader stepped toward her and stopped. "There are too many of us, Maiden. Too many and too much at stake. We can't let the Sixth and the Maiden meld."

He lunged then, not toward her but toward Caden. Fate screamed and ran toward the knot of men. "Caden!" She screamed out his name and threw herself into the fray.

Caden grunted as a blade sliced into his side. He parried and lunged, then felt the wet give of his blade as it slid into flesh. As he pulled it free, he glanced around. One Guard down, another wounded but still fighting. And the third, God, the leader of the trio held Fate down and was throttling her. He lunged for her again, but a bullet grazed his leg and he went down.

God, help us.

She clawed at the hands around her throat. The Guard muttered something but Caden couldn't make it out. He tried to stand but his leg wouldn't let him, damn it. He started crawling toward her, knowing he wouldn't be in time. Her face, normally pale, now suffused with color. Frantically, he called out to her mentally. *"Fate, fight him! Knee him in the balls, kick him, and scratch him. Anything, baby. Anything."*

Her hands came up in a feeble movement, strangely uncoordinated and Caden knew if he didn't do something, he'd lose her. He took a breath and then focused all his attention, all his power, and all his belief on her. A surge of—something ran through him, as if

~ ☾ ~

he'd gotten a mild shock, then he fell to the ground,
exhausted. He could only watch her as she battled for
her life.

In her job so far, Fate'd accompanied dozens of souls
to the portal of eternity, but she hadn't seen beyond the
door. Now, she would have the opportunity. No. She
wouldn't enter eternity. Her soul would be someone
else's and she'd be lost.

Oddly, she didn't feel panic at the thought of losing
her soul, losing her opportunity to exist forever. Instead
the only feelings that ran through her consciousness
were puzzlement that it took so long to die, and regret.
She'd leave Caden and he'd blame himself for her
mistakes. But he would live.

Her vision faded as she tried to grasp one more iota
of oxygen the Guard denied her. The hands she'd tried
to raise in response of Caden's mental plea flopped to
the ground, useless and weak. So, she'd learn of death
and the darkness...

It started as a prickle of sensation and she studied it,
intent on preserving her awareness as long as possible.
A twinge of heat, a buzz of electricity that grew into a
surge, then flooded her system. She recognized it even
as it inundated her with a strength that wasn't hers,
couldn't have been hers.

She felt Caden with her, yet not present. His mental
voice wasn't there, but his power ran through her to lend
strength to her arms and hands. She pushed the Guard
away with a lunging thrust and then in a fury of
movement found the pistol that lay at her side. His eyes,
widened with shock as she pulled the trigger and ended
his life, freed his soul.

She turned onto her hands and knees, still trying to
find air to breathe and searched for Caden. The mist

~ ☾ ~

that covered her eyes faded to a sharp focus and she saw him, lying in the midst of the other Guards.

They were dead; one lay in a pool of blood, the other lay to the side of Caden, his neck bent at an unnatural angle. And Caden's eyes were on her, his face white and drawn.

She didn't bother to stand. She didn't trust her legs anyway. She crawled to him as a man stuck his head out the back door of the restaurant. "What the hell?"

"Call an ambulance. He's hurt!" She husked as she sat beside Caden and stared at him.

"Fate." His voice, rough and grating, sounded like heaven.

"I'm here. Where are you hurt?"

"I'm okay. Just a graze on my leg and a cut on my side." He waved a hand toward his body and then let it fall on her bent legs. "You're okay?"

She nodded, her hands already smoothing over his body, trying to find his injuries. "Thanks to you. Have you lost a lot of blood?" His vague descriptions of injuries didn't explain his pallor.

He shook his head and inched forward until he could lay his head on her lap and pushed his head into her stomach. "No, just a scrape. I think the bullet numbed my leg, but it's not bleeding too much or numb anymore. I sent you a message."

She smoothed his hair back from his eyes. "You sent me more than that. Did you mean to?"

"Yeah. At least I hoped to. Never been done before. May need to keep it to ourselves..." His voice faded out and he slumped into her lap. Fate's pulse jumped until she noticed the color creeping back into his face. She slid her hand to his neck and felt for a pulse. While a little fast, it remained strong. And Caden slept in her arms.

She held him, her eyes and ears alert for any sounds.

~ ☾ ~

As the noise of the crowd that now surrounded them and distant sirens played around her, she sat, her fingers in his hair and pondered on the Guard's last words as he tried to kill her.

"You won't mate and meld with the Soldier, Maiden. You won't destroy our future."

~ ☾ ~

Chapter Thirteen

Caden groaned at the sight that greeted him when he woke. Fate stood beside him, but she wasn't the source of his unease. Mentor Donan waited at the end of the bed, his expression unreadable.

He tried to find a comfortable position in the hospital bed, his back already sore and twisted from the mechanics of the folding bed. "Did the doctor say when I could leave?"

Fate curved her hand around the rail and smiled. "You were right. It's a graze on the leg. The doctor said your numbness turned out to be an immediate reaction to the wound. And your side just needed a couple of stitches."

"After you talk with the police, you'll be free to go." Donan's emotionless voice told Caden everything he needed to know. Don't give anything away about the Guard and the Soldiers. As if he ever did in his dealings with the police.

He nodded. "I'll talk to them."

Fate stepped a millimeter closer, "They started to ask me some questions, but I wanted to wait until you were awake." She sent a silent plea for a story to share with the police. Caden answered with a scenario about the trio coming on them as they exited the restaurant, intent on robbery. He could feel her absorbing the story as he laid it out for her consciousness, just as he sensed Donan monitoring her.

She nodded, smiling at both of them. "I'll let them know you're awake. You'll probably see them in a few minutes."

~ ☾ ~

Long enough to talk with Donan.

His leader waited until Fate closed the door behind
her before taking her place by Caden's bed in the cubicle
of the emergency room. "You were lucky."

Caden nodded, eyeing his mentor and opening his
link with him. *Fate sensed their presence, as well as
their position. Not exact, but close enough to give us a
chance.*

"Yet you almost died. And she has bruises on her
throat that look like she may have barely escaped
herself."

Caden met intent Donan's gaze. "She told you about
the fight, didn't she?"

"Yes, but I have a feeling she left some things out.
Like how she got the bruises."

"Did you scan her?"

Donan's flat effect failed then and Caden experienced
a flicker of pride at the fact that obviously Fate blocked
his mentor. *"She shielded from you? No easy feat."*

"She's clearly Selene's student." Donan drew a breath.
"You will have to find another refuge. Your cabin will be
overtaken by the time you arrive."

Caden gave his assent to the idea. He knew a couple
other places he could take Fate, even Donan didn't know
of them. "I'm going to be able to leave tonight?" This he
uttered vocally.

"Yes. Right after you talk to the detective. But take
care not to open your stitches." Donan added, "You'll
need your strength. Use your power to heal as quickly as
you can."

Caden kept his shield up as he wondered if he'd used
his reserves earlier. If so, he'd have a hard time
accelerating his healing.

***

Fate waited at the emergency room's exit for Caden to
be released. As she did, the battle played out in her

~ ☾ ~

mind, over and over again. What happened to them, how they'd escaped being killed remained clear. They'd been outnumbered and out-gunned and yet she and Caden were alive and the Guards dead. But did she make matters worse?

Caden wanted to give her some peace by taking her to the restaurant, she knew. Though he never came out and admitted it, he realized she experienced a little house madness during her forced hiding. Could it be her fault he'd taken her to the small restaurant and opened them up to attack?

And did she make him more vulnerable by turning and running toward him when the Guards surrounded him? A sick feeling washed over her at the thought that she could be responsible for his wounds.

A slight sound caught her attention and she turned to see him walking slowly toward her. No wheelchair for him, apparently. A stern faced nurse walked behind him and to her rear, an abandoned wheelchair.

He looked fine, to the outer eye. But he moved a little slower, with more care. He'd spent a lot of energy, sending her his extra power. Would he have enough to spare for healing? And would he be better off if she left him?

"No." The voice came through to her mind loud and clear. Once again, she hadn't been able to block her thoughts and emotions against him.

She smiled encouragingly, "You all set?"

"Yeah. You have my truck?"

Fate's smile altered from a forced one to one that felt more natural. "I didn't bring the truck, Jake has it. Before you ask, he said he'd take care of it. I have another car."

He placed his hand on her lower back then started through the exit. "Good. We need a different vehicle anyway. What did you get?"

Fate indicated the SUV parked in front of them and

~ ☾ ~

after a long look at it he nodded then held his hand out for the keys. She balked. "I'm driving."

"You don't know the way."

"We're not going back to the cabin?" She didn't bother masking the disappointment in her voice. Though she'd been a bit stir-crazy, the cabin still held appeal as the place they'd finally come together.

"No. It's too vulnerable. So, keys?" He waggled his fingers at her and she dropped them in his hand.

They made short work of exiting the parking lot and Fate kept a mind open to dangers until they were out of town. She didn't realize how tense she'd been until she drew a deep breath and glanced around her.

They were deep in the country, now. In the fading light of day, she could make out fields and some rolling pastureland. In the distance mountains rolled and abutted against the sky. "We're going to another cabin?"

"No. I have a friend with a house we can use for a while. It's in the mountains." He motioned with his head toward the mountains in the horizon and continued. "It's out of the way and gated, so we should have some warning if anyone tries to sneak up on us. And no one else knows about it."

"Even Donan?"

"Even Donan. He tried to scan you, you know."

"I felt it. He didn't pick up anything, did he?"

Caden smiled and she sensed his pride. "Not a thing."

"He admitted trying to read my mind?"

"Not until I questioned him about it. He saw your bruises," Caden lifted a hand to her neck and smoothed away the collar of her sweater, then lightly skimmed the purpling bruise on her neck. "God, I'm sorry I couldn't get to you in time."

She covered his hand with her own, "You did. If you hadn't sent the power surge to me, I wouldn't have been able to fight the Guard off. Are you okay?"

~ ☾ ~

"You mean from the surge? Yeah. I'll have to take it easy for a couple of days but other than that, I'll be fine."

"And your wounds?"

"Should be sealed by tomorrow, completely healed within the week."

If no other attacks happened. Something tells me the Guard has stepped up their attacks and numbers for a reason. "Will we be able to train?"

"Yeah, I need to stay limber." He threw her a quick grin. "You'll like the new place. It has a gym."

Unbelievably, they talked about other things during the rest of the drive. Caden ribbed her about her choice of clothes. The scrubs were a replacement for the blood soaked jeans and blouse. The sweater she wore over them she'd retrieved from the lost and found bin at the hospital. Fate tossed the other clothes in the trash, not wanting a reminder that she'd literally held Caden's life in her hands, there for a while.

Though dark by the time they reached the house, she could make out a two-story structure. Tucked into the side of a mountain, the stone and cedar house looked in the gloom of night as if it as if it'd sprung up from the forest itself. Yet, inside the place seemed to have every modern convenience.

The recessed lighting glowed softly. Totally at odds with the cabin they'd left with its simple, clean lines, this house definitely featured more modern features. With overstuffed couches, paintings and wall sconces decorating the walls, and high-end appliances, this house provided everything desired. She glanced around as Caden dropped into a chair in the sumptuous living room, letting a black case fall to the floor beside him. He swiveled his head toward her and held out his hand.

When she got to his side, he pulled her onto his lap.

"Caden! Be careful."

His eyes drifted shut as he braced her with a hand on

~ ☾ ~

her hip and the other on her thighs as they rest on his legs. "I'm fine. Just tired. What do you think of the house?"

"It's fine."

One eye slatted open. "Fine?"

She smiled and leaned gingerly into his chest. "It's a little too decorated, for me. I like comfortable, like my apartment and your cabin. But this is good."

He chuckled. "I'll not tell my friend what you said. He'd have to start all over with the decorating."

"Why?"

"Cause he's a perfectionist, and his wife has more time on her hands than she knows what to do with." His eyes drifted shut again and Fate lay against him, letting him rest and listening to him breathe.

Several minutes passed before he stirred, then ran his hand up and down her back. "You want to talk about today?"

She sighed. Tempted to ignore his question and continue in her peaceful interlude, Fate knew she needed to share the Guard's threats with Caden. She started to sit up but when he grunted a negative she remained lying in his arms.

"I'm sorry I ran toward you, instead of away."

He squeezed her thigh, "I understand. I would have done the same thing. The Guard that attacked you, he said something to you, didn't he?"

She nodded into his neck then repeated the Guard's threat. "What could he have meant? A melding and the destruction of the world? That doesn't make sense. Two people having sex can't mean the end of the world."

"Maybe he didn't mean it literally. Jake mentioned a similar tale, only with a more positive slant." When he filled her in on Jake's historical research he didn't prevent her from sitting upright.

She stared at him, perplexed. "You mean we're the

~ ☾ ~

people they're talking about in the prediction or
prophecy or whatever?"

"Or legend. Yeah, they seem to think so, and
apparently, so does Jake. Has Selene mentioned
anything like this to you?"

She shook her head, her hair falling about her face. "If
she knows anything about it, she hasn't shared it with
me. Does Donan know about it?"

"He probably put Jake on the research kick."

"Do *you* think we're the couple of the legend?"

He didn't answer for a time and she began to think
he'd fallen asleep again. Then he met her gaze with a
steady one of his own. "I'm sure of it."

Her heart pounded in her chest. "So, we kill the
Guards and go our separate ways."

He slowly shook his head. "We find out what the
legend means."

"But if it does mean the end of everything?"

"Honey, it isn't the end of *our* world. It's the end of
the Obsidian Guards' existence." He straightened and
shifted her to his side and Fate stood. She stepped away
to give him room to move as he came to a stand but he
hauled her back with a kiss. "We need to find out some
things. Come on."

He tucked her hand in his and leaned over to retrieve
the case. Then he towed her to the sofa across the room
and sat down, pulling her down beside him.

She sat quietly as he set the case on a glass-topped
table and opened it. Her eyes widened slightly at the
sight of the assortment of knives and pistols in the foam
lined case, but his attention focused on the thin folder
he removed, along with an older, thick book that lay
wedged in with the weaponry. "I didn't have much time
before we left the hospital so I called Jake and he
brought this stuff to me."

He closed the case with a decisive click and leaned

~ ☾ ~

forward to tuck it under the coffee table. On the table itself he placed the book and file. "This is the legend," he indicated the thick, water-stained, leather bound book, then the folder, from which he removed a small flash drive, "and the research. Too bad I don't have a computer."

She glanced around at the ultra modern house and muttered, "There's got to be half a dozen in this place."

Caden grinned then chuckled. "You're right. I'll use one of the computers here then do a sweep on it." He gave her the book. "Jake said he marked the place where the legend is mentioned. You look at that and I'll check on his research."

As he leaned forward over the file, Caden grimaced and ignored the look Fate shot at him. She decided to let him work for a while. They couldn't let up on this now. It was too important. *He* was too important.

They read in silence for a while then she huffed a sigh of impatience. "I hate this veiled language. Listen to this, 'The Maiden is fair and searches for truth, the Soldier brave but craven. When mated, the Soldier will dominate the Maiden. Then the world will change, the winds will blow. The new will come the old we will no longer know.'" She made a disgusted face. "Not only were they cryptic, but they were lousy poets, too."

Caden grunted then added, "But it makes sense. Think of your love of books. It could be construed as a search for truth. Your job, you didn't pick a job like nurse or something like that, like most Maidens. You picked something that fell in line with your true calling, helping families when someone died."

"So? You're not craven."

Caden grinned and shot her a lustful glance, "In the opinion of a Soldier Monk, bound to sexual abstinence? I'm definitely craven, babe."

She still wasn't convinced, so he turned his attention

~ ☾ ~

to the folder. "I'll have to check Jake's facts on the flash drive, but it looks like there's a connection between me, a sixth son Soldier and you. Jake said you were the direct descendent of the founder of the Maidens. Is that true?"

She looked up from her reading, startled, "I don't know. My mother died when I was eight and Selene hasn't mentioned anything. Wouldn't she tell me something like that?"

Not if she wanted to keep you in the dark. The savage thought startled him, but something hidden, almost subversive seemed associated with the knowledge withheld from Fate and he didn't like it. But one thing came through clear as she read his thoughts. She wasn't going to be the sacrificial lamb.

He closed the file and tossed it to the table then stretched his arms over his head. "I'm beat. Ready for bed?"

"You're not hungry?" She eyed his body as he stretched and relished the rise of want. Maybe he wasn't that tired.

"You?"

"A little. Besides, you need to eat and drink something if you're going to heal properly." She stood and held her hand out to him. "Let's go see what this fancy house has in the way of food."

They did find some food. Caden must have taken the time to make more than a phone call to Jake, Fate mused as she chopped vegetables for an omelet from the fully stocked refrigerator. She ignored the more substantial offerings like steaks. Tonight, they'd eat light and rest.

He made toast and coffee while she fixed the omelet and they ate at the small table settled in a nook in the corner of the kitchen. As much as she liked the looks of the house, she could never feel at ease in this obviously

~ ☾ ~

rich atmosphere. With cherry cabinets, granite counter tops and what looked like marble flooring throughout the lower floor she felt like a true visitor. What lay upstairs, she wondered, velvets?

She stabbed at the food in front of her for a few more minutes then gave up eating the rest of her omelet and watched Caden polish off his. She grinned as he eyed her plate then slid it over to him and chuckled as he finished the remaining half omelet she'd left.

After he'd finished, he sat back and sighed. "I guess I was hungry."

"I guess you were," she purred, satisfied. Her old persona would have laughed at the picture she presented now. A woman happy to provide food for her man. *And what a man he is.*

He stood and picked up their plates, carrying them to the sink. He dumped them into the basin and turned to her, dark intent in his eyes. "Time for bed."

"I need to..."

"Time for bed," he repeated and advanced.

Fate returned his smile but put out a hand to indicate the dishes. "But I need to clean up."

"Tomorrow. Time for bed." He draped an arm over her shoulders and led her to the staircase.

Once upstairs, he didn't waste time showing her around but hustled her into a large bedroom. Fate looked around. No velvet curtains, thank goodness, but silk draped on the windows. "Is this a vacation home?"

"More like a business home. It belongs to an old client. He uses it for retreats, meetings, and things like that. Only uses it a couple times a year, from what I've heard." Caden drew the drapery together before turning on a bedside lamp. He then walked to the door and flicked off the overhead light he'd turned on when they entered the room. Then with a swipe of his hand, he closed the door to the room.

~ ☾ ~

His smile held promises of a long, heated night and she smiled as he advanced, unbuttoning the top three buttons of his knit Henley shirt.

"You do realize I have no clothes, don't you?" She gestured toward her own mismatched outfit.

His grin widened, "We'll have to make do, I guess."

She laughed at the frankly lascivious look in his eyes. "That's fine for tonight, but what about tomorrow? You don't have any clothes either, if you'll recall."

He shrugged. "I'm not expecting visitors. We can scrounge around for clothes in the closets. If we don't find any," he pulled the loosened shirt over his head, displaying the chest she loved so much, "we'll have to make do."

When he closed in on her Fate allowed herself the luxury of draping her arms around his waist and leaning into his kiss. She hesitated a moment at the feel of the bandage at his side, then smoothed her hands along his back before bringing them to the front of his jeans. She opened the belt at his waist and loosened his pants at the same time she felt the tug of his fingers at the drawstring of the scrubs she wore.

He didn't have to push the pants off her waist as she did the tighter jeans he wore, but she made short work of his jeans and in no time he stood naked. She lifted her arms over her head to assist in taking off her shirt.

She stepped back as he pressed into her, his erection nudging against her midriff. The back of her legs hit the bed and she fell. For once and for all, to fall for this man. She finally admitted her love for him.

Caden followed her down onto the bed, one knee beside her and the opposite hand bracing him. Fate opened her eyes and caught a slight wince as he supported himself over her. "We can't do this tonight."

"The hell we can't," he growled and flopped onto the bed at her side. Instead of lying there, resting, he tugged

~ ☾ ~

her until she lay on top of him. "You get to do the work, though."

She sucked in a breath at the feel of him. His knees bent over the edge of the bed, but she could still feel his chest hairbrush against her sensitive nipples, his erection press insistently into her stomach, and his hands on her butt. She sighed and smiled at him then pressed a kiss into the notch at the base of his neck. "You're sure about this? It won't hurt you?"

He grinned, "If we don't do this, I'll definitely hurt, all night."

She leaned in and kissed him, a brief peck, then levered herself off him. At his look of confusion, she smiled. "We need to get more comfortable."

He glanced down at himself and laughed, "I'll not be comfortable for a while, honey."

"But I can't reach all of you, with your legs hanging over the bed." She gestured toward his lower half, then scooted off the bed and started to pull the covers away.

He grumbled about losing the momentum but stood and helped her fold the covers at the bottom of the bed afterwards. He slowly crawled to the middle of the bed and lay down, then propped his arms behind his head. She shook her head at the satisfied, yet hungry look in his eyes. Somehow, despite the gravity of their situation, he could find the joy in loving her.

She lay beside him. Her hand rested on his chest as she leaned over him and gently bit his lower lip. A growl rose from his belly, and he started to lower his hands, only to raise them and lace them together again at the shake of her head.

"You wanted to do it this way. It's my turn to torture you." She ran her tongue lightly along the seam of his lips, and then captured his sigh as he opened his mouth to her. She propped one hand on the bed beside him and ran the other one along the fine line of hair that ran

~ ☾ ~

from the sprinkling of dark hair around his nipples down. She explored his mouth, playing chase with his tongue as she ran a hand down the narrowing line to his groin, where the hair grew heavier.

Her hand closed around his erection and she murmured soft words at his jerk and moan. "Did I hurt you?"

"Babe, you'd never hurt me holding me like that." His hand lowered to cover hers as it gripped him and gave a squeeze, a silent request for more. She nudged his hand away and he gripped the sheet in his fist.

"No, I mean when you jerked. Did it hurt your stitches?"

"Uh uh." He followed the denial with another moan as she began to caress him, her hand moving in slow rhythm. Soon, she felt the moisture of his readiness and she leaned down in anticipation.

Instead, his hand came from the sheet and grasped her hair. "No. I want to come in you, not your mouth."

She rose up and eyed him, impatient to taste him, but aware of the thrum of desire that ran beneath the words he spoke. In their unspoken communication, she could feel the need, the burn that pounded through him.

She kissed him once more as she straddled him, taking care not to lean on him, rather on the bed. He released the sheet and she felt his hand between them, separating her then finding his way into her. She sighed as he ran his hand up through the soft hair covering her groin and to her waist.

She set a slow pace, using her newly toned leg muscles to raise and lower herself, trying to prolong the sensation of having him brush against, then glide inside her. Something felt different, more intense. The smooth, yet rugged feel of him inside her, slightly damp, sent her higher.

She stopped in surprise when she realized the change. "Caden, the condom." She gasped.

~ ☾ ~

He bracketed her waist with his hands and lifted her.
"Forget 'em."

"But—"

His eyes opened, brilliant and dark. "I want to feel
you, not a barrier between us."

She bit her lips at the sensation of the pace he forced
on her, slow and irregular. "But with no condom..."

"You're mine. *Mine*. Any baby we make will be mine,
too." He groaned and gripped her waist harder. She'd
have marks on her after this, but Fate couldn't care as
she took his hint and increased the pace, moving on
him, over him in increasing speed.

Soon, she cried out and stilled. Caden followed her
and she felt the rush of his orgasm, both physical and
psychic, wash over her, triggering another spasm in her.

She collapsed onto his chest, her breathing ragged
and short. He folded his arms around her, squeezing her
in a tired pulse of feeling then letting his arms loosely
encase her as their breathing eased.

Caden didn't want to move, nor did he want to think.
He refused to consider the ramifications of unprotected
sex with Fate. Yet the thoughts of her having his child, of
spending the rest of his life with her, were so compelling
he ached for it.

She'd managed to enter a heart that couldn't be
breached, or at least that's what he'd thought. What he'd
been taught his entire adult life.

He shifted a bit, his leg aching from the tension he'd
been in. Fate murmured and started to shift away from
him. "No, stay." He turned on his side, still inside her,
and tucked her into him, face to face.

Her hair covered her eyes and most of her face and he
smoothed it away so he could read her expression. She
looked totally satisfied with her life right now and he

~ ☾ ~

prayed it would stay that way. Somehow, someway, he would keep her.

She raised her face for his kiss and then buried it in what must be her favorite sleeping position, in the curve between his neck and shoulder. He tightened his embrace and finally spoke the words he'd been fighting for days.

"I love you."

She nodded her head against him, forcing him to lean away and tilt her head up with his finger. Tears glistened in her eyes as she smiled and responded. "I know. I felt it."

"So?"

"Didn't you feel it from me, too?"

Caden grumbled, "Maybe I did. But I need to hear it too. Say the words."

"I love you. I want to stay with you, even if Selene tells me I can't be a Maiden anymore."

Caden tucked her back into her place. "Is that what happens with Maidens who fall in love?"

"Yes. It doesn't happen often, but it happens. Usually, they're cut off from the community. Selene says it's the just and right punishment, separation from the kinship of the Society." She ended the sentence with a scoff that told him what she thought of the idea of separation from the Maidens' Society in comparison to being separated from him. "Isn't that what happens with the Soldiers?"

"No." He didn't want to talk about it.

She reared back, her face serious. "We *need* to talk about it. Tell me. What happens to a Soldier who falls in love?"

"Excommunication at the least, but more, depending on the level of the Soldier."

She waited until he continued. "If the Soldier is a regular warden of souls, the kind who goes in with another Soldier to fight, then excommunication is the

~ ☾ ~

punishment. Nothing more. Some of those Soldiers have even succeeded in their old cover jobs, police, and security services, that sort of thing. For a Soldier who has a more senior position—"

"Like you."

"Like me, those Soldiers face more stringent discipline."

When he stopped she disengaged herself from him and sat up, her pale body momentarily distracting him. "Caden? What happens?"

"Removal of powers. Torture. Death." He kept his voice even though his mind ran through the possibilities of his entanglement with her.

She must have picked up on it because the faint tint of rose in her face from the lovemaking faded swiftly, replaced by a pallor he'd not seen since her Maiden job. He levered himself up on one elbow and reached for her with the other hand.

Fate backed away from him, her eyes stricken. "You could die because of me?"

"No. I could die as a result of the Guard's activities. I could die from a car wreck. I *won't* die because I love you. I won't let that happen and neither will Donan."

She scurried off the bed and turned in a circle, evidently looking for her clothes. Caden followed her more slowly, the insults to his body making themselves known. He found the top to her scrubs and handed it to her then struggled into his jeans and shirt as she retrieved the pants herself.

He didn't stop her when she ran into the bathroom and slammed the door. Instead, he found another bathroom down the hall and went inside to shower.

***

Fate threw the clothes into a heap on the floor of the sumptuous bathroom and sank onto the toilet seat, stunned. She'd never wanted to fall in love, never

~ ☾ ~

thought she'd face the prospect of leaving the Maidens for the love of a man. Now, she knew she could face the separation from Selene, the community she'd known since her teen years, without a backward glance, for Caden.

But what would he face? The images that rushed through her mind were vague, blurry at the edges. He'd remembered things from lectures and conversations, not from reality, but the pictures in his mind were more than enough to make her nauseated. For him to love her, to commit to her and a life with her, he'd face death. She knew Donan's respect for him, his desire for Caden to do something important in the Soldiers' organization. When he'd tried to read her mind she'd gotten a glimpse of his in return. She clearly wasn't included in his plans for Caden.

She made herself stand and turn on the shower, determined to figure out a solution to the problem. He *couldn't* die because of her. She'd give him up first.

She showered quickly then dressed in her borrowed scrubs. If she could find the car keys she could be away from the house in a few minutes. She'd heard the sound of another shower running nearby, so maybe she could sneak out before he became aware of her absence.

She opened the door to the bathroom and came face to chest with him. Caden leaned against the doorjamb, his arms crossed across that firm chest, now covered by a different shirt than the one he'd worn to the house.

"You aren't going anywhere." He ground out the words and then cupped her shoulders with hard hands, giving her a little shake. "Do you understand me? *Nowhere.*"

She tried to hold in the tears but one spilled over her lashes. Caden cursed and pulled her to him. Fate breathed in his scent, soap and a faint citrusy smell, with the underlying scent she identified as Caden. She

~ ☾ ~

sighed into his chest, knowing she'd not be able to leave him.

"I'm sorry, baby. Did I hurt you?"

She glanced up at him, confused then shook her head. "Where did you find the clothes?" She ran her hand over the flannel shirt. The faded colors testimony of its age and wear.

He draped his arm over her shoulder and led her to the living room where he dropped onto the sofa and pulled her down with him. His position on the couch told her of his fatigue more than anything. He lounged with his head back and his feet on the expensive table in front of the structure. "I found a few shirts in a laundry room. Looks like something the guy used to wash his car. They were folded beside the soap and bucket. I found you one like mine, but it's missing some buttons."

She shrugged and tugged at the hem of her own shirt. "It's something to change into while this washes."

He nodded. "Fate, I can't lose you. I *won't*."

She let her head fall back onto the back of the couch, then swiveled it to look at him. "Donan has big plans for you Caden. He won't let you go without a fight. Even if the fight is with you."

His expression darkened. "How do you know Donan's plans for me?"

"I sensed it when he tried to read my mind at the hospital. We threaten him. I didn't realize why then, but I think he knows there's a strong connection between us."

He turned his gaze toward the ceiling. "Donan told me about the Soldiers and Maidens' history and the reason they split from working together."

"You mean about the Soldier and Maiden who chose their love over souls?"

He looked at her. "Selene warned you too?"

"Just since we, um, you know. I don't think she knows

~ ☾ ~

anything, but she "warned" me of the situation."

He shook his head. "I don't think that's the only reason Donan is worried. He does know about our ability to communicate. But I got the impression last time we talked, really talked, that he wanted to tell me something else. He probably put Jake up to the research... Oh, holy damn. He knew of the legend." Caden looked at her then, "He knows if we made love we could become a pair."

She sat straight. "And then?"

He shook his head. "Hell if I know. He may want to use it in service of the Soldiers or he may string me up and cut off my balls. But we have to talk to him, and to Selene. If he knows about the legend then obviously so does she. I don't want to be out of the loop any more than we are already. We need to plan."

He started to get up but her hand on his arm stopped him. "We need to plan for the Guard first."

He looked at her intently then leaned back again. "Why?"

She shook her head. "I don't know. But the attack at the restaurant acted only as a warning shot. Don't ask me how I know but there's another attack coming, soon."

His eyes narrowed on her but she knew he didn't doubt her. "Okay. We plan for the attack."

~ ☾ ~

Chapter Fourteen

They'd planned, trained and tried to avoid thinking about Donan's retribution over the next few hours. Caden pushed himself and Fate farther than he knew he should. His side ached from training, but he'd focused his healing energies on it and the wound in his leg as much as he dared without draining his reserve energy.

If he became too fatigued, he'd be of no use to Fate in a battle. He trusted her radar for the Guards, and she expected another battle with several Guards, and soon.

The next morning, after a workout that left him gasping for breath, he made her go with him to the field behind the house. There, he set up a small target and showed her the handgun with silencer attached. She looked on as he explained how to thumb the safety on and off, how to advance shells into the chamber and the process of firing. She took the gun from him, her face drawn and tight, and aimed for the target. Caden shoved aside the desire to help her fire, instead he forced himself to critique her and push her with each shot.

"Don't lock your arms. And don't consciously aim. You'll end up shooting beyond your target. Don't jerk the trigger, squeeze."

She dropped the hand holding the pistol and whirled on him. "Don't aim, don't jerk, and don't put your arm out. What am I supposed to do, throw the thing at the Guard?"

He stepped behind her and lifted her arm once more. He could feel the fatigue, the faint tremor in her muscles as she took a breath. "Once more. Hold the gun steady

~ ☾ ~

with a slightly bent elbow. Look at your target and line up the gun with your eyes, no squinting or aiming. Then squeeze." He removed his hand from her arm and watched as the gun coughed a shot and a neat hole appeared in the target, her first hit.

She fired off four more shots, each hitting the target and then again dropped her arm and turned to him. As she handed him the pistol she shook her head. "We can practice all day and it'll still be a lucky shot if I injure one of them."

He reloaded the gun then thumbed on the safety and stored the pistol in the back of his jeans. "A lucky shot is all it takes. Now you're not scared to fire it, like before."

She glared at him. "How did you know?"

"I know you." He kissed her and then led her to the target and bent to retrieve spent bullets from around the area. She helped and they finished clearing the area in a few minutes. He hefted the straw bale onto his shoulder and headed back to the house with her trailing him, bending to pick up a spent shell every now and then. He mentally shook his head. In the course of a few days, she'd gone from a victim to a woman with power over her world. She didn't blink at the thought of shooting at a person, fell into the subterfuge of hiding target practice from civilians, and blithely discussed a plan to draw out Guards.

Damn, could he ask for more in a woman?

They planned a trip, another foray into unprotected territory. Fate couldn't predict where the attack would occur. Only that it would involve more than one Guard. Caden faced the dilemma now of whether he put her at risk by coming out into the open. And how much did he tell Donan?

She changed from the flannel shirt she'd used to train and practice shooting in and back into the now clean scrub top. Caden smiled at the thought of her frowns, as

~ ☾ ~

she'd put on the scrub bottoms that morning. She'd
washed their clothes in the night and announced them
ready to burn when they gained access to a more diverse
wardrobe. He couldn't agree more. Burn all her clothes.
He'd be more than happy if she didn't wear any ever
again.

He stowed the bale back in the storage shed then
entered the house where he found Fate tidying up the
kitchen. She tossed a paper towel into the trash and
wiped her hands before turning to him. "Everything is
the way we found it, except for this." She indicated the
small bag of trash they'd take with them as they left.
"We won't be back, will we?"

He shook his head. Either way, they'd spent their last
night in the up-scale vacation home. "Ready?"

She nodded her head and shouldered her purse. He
tied the trash up and carried it to the car, along with his
own satchel. They didn't talk much on the way back into
town. But, it didn't matter, as both minds were open to
the other, and each tried to boost the other for the battle
ahead.

First they went to her place of business. Fate
introduced Caden to the women she worked with and
put in her resignation at the same time. She'd never
work there again. The job secured through the Society
wouldn't exist for her after she spoke with Selene.

As she gathered the few things she wanted from her
desk, she watched Caden survey the office, never off
duty. Except with her. Alone with her, he relaxed,
smiled, even joked. He even became jealous of time
spent away from her.

She knew the risks she undertook, but really, when
she thought of life away from him, there wasn't much of
a risk at all. The thought that they may repeat the

~ ☾ ~

actions of that couple long ago, choose love over souls, occurred to her, but she dismissed it. First, she couldn't imagine either of them putting themselves over a soul, and two, if it did happen, she'd face the consequences with Caden.

He allowed her time to gather her things and for her work friends to check him out. She didn't appreciate that too much, though she understood. Then he hustled her out of the office and to the truck Jake delivered to her office. She broached the subject of retrieving her car. "Not today. We're taking a risk coming out into the open, as it is."

"Isn't that the plan, for us to look vulnerable to attack and draw them out?"

He smiled and reached for her hand. "I know and I'm trying. It just goes against the grain for me to put you out there, you know?"

She squeezed his hand and let it rest on her thigh. "But if we don't we may never see the end of this. We may never be able to have a life of our own."

He grunted in reply then started the truck. "To your Guide's house?"

She nodded and sat back against the seat and tried to prepare herself for the upcoming meeting. She needed to talk to Selene, find out what she knew and discover the ramifications of the decisions she and Caden made. She looked at him as he drove, steady and silent, his hand enfolding her own in its strong grasp. She wouldn't change her mind, unless for his sake.

"Don't even think it, honey. We're in this together, no matter what. Right?"

He'd read her mind again, drat him. "If Donan decides your defection deserves torture, or worse?"

"I'll face that when I have to. Besides, I don't think it'll happen."

"What happened to them? The Soldier and Maiden

~ ☾ ~

that chose their love over the souls?" She looked at him but got a shrug as a response. "Selene didn't tell me, either. I guess that means they died."

"Or disappeared. They might have had eight kids and died peacefully in their beds, honey."

Fate smiled, as she knew he expected. *How did they die?? And will I be able to die peacefully as well?* Even as the thought occurred to her, she knew the answer. She couldn't imagine living without Caden and if that meant she died with him, so be it.

They drove on, silent, each searching for Guards and simultaneously seeking strength from the other.

When Fate saw the exterior of the Retreat, she took a deep breath then sighed. As soon as they entered, she turned to Caden. "I want to see Selene alone."

He stared at her. "She needs to see us together, Fate. As a couple."

Fate raised her eyebrow. "I'll be surprised if she doesn't already know about us. Besides, if she doesn't, seeing you when I tell her about my decision will be a slap in the face." When he opened his mouth to argue, she shook her head, "Please. I need to go in alone. And you *will* be with me, you know."

"Fine. Call me if you need me. I'll make myself comfortable," He finished with a grimace at the delicate armchairs in the small reception area slash living room. Fate smiled and entered the hallway toward Selene's quarters. In her mind she could hear his grumbles and mutterings about the seating and realized he did it to calm her fears.

She sensed her teacher's presence as she neared the inner room that served as Selene's study. At her knock, a voice murmured permission to enter. She slid the pocket door open and stepped inside the room, unsure of her reception.

Selene sat in her familiar pose of crossed legs and

~ ☾ ~

hands at her knees. She appeared serene, but appearances could be very deceiving. Fate made her bow of acquiescence and waited. Selene motioned for her to sit and Fate sank down, grateful she didn't have to rely on her legs to support her.

"You've made a decision." Selene didn't prevaricate.

"Yes. Caden and I've decided to draw the Guards out into the open. I've been a victim too long."

Selene stood and walked to the small table that rested beside a chair. She retrieved a necklace, one that Fate remembered displayed in a glassed-in tray. Now, Selene draped it around her neck. At the center of the simple gold chain a large amethyst stone in a gold setting. The necklace fell to rest mid-chest and Selene then returned to her original position.

"You realize if you draw out the Guards, you risk your life, your soul."

"As well as Caden's. Yes. We've discussed this and still, it has to be done. Or my life will be one of constant fear."

Selene appeared surprised at her statement and maybe it seemed a little over the top but it aptly described how she felt now. A tingle bloomed in her mind, signaling her teacher's probe. For the first time ever, she blocked the attempt. Selene's eyes widened slightly at the block but she didn't say anything. Instead, she asked some questions about the plan. Fate highlighted only the facts she and Caden agreed to release to their leaders.

"It sounds well planned, but I still worry for you." Selene's concern came through in her dark eyes and Fate relaxed a little. The woman who'd served as a surrogate mother surfaced.

"I know. We're being careful."

"Now, what of the other?"

Fate feigned confusion. "The other?"

~ ☾ ~

"Your decision to have an emotional connection with this man." Selene didn't bother to hide her distaste. Fate remembered when it as her own initial reaction as well. Before Caden.

"He's worth being divided from the Society."

"You're certain? The Society has been your home since you were fourteen, Fate. Your mother chose this life, as well as your grandmother. To leave it means you're turning your back on their lifestyles, as well as your own. And for a Soldier."

"No, it means I'm embracing another lifestyle." Fate rose from her position, suddenly too restless to remain still. Caden's gentle but firm intrusion into her thoughts calmed her. She focused on her goal, to have Selene understand her decision. "I didn't expect this to happen, didn't ask for it to happen."

"Yet, you were open to this man's seduction." Selene almost sneered.

"And he to mine," Fate shot back. "You do realize he faces more consequences than I do, don't you? He doesn't have to just worry about excommunication. He has to worry, *we* have to worry about injury to him, loss of his abilities, more." She broke off, unwilling to voice the last, worst possibility.

Selene stood and approached Fate then folded her in a familiar embrace, comforting. For an instant, Fate felt like a young teen again, faced with decisions she couldn't understand and asking her teacher, her friend, for support. The difference now, Caden lived in her mind, in her life.

She eased away from Selene and looked her in the eye. "I understand your concern, but this is what I want, what I'm meant to be."

Selene's eyes darkened and she started to say something then stopped, her mouth in a firm line. "Perhaps. I need to consult our Prioress about this, Fate."

~ ☾ ~

Fate couldn't hide her gasp. "The Prioress? Why?" Other women left the Society and the Prioress hadn't been consulted.

"Others are not you, my child." Selene clearly picked up on the thought and Fate checked her block to make sure it remained secure.

"But it's my decision. Consulting the founder of our order won't change my mind."

"But it may ease mine." Selene gestured toward the mats where they'd sat earlier. "Please. It may take a while to make contact with our founder, so I'd rather be comfortable." Selene positioned herself on the floor and closed her eyes, her hand wrapped around the stone of her necklace.

A short visit apparently out of the question, Fate sank back onto the mat and tried to calm herself. She sent a call out to Caden that he should try to sit in the awkward chairs a bit longer and he grumbled in her mind again. The short respite didn't lessen her worry, though and she bit the inside of her lip. Considering the difficulty in convincing Selene of her decision to leave the Society, how did she expect to do so with the founder of the order?

A low sound emanated from Selene and Fate sat straighter. She'd heard of the Prioress's visits, but never witnessed one. The founder, long dead, visited the head of the Society only if called and Selene used her necklace to do so, apparently. The Prioress could present herself through visions to the audience or through mind talk. Fate wondered if the block would hold—

"It doesn't, child." The strange voice barked in her mind and Fate flinched from the pain that accompanied it. *"Your discomfort will decrease with your lifting of blocks."*

"It's nothing." Fate didn't doubt the Prioress could see beyond her block, maybe even into Caden's link, but Fate refused to totally relinquish control.

~ ☾ ~

A chuckle sounded in her mind and the founder's voice softened slightly. *"Now I understand why Selene wanted my presence. You are strong, Fate Halligan."*

"Strong enough to leave the Society." Fate countered.

"But will your power be able to withstand the task ahead of you?"

"What task?" Caden? Would he be injured, or worse?

"You must be willing to face the worst possible outcome of your decision. You must be willing to take on the responsibilities of your decision. Are you that strong, my girl?"

Could she lose Caden? If she lost him, would her decision to leave the order be for naught? Would she be willing to lose her own life?

She felt Caden's panic for an instant. He heard her hesitation and Fate experienced the stain of guilt. He would give up everything for her and she stalled? No.

"I made my decision. I stand by it, Prioress. Regardless of the consequences."

"And if the consequences are the end of the Society as we know it?"

Fate exhaled, shock bringing her eyes open wide. *"That's impossible! I'm one person, and so is Caden. We won't bring down the Society."*

"Did I say you would defeat the Society?" The stiletto tone returned with a vengeance. *"You are not strong enough to bring us down. The Society de la Morte has been in existence since time, and will continue."* A pause followed and Fate began to think the founder left her mind then the Prioress continued. *"But the decision you make will change us, mayhap for eternity."*

She didn't believe it. Couldn't believe it. The Prioress attempted to scare her for some reason and it worked, in spades. Still, Fate drew in a breath and repeated her decision.

"So it is." Another pang of heat rose in her mind

~ ☾ ~

followed by a void. Fate felt like collapsing onto the floor. She'd remain upright long enough to get to Caden. He'd help her figure this whole mess out.

She didn't realize her eyes were closed until she opened them to find Caden squatting before her, his face drawn and tense. "You all right?"

She nodded and looked at him in confusion. "When did you come in?"

"Summoned by your 'Prioress'. I've been here the whole time." He couldn't have looked more grim as he helped her to stand. Fate glanced down at Selene. She sat still, her face set and eyes closed. She lingered with the Prioress.

"Let's get out of here." Caden wrapped his arm around her waist and led her to the truck, ignoring the mutters and gasps of Maidens and Latents they passed. Fate didn't notice much about the surroundings, though she figured she'd never be in the house or see any of the women she'd lived and trained with for over half her life.

Caden carefully deposited her into the truck. Fate waited until he'd started the vehicle before she spoke. "You were there? In my head?" At his nod she frowned, "Then why didn't I sense it? You seemed farther away."

"The bitch wouldn't let me any nearer." Caden growled.

"Selene?"

"No. Your Prioress. I tried to join your consciousness, to help with the argument but she forced me out. I could only stay and listen. I got one second to send a message when she tried to talk you out of staying with me."

"I heard you then. You do know I love you, right?" She wanted more than anything to still any fears.

He glanced at her, cursed and then pulled the truck to the side of the road. Fate gasped when he pulled her into his arms and kissed her. His mouth took hers, hard thrusts and nips at her lips before he pulled away and

~ ☾ ~

buried his face in her neck. "God, I was scared to death she'd talk you out of it."

She arched into him as much as she could in the space he allowed her, her arms around his neck and her head arched up as he planted kisses along her neck. "I almost did. You may die and I don't think I could..."

He pulled away far enough to meet her eyes. "I won't. I'll figure something out. And we *will* make it."

She nodded, her eyes filling with tears.

He thumbed one off her lashes. "We will, Fate, I promise."

She drew away then and pushed at his chest. "Let's get to Donan and talk to him, okay? We don't need to be parked here like sitting ducks."

***

He pushed away and took his place behind the wheel then put the truck into motion again. He'd never been more frightened in his life than when he heard her mind talk with the Prioress. His training, his experience, didn't in any form prepare him for this battle.

He'd just taken a turn toward Donan's Refuge when he sensed the Guard. Fate's hand shot out and her nails dug into his forearm. "They're here."

He didn't bother looking at her, he felt her in his head, giving him the location of the Guards. "How many, honey?"

"Too many. I don't know," she replied, her voice tight with tension. "At least four, maybe more. I think they're trying to box us in or something."

Caden put out a mental call to Jake. Maybe he could get there in time. He turned sharply away from the Guard's direction, only to see a construction blockade at the end of the small residential street. "Damn it!"

He started looking for another turn when Fate's scream cut him off. "Caden!"

A jolt from the driver's side pushed the truck a little

~ ☾ ~

to the right and he shot a look over his shoulder. A black
SUV rammed them on his side of the truck, near the end
of the storage bed. Caden struggled with the steering
wheel, trying to force the vehicle in a straight line. Hell,
he couldn't get the man off them. Scraping sounds and
grinding metal accompanied the drag on the truck as he
fought to keep control.

Another scream from Fate and a second, harder jolt
gave him more information than the push they got. He
frantically looked in front of them. Two more SUVs
swerved into both lanes in front of them and were
slowing, trying to hem him in. No construction workers
were in the area, no people that could help them. Damn,
he'd driven them into a trap.

"Hold on, baby." He jammed his foot on the gas and
shot ahead of the two cars that tried to hold them back.
Then, with a sudden movement, he whipped the steering
wheel around and the truck into a spin. With every
ounce of will on the turn, he hoped against hope he
could get them out of the dead end.

Fate didn't utter a sound now, only held on to the
door. She fought to keep her mind open to the dark
intent the Guards uttered. Caden cursed luridly and
stomped onto the brake, his arm shooting out and
catching her as the momentum of the truck's sudden
halt threatened to send her into the dashboard.

Fate bounced back against the seat and tried to
catch her bearings. The two black SUVs were parked
cross-wise in the road, blocking them from going any
farther.

Caden leaned forward and pulled the now familiar
black case from the glove compartment and dropped it
in her lap. "It's loaded." He opened his door.

Fate scrambled to open her door and carry the case

~ ☾ ~

with her. "Caden!"

He ignored her and advanced on the cars, his hands loose at his side. She unzipped the case, her fingers awkward and fumbling. Once open she pulled the gun free from its foam form and let the case fall to the street. She walked forward, her hands shaking but determined that he not face the Guard alone.

She'd almost made it even with him when he extended an arm and stopped her. "No. Behind me."

Four men, now familiarly dressed in black and with expressions of pure hatred, exited the cars. When they saw her gun one hesitated. They started walking again when the apparent leader barked an order at him. Fate lifted the gun and pointed it. "Stop right there. Move the cars, now."

The leader lifted his hands and kept coming. "We won't hurt you. Only want to talk."

"Like you've talked before? When one of you cut her?" Caden stepped near Fate, his body blocking everything except her gun hand. She tried to keep her breathing steady.

"A mistake. We don't want the Maiden killed."

Fate lowered the gun and shot at the leader's feet. The bullet sent up dust and asphalt, but only served to slow him a bit. He continued his advance and began to talk low to his men. They spread out and Fate cursed under her breath.

"Now what?" She asked Caden.

"Aim for the leader. I'll take care of the others."

She nodded, though he couldn't see her. She let another shot go to the other side of the leader's feet and stopped when Caden's inner voice came through urging her to conserve bullets.

Caden stood beside her one minute and the next sprinted to the right and tackled a Guard who'd managed to advance to within a few feet of her. Fate

~ ☾ ~

glanced out of the corner of her eye at him. Her first
mistake.

When he tackled her, the Guard didn't take care of
her head, or of the asphalt that she landed on. Fate
bounced, her head narrowly missing the hard surface
and she fought to keep her wits about her as she
scratched and clawed at him. She fought instinctively,
kicking and pushing at him with her hands. She found a
vulnerable spot and pushed then tried to ignore the
squish and wet feel of his eye as it collapsed into her
hand. A howl followed and she sprang free.

She tried to regain her feet. She'd lost the pistol when
another man tackled her at the knees. This time, though,
she went down in a skid, her hands taking the brunt of
the impact. She twisted to face her attacker and started
her battle again. In the back of her mind, she searched
for Caden. Her second mistake.

A blow to the side of her head stunned her for an
instant and she fought the blackness that rose in her
vision. Fate got a momentary glance of Caden. He'd
gotten to his feet and ran toward her when another
Guard struck him from behind. Her mind filled with the
horror of seeing him fall, the last thought in his mind of
her. She felt the blow to her face when the leader of the
Guard struck her but now, it didn't matter.

Without Caden, nothing mattered.

~ ☾ ~

Chapter Fifteen

Fate woke with the thought of if she'd just worn the seat belt in the car she wouldn't feel like a truck hit her. The cold floor she lay on seemed to be an enclosure, like a basement or bunker of some sort. She shifted her weight to relieve the ache in her hip only to gasp. Her arms were behind her and pain burned through her with each attempt to free herself. No matter how she tried, she couldn't move them. Combined tears of frustration and pain welled in her eyes and she blinked to clear them before twisting again.

As she moved, her head cleared and she remembered. The truck rammed, the Guards attacked and Caden fell. Frantically, she tried to link with him, only to have darkness and silence greet her. Fate made herself breathe, at least for now.

"Maiden Halligan. Greetings." The voice came from the darkness around her, audible yet low and even. She strained to locate the direction of the voice, to see if she could discriminate any other sound. Nothing but the sound of her own breathing and the hum of a tiny light suspended from the ceiling a few feet away. She wiggled her hands more, now feeling the cords that secured them.

"Don't bother to try to free yourself. My Guards are quite adept at bonds." Try as she might, Fate couldn't distinguish if the voice came from a male or female.

"Why am I here?"

"To serve my purposes." The voice advanced and a slinking sound, almost sliding accompanied it. Fate strained to look with her eyes.

~ ☾ ~

Nothing.

Could she see more with her inner mind?

"Your purposes? Isn't the Obsidian Guards' purpose to steal souls and take powers?"

"Ah, but that's the old purpose. We've moved into a new age, *my* age. You, My Maiden, have something more valuable than a soul and powers. I mean to have it."

Fate closed her eyes and called on every resource she'd been taught. At first nothing but the usual static of dying souls sounded in her mind. Then, gradually, a face, a presence coalesced in her mind. A woman, ageless but evil, with long yellow-white hair flowing about her, stood in the center of a dark circle. Around her knelt Guards, but not in obedience. For her, they swore to die, their goddess.

Arkane.

Fate drew in a breath at the nausea that rose in her throat. A body lay at Arkane's feet, its face and figure obscured by bloody cloths, this future vision of her death. More terrifying, the tiny form lay in Arkane's arms. An infant, obviously newly born, lay still and silent.

Fate's child.

Caden's son.

She gasped, her eyes flashing open. The image hung in her mind. Arkane wanted the unborn child she carried.

"You've seen the future, Maiden. Give in to me." Arkane's voice hissed now as she advanced and stood over Fate. The small light highlighted the silver in her hair. Fate tried to wrap her mind around what she'd seen, what she knew to be true. She studied the enemy who'd made her life hell for the past weeks.

She wasn't as tall as Selene, or Fate for that matter, and her manner not regal or powerful as Selene's. She

~ ☾ ~

stood slightly hunched over, as if the mass of hair she carried weighed her down. Fate fancied that she could see the individual strands stir, as Medusa's hair must have moved. But, no, she gave the woman too much presence.

"You won't kill me."

"Not for a time, no."

"When my child is born?"

"His soul will be mature and I will harvest both your soul and his. The power that affords me will make me almost invincible."

Almost. What price did she dare pay for almost invincible power? The innocent bystanders like Beth. Caden. What price remained yet to be paid? Her baby? Caden's child?

No.

Fate put the agony of Caden's absence from her mind. She must focus on their child.

"Why not kill me now, take his soul before he becomes a threat?" *Please let this work.*

"He will not be of use to me until his soul matures, at birth. Do you not know anything?" Arkane hissed in derision. "Selene is as useless as ever. The soul isn't mature, isn't ready for harvesting until birth. The trauma of birth awakens the powers, the ability to interpret pain and joy and vengeance," she finished, bowing to emphasize her point. Fate drew away as some of Arkane's hair brushed against her.

"So, I'm to be jailed in this cell until my child is born."

"No. His soul will be scarred if we mistreat you. Unfortunately, you must have other accommodations." Arkane gestured into the shadows and two Guards stepped forward. "Take her to the room adjoining mine."

Fate made sure to give the Guards a tough time getting her anywhere. She refused to stand and walk, then when one raised a hand to strike her, Arkane

~ ☾ ~

reduced him to a crumpled mass of howling flesh with a motion of her hand. A third Guard scurried forward and between the two of them, the Guards picked Fate up under her arms and hustled her to a room. Once there, one Guard held a knife at the ready while the second cut her hands free.

The room wasn't luxurious, by any means, and Fate again got the impression that it lay underground. But as she roamed around the room, she started inventorying the items she could use as weapons or as a means of escape. Arkane may have denigrated Selene's training, but she didn't take into account the important changes in Fate's life.

Caden left her with knowledge that she could use now.

She sent another, desperate message to him, unable to accept that he might be gone from her forever.

"Caden, where are you?"

***

Caden groaned, aware of the rain on his face. No, not rain. Water.

"Let's go, man. Wake up." Jake shook him and Caden moaned, his head about to explode. The grit of asphalt and gravel bit into his cheek but when he tried to raise his head it spun to the point he felt like vomiting. Then he tried to sit up.

Bad idea. He decided on vomiting instead. After he'd crawled free of the mess he finally made it to sitting.

"Damn, man. You made the concussion club this time." Jake knelt beside him and probed the spot on the side of Caden's head, bringing another wave of pain and nausea. Caden waved him away and opened his eyes. His vision wavered then settled into clarity. One black SUV still sat sideways in the middle of the road. Two Guards lay in the street, near the truck. Jake's own truck sat, skewed, in the midst of the mess. One of the lesser Soldiers stood near the chaos in silent watch.

~ ☾ ~

Caden surveyed the scene then turned his head to search. "Where is she? Is she hurt?"

He reached out to steady himself as he tried to stand and Jake lent a hand. Caden weaved a bit then turned, looking for her.

"Fate? Where is she? Damn it, Jake!" He spun around as fast as his body would allow and stared at his friend.

"They took her, Caden. I got here too late. She's gone."

"No. Damn it, no!" His words ended in a howl of agony and Caden started toward his truck, stumbling, and his hands in his pocket as he fumbled for his keys.

He didn't make it to the truck before Jake stopped him. "You can't drive."

"The hell I can't. I have to find her."

"Where? Where is she? Do you know? Does anybody?" Jake pulled him in the direction of his own truck, even as he gestured toward Caden's vehicle. The silent guy nodded and headed toward the other truck. Along the way, he stooped and grasped a black case and another object off the ground.

"He doesn't have my keys." Caden dug in his pocket, vaguely aware he searched for something but not sure what.

"He'll manage." Jake pushed Caden into the truck. "We have to clear the area before someone finds the bodies."

"I have to find Fate."

"We will, buddy. I'm taking you to Donan. If she's alive, he'll know where she is." Jake hustled Caden inside and started his vehicle. As they drove away Caden saw more Soldiers arriving to clear the area. In less than five minutes, any evidence of a battle would be erased. Any witnesses would have their memories erased and no ordinary world inhabitants would be aware anything happened.

~ ☾ ~

Caden swallowed another surge of nausea as his head dropped back onto the headrest of the seat. Fate had to be alive. He'd know it if she wasn't.

By the time they arrived at Donan's Refuge, Caden got his headache under control, or at least didn't feel like relieving himself of his internal organs every time he moved. His entrance into the house held no ceremony but all of the inhabitants of the building looked on, as if they'd been forewarned. Jake paced beside him, opening doors and generally glowering at anyone who approached them.

He made it to Donan's study and sank into a chair then put his head in his hands. He'd tried to reach her to no avail. *Where is she?*

"She's still unconscious." Donan entered, followed by—

"Selene?" Caden started to stand only to fall back into the chair at her gesture. She circled him and he sensed her studying his head before she went to the door of the room and opened it then called for water and ice. Then she came and stood beside his mentor and glanced toward Jake.

"He stays." Caden needed someone who'd back him up. He may shock the hell out of his friend, but Jake would understand. Or at least watch his back.

"Very well. We must plan, now." Selene's steady gaze assessed him.

Caden started to fill them in on what happened in the ambush and this time Donan interrupted. "We know. We sensed it as it happened."

His gaze sharpened. "So you know where Fate is."

Donan nodded, his expression grave.

"She's not dead." Caden ground out. "I'd know it."

"So, you admit to an emotional attachment." Selene spoke as she sank onto a mat cross-legged and serene.

"You know we're connected emotionally as well as

~ ☾ ~

psychically. Fate talked to you about it." If they'd stop this shit he could get on with finding his mate.

"Yes, but she could have been fooled."

"She wasn't. I'm committed to her." He looked at Donan. "Willing to accept any consequences."

He heard a curse behind him as Jake took in the ramifications of his statement, but didn't take the time to send any message to his friend. "If you agree to help me, I'll accept anything you can throw at me."

"Even death?"

"Even death, if you think you can kill me." He glared at the woman who'd given Fate so much grief. "Now, are you going to help me or not?"

"We are." Finally, Donan spoke.

"Where is she?"

"In the Hold of the Guard."

"The Hold? The headquarters."

"More than the headquarters. The Hold is an underground bunker for the Guards, their extra weapons, and the leader of the Guard. It also contains the powers that have been stolen. Arkane uses the powers as bargaining chips to control her forces."

Caden gritted his teeth and forced himself to stay calm. "Did you know of this Arkane all along?"

Donan shook his head, his expression now cold. "No. We thought Arkane long defeated, dead. Apparently, she's been in hiding for years. I only became aware of her when she appeared to her Guards, the ones you managed to kill in the ambush."

"So, she has Fate." Caden heard someone enter the room. Donan's eyes shuttered, as did Selene's. Caden could feel the curiosity emanate from the lesser Soldier as he placed containers of ice and water on a table, along with a stack of cloths, before excusing himself.

Selene stood and withdrew a towel from the stack and dipped it in the water. She approached Caden with the

~ ☾ ~

towel and he realized her intention to clean his wound. "Never mind. It'll keep."

"I can clean your wound while we plan." She ignored his hand as he tried to bat her away and instead started to dab firmly at his head. He hissed as her ministrations brought new pangs, then sighed at the application of ice to his head.

He turned his attention to Donan. "How much time do we have before they try to kill her? And why didn't they kill her at the scene?"

Donan's shuttered expression didn't change, but Caden caught a gleam of, what? Worry? Unease? "She is in no immediate danger."

"Why? They've been after her for weeks. Why stop now? We need to get to her before some idiot tries something."

"No. She isn't going to be injured for now." Selene stepped away from his head and laid the dirtied towels on the table before assuming her position again. "Even if they keep her for months, she won't be harmed."

"Months?" *Oh, hell no.*

"She won't be killed until the child is born." Selene watched him as she delivered the last words.

Caden ensured his head injury didn't make him lose consciousness. But as the impact of Selene's words hit him he almost keeled over. "Fate's pregnant?"

"With your son." Selene finished.

"My son."

"The Soldier's Legend, the Prioress's Predictions, they concern your son. The product of the Sixth Son and the Descendant of the Prioress. The one who will change the world of the Society and the Soldiers."

"Change it how?"

Donan smiled archly. "You and Fate have started the change by working as a team. Your connections are the start of a larger connection between the Soldiers of Light

~ ☾ ~

and the Society de la Morte Maidens."

Jake, a silent sentinel until now stepped forward. "You mean the connection Fate and Caden have is something other Soldiers and Maidens may achieve?" At Donan's nod he shook his head. "No wonder the legend warned of our world ending. It means ending dichotomy between the Society and the Soldiers."

"Has ended, as of today." Selene affirmed. "We worked as one entity before the schism and now must relearn how to work as one. Saving Fate will be the first test of that cooperation."

"Well, hell." Caden muttered. They intended to use Fate as their guinea pig, damn it.

***

Fate finished her work on a rudimentary knife just as the lights went out of her room. "Guess it's time for bed," she grumbled. Arkane warned her in one of her uncomfortable visits during the day that no one else would venture in the room. Instead, a steady supply of water and food regularly appeared through a slot midway up the wall of the room. Now, as she felt her way to the bed, she wondered, even if she made a knife and a spray she could use to blind a Guard, if the men didn't show up it wouldn't do her much good.

She rejected the possibility of disarming Arkane. The woman scared her, more than any being or dark force could. She kept a constant headache brought about from erecting barriers and constantly reforming them against Arkane's persistent attacks. Now, she dare not sleep in case she lower a barrier and provide the monster an entrance to her mind and secrets she didn't know she kept.

She lay on the bed and allowed herself the luxury of thinking of Caden. She'd put him out of her mind all day, and concentrated instead on the prospect of escape and finding a way to protect her child. No clear plan

~ ☾ ~

showed itself, though and she fought back tears at the
futility of her situation.

"*Caden,*" She whispered into the night, desperately
wishing for his arms around her, his wry sense of
humor.

"*Fate, baby. You okay?*" His voice came through to
her mind clearly, and she sat up on the bed, her eyes
wide and unseeing in the darkness.

"*I'm fine. Scared, but fine. And you? I saw you hit.*"
Anguish filled her at the memory of his fall.

"*I've got a hell of a headache, but I'm good. Where
are they keeping you?*"

She gulped back a sob, intensely aware that though
no Guards showed their faces, they watched her
constantly. She lay back down on the bed and wrapped
her arms around her middle.

"*I'm not sure, but I think it's an underground shelter
of some sort. A woman, the leader of the Guards, I
think, is keeping me here. Her name is Arkane.*" She
sent a mental picture of the physical Arkane, as well as a
warning that the Guards' leader's psychic abilities were
equal to her own.

"*I doubt that. You have something she doesn't have.*"
Caden whispered in her head.

"*What?*"

"*Me.*"

***

Caden didn't want to close the mental link with Fate,
too aware of a push to his mind as well as her warning.
Even now, Arkane tried to break into their link, to use
their connection against them. He assured Fate he'd
return and then spun around to face Selene and Donan.
The two of them sat at a table, a topographical map
between them. Somehow, they united their powers and
attempted to locate the Guards' bunker.

"Any luck?" He strode to the desk and glanced at the

~ ☾ ~

map, wondering if the information Fate passed on would help.

"Not yet, but we will get the location. I'm sure of it." Selene leaned back in her chair and rubbed a crease in her forehead. For the first time since he'd met her Caden sensed age on the woman, as well as stress. Fate's capture weighed on her.

Donan pressed forward, his eyes on the map. Caden passed a cursory glance over the layout then studied his teacher. If anyone could pinpoint the Guard, it would be Donan.

Behind him, Jake spoke with several Soldiers. His friend handpicked men to accompany them to the bunker and to free Fate. Caden knew most, trusted Jake to vet the rest.

"I have it." Donan looked up into Caden's eyes with a gleam of triumph in his own. "I know where she is."

"Where?" Caden demanded.

"Here." Donan pointed to an outcrop of hills near Hilldale, a town about sixty miles west of them. "It's a straight shot into the mountain."

"She isn't underground like she thought; she's in the mountain." Caden murmured as he started to take notice of the terrain around the bunker. Jake joined him and Selene and Donan separated themselves from the pack of men. He put them from his mind. Now, he turned to his strength, he planned for battle.

"Jake, we'll need a couple of separate forces to take out any Guards on the exterior. And one main force to go in with me."

Jake nodded then narrowed his eyes at the map. "It's a rough place. Natural fortifications, here and here." He pointed out outcroppings of rock and abutments in the hills. "We may need more men."

Caden shook his head, "No time. We need to get in as soon as possible."

~ ☾ ~

Jake turned his eyes on Caden. "I thought Donan said Fate isn't in any physical danger right now. We can wait, plan a couple days."

"No, we don't. She may not be in physical danger, but the leader is bombarding her psychically."

Selene stepped forward, "That's why I haven't been able to connect with her."

Caden shrugged. "Maybe. I got through but only for a short time. I picked up on someone trying to butt in." He leveled a gaze on Selene but didn't get much of a reaction, then continued. "Fate's in pain. She constantly has to change and reinforce her barriers and she's getting tired. Eventually, Arkane's going to break through."

"We'll all be at risk." Selene finished, her voice grim.

"I don't give a damn about the rest of us. If Fate breaks it'll be for only one reason. She's too tired and too damaged to fight."

"So, we go in with what we have." Jake asserted and leaned forward to study the map for a better route in.

***

Fate paced the room. She'd measured the area, thirty-four paces by twenty-two paces. She figured she'd made the trip enough to do a mini marathon, but her nervous energy wouldn't allow her to stop. She massaged her temple absently, adjusting the barrier once again. She'd almost lost the wall when she dozed off during the night, but came awake with a taste of evil in her head, slamming down a block in an instant.

She was tired, beyond exhausted, but couldn't stop walking. If she stopped walking, she might sit, and if she sat, she might fall asleep.

Everything rested on her staying alert.

"Fate." His voice came through her mind, sliding under layers of barriers she'd built against Arkane. Fate almost collapsed with relief.

~ ☾ ~

"I wasn't sure you'd be able to get through the blocks."

"I'll find you anywhere, baby. How you holding up?"

"Okay." She didn't elaborate. Though she didn't open her mind up enough to feel him, he knew of her struggles with Arkane.

"You won't have to fight much longer."

"Caden?"

"Just be ready. When I ask you to open, do it, okay? We'll need to do this together."

She turned away from the door and slit in the wall, sure they'd be able to see the mingled relief and worry in her face.

She did sit then, her legs wouldn't support her.

Minutes passed, minutes that felt like hours. In the distance, she thought she heard shouts and thuds, but then again, it could have been the pounding of her pulse against her temples. She wasn't mistaken, though, when she heard the scrape of a key in the door.

Arkane opened the door and entered, not bothering to close it behind her. Her face, usually composed and cold, suffused with color, her skin blotchy, making her ugly. "Come on."

She reached out and grabbed Fate, her nails digging into Fate's arm as she dragged her off the bed. Fate followed, unsure if she should fight or not. She'd gotten out of the locked room, sure, but where now?

They went down another hallway, one in which the sounds of their footfalls bounced back. Fate glanced around but saw nothing but cinderblock and mortar, giving her the impression of a lit cave. They must be going farther underground, though they didn't descend. The bunker must be inside a mountain. Suddenly, Arkane stopped, her hand dropping from Fate's arm. Fate ignored the pinpricks of pain the nail bites left behind, instead she looked at the door before her with dread.

~ ☾ ~

Inside lived panic, pain, and misery. Even with the myriad of barriers she built, she sensed voices calling out for help. Her help.

Arkane isolated a key from a ring she retrieved from a pocket and inserting it in the lock, gave a savage turn. She twisted her head and glared at Fate. "In."

Fate retreated a step. She couldn't go in. She shook her head and gasped as the older woman once again reached out, seized her by the neck and pushed her into the room. Fate sprawled onto the dark concrete floor, vaguely aware that Arkane followed her in and shut the door.

"You think you can fight me. You think your control is stronger than mine." Arkane bent over her, spittle spraying from her mouth as she ranted. "Your lover won't make it to you in time, Maiden. If I can't have both your soul and that of your child's I'll settle for severing the connection. I'll settle for your soul, your powers."

~ (~

Chapter Sixteen

Arkane moved with shocking speed toward a cabinet set against the far wall of the room and started rummaging through it, muttering to herself. Fate crab walked a few feet to the wall near the door and braced against it to come to a stand. She edged to the door and twisted the knob.

Locked.

With the wall at her back she surveyed the space around her. The room shone with a low level, eerie glow. A singular bulb put out meager light to the corners of the room. There were several cabinets, some with glassed in doors, others made totally of coarse wood, ranged along every wall.

Fate saw what looked like chemists' trays ranged in the glassed in cabinets. Inside the shelves were lined with slender vials, sealed with stoppers and containing a substance. The contents of the vials looked like liquid, yet solid and some of the vials fairly vibrated with the motion of the substance, as if small waves rocked it to and fro. Others lay quiet and still.

Fate knew instinctively these were stolen souls. Not yet absorbed and depleted of the powers that made each man and woman unique, but trapped for how long? She shivered with the knowledge of the souls' torments. If she survived, she'd find a way to set them all free. Their voices sounded in her mind and she forced herself to build another wall against them, knowing if she didn't she'd be too distracted to face Arkane. She needed to focus on her survival.

~ ☾ ~

Arkane's shout brought her attention to the woman in front of her. Red suffused her face, framing eyes wild with her own warped reality.

"You hoard the souls of innocents."

"So? I save them for when I need them. Each of them serves a purpose, my purpose. As will you. You, I won't save," Arkane advanced, a blade gleaming dully in her hands. "You I'll use to defeat your lover."

She pounced then, though she fell short as Fate sidestepped her. Fate didn't want to leave her only means of escape, the locked door, but she didn't have a choice. Arkane waved the knife she held wildly, swiping at Fate who managed to dodge the strikes with inches to spare. As she did, she frantically glanced around her, trying to find something, anything to use as a weapon.

No spare pieces of cutlery, bowls or sharp objects were apparent. Only the knife Arkane wielded. Fate danced out of the way of another swipe and bounced into one of the cabinets. Glass tinkled behind her and she inched farther along toward the cupboard Arkane been rifled through earlier.

Her mind awhirl with voices, barriers and the incessant battering of Arkane, Fate almost missed Caden's call. *"Fate. Where are you? We're in."*

"I'm in a room, down a hallway." She sent a mental picture of the room and the route, though she wasn't sure the hallway looked any different than any other hall in the complex.

A burning gash opened up on her arm as she threw it up to defend herself and she cursed before lurching out of Arkane's path once again. She bumped into the cabinet behind her, causing more of the vials to clatter together. Could she use them against Arkane?

Even as the thought occurred to her, she rejected it. It could have been the beginning of the path Arkane chose. One small misuse led to another and now, she disrupted

~ ☾ ~

countless lives. Fate wouldn't do that, no matter what.

"Fate! Where the hell are you?" Caden's frustration came through loud and clear, almost audibly and she barked a grim laugh.

"In a room with a thousand trapped souls." She muttered under her breath and dodged another blow.

Arkane's breath came in gasps and Fate silently thanked all her trainers through the years for her endurance. "Been taking it a little easy on the workouts, Arkane?"

"You bitch! You and Selene think you have all the power. She always gloated about her abilities. I wasn't good enough. They made me a Latent."

Fate's shock slowed her to a standstill. "You were a Maiden?"

"No," Arkane spat. "A Latent. I didn't have the level of energy the Society demanded of the Maidens. The Prioress didn't think me adequate. But now," she lunged for Fate once again. "Now, I have more power in this room than the Society will be able to battle in a thousand years. I'll be here. To rule."

Arkane's blade, aimed for Fate's neck, missed the mark. Instead, Fate blocked with her hand and suddenly felt the solid hilt of the knife, surrounded by Arkane's boney fist. She wrapped her hand around Arkane's and pushed, bringing her other hand up to assist. As she fought Fate sent out a call. If she didn't take the blade from the woman, she wouldn't make it.

***

"Damn it!" Caden halted at the end of another dead end. A shattered door led to an empty room. He wheeled and started sprinting down the hall in search of another corridor to search.

Behind him, Jake pounded. "Caden, we're wasting time."

"I know," he bit out. "But she couldn't tell me any

~ ☾ ~

more details. Just that she was in a room 'with a
thousand trapped souls'." He veered to the left and
down another hallway, blank cinderblock walls and bare
lighting the only features.

Jake's hand shot out and grabbed Caden's shirt collar.
"Hold it. You said a thousand souls?"

"Yeah. So?"

"If she's in a room with souls, maybe the Maidens can
locate it. Maybe Selene can."

"Damn!" Caden backed up against a wall and opened
his link to Donan. He relayed the facts to his mentor and
waited.

A second later, Selene's voice filled his mind. *She's in
a room to your right, down a corridor. Filled with a
thousand trapped souls.*" Her voice trailed off in horror,
sorrow and something Caden didn't wait to analyze. He
could find Fate now.

He doubled back and ran down the hall. Jake
followed, yelling behind him. "We need
reinforcements?"

"No. I'll take care of Arkane myself." Caden bit out,
seeing a passageway ahead and to the right of the one
they traveled down. He started down it and saw a door,
closed and secure, at the end of the hall. He picked up
his speed and reached behind him to pull his pistol from
his back holster. He'd not waste time with this bitch.

He kicked at the door but it didn't budge. Jake added
his efforts and with a few more kicks, the door hung
askew on its hinges and he rushed in.

He didn't take the time to look at his surroundings,
other than to make sure there were no other Guards
inside. "Fate!"

He couldn't see her face as she struggled with a much
older woman. They struggled against a cabinet, their
hands hidden between them. Caden saw the effort in
Fate's body as she battled for something.

~ ☾ ~

"Knife." She grunted as she gave another heave at the woman then broke away, scuttling backward to clear the way for Caden. Or so he thought.

Arkane stood, her hands wrapped around the hilt of a knife Caden recognized. The Guards' ceremonial Soul Taker. The knife appeared to be buried in the woman's midriff with only the hilt visible. As he lurched forward, toward Fate, Caden watched the older woman slump then fall to the floor in seeming slow motion.

Fate stumbled slightly and Caden rushed to enfold her in his arms, his attention totally focused on her now. In the background he could hear Jake talking, but he didn't pay attention. All his focus remained fixed on the woman in his arms.

"You okay?"

Her nod into his shoulder reassured him slightly, but he wanted to strip her down and inspect her from head to toe. He wanted inside her head to assure himself that Arkane hadn't damaged her psyche. Fate stirred against him and Caden briefly shut his eyes, overcome by relief. In that instant, though, he realized his mistake.

He turned toward Arkane's body in an attempt to keep her in his sight and the vision in front of him horrified him. Arkane somehow managed to regain her feet. She now stood braced against a cabinet, a bloody apparition, her silver hair tipped in her own blood, the hilt of the Soul Taker blade still visible in her abdomen, Jake between her and them, his stance one of defense. She'd somehow gotten the glass door of the cabinet open and now clutched several vials in her hands. In a low but carrying voice, she incanted some words Caden couldn't make out then smashed the vials against her chest, making them shatter against her, their contents staining her clothes.

In an instant Caden realized the contents of the vials. He reached out in a futile attempt to halt the

~ ☾ ~

destruction. At the same time, Fate's hand shot out and
clasped his, and she turned in his arms, her eyes on
Arkane. "No!"

The thread of power he felt in her hand matched one
he called from his psyche. He could feel them intertwine
and grow in strength, until he vibrated with the
sensation. He knew, because Fate knew, the only way to
stop Arkane once and for all.

In the next instant the stain on Arkane's clothes
danced away, writhing darkly, then lightened in color.
As the power departed from them Fate and Caden
retreated into the place where only Maidens went. A
portal opened, bright and shining. The souls started to
move toward the opening, each of them displaying
myriad of colors, from pink to yellow, burgundy to every
shade in the rainbow, including a bit of darkness. They
watched as one as the souls dissipated in the air and
then entered the portal, followed by each and every one
of those Arkane shattered. As the released souls entered
they uttered a sigh of joy and relief from pain. The souls
were finally at peace, save one.

One soul remained in the air around them, Arkane's.
It hovered near the edge of consciousness. "I won't go! I
am the Power, I have all Power."

"You must go," Fate silently averred to Arkane. Caden
still held her, but now he wasn't an observer, as before,
but an active participant. He turned so he could see
Arkane more clearly.

The other souls he'd seen, both in his work and that
of Fate, appeared cohesive, almost corporeal. Arkane,
however, manifested as a scramble of forms, of dark
colors, of sickening hues. Great gaps appeared in her
form, with opaque voids behind them.

"You've failed, Arkane. Your power wasn't real, but
that of others, and not yours to hold." He knew these
things, but still it surprised him when the words came

~ (~

from him. "Your only hope is the portal."

Arkane sneered and butted against the edges of consciousness as she tried to leave the area. Fate and Caden's combined force kept her contained. She hissed her frustration.

Fate eyed the morass of souls contained in Arkane. "If I must, I can portion out the souls on this side of the portal, Arkane. On this side, you'll have intense pain. On the other side, none as the souls depart yours."

Arkane's scorn grew. "You have no idea of what happens on the other side, Maiden."

Fate separated herself from Caden and he momentarily wondered if that would make him an observer once more. No, he continued to be active. Still more than aware of the combined power that emanated from them.

Fate stood just in front of him, her attention on Arkane. "I am not the only Maiden to encounter you, am I, Arkane? You've battled Selene as well as me. Before us, the Prioress."

"Yes, and I defeated her!" Arkane's soul pulsed with colorless rage.

"You think this, Latent?" Another, disembodied voice rose from all around them. Caden's consciousness glanced around, in search of the speaker. Finally, he realized it came through the open portal.

Arkane shrank back, "I defeated you. I sent you to eternity!"

"I reside here, but you did not defeat me, as you see." A mist drifted in through the portal, soft and warm, though not weak, as Caden would imagine soft and warm would feel. No, this soul embodied power and regality. All aiming for Arkane.

"You can't harm me. It's against the Maiden's Call."

"So, it is. I wrote the call for the purposes of protecting souls from retribution. I will not harm your

~ ☾ ~

soul. Merely allow Fate and Caden to free those trapped within you, ensnared by you."

Caden felt Fate join with him again and knew his task. He focused—they focused—on separating the entities inside Arkane. As he worked, surprise and disgust swept over him at the multitude of trapped essences.

She fought, writhed as one by one, they separated the poor souls and sent them on to the Prioress, who directed them into the portal. The time spent on the task could have been an instant, could have been days. Caden didn't feel a drain on his power, on their power.

Finally, the last trapped soul floated free. As it entered the portal, a gust of joyous wind ruffled through the area, clearing the way for one more soul to enter. Fate stepped forward. "You have been freed of your powers, of your greed, Arkane. Enter the portal."

"I'll be punished." Arkane's voice sounded reedy and frail now as she cowered in the corner of the area.

Caden and Fate began to shrink the enclosure, bringing the portal closer to Arkane and them. The Prioress's essence monitored all silently. Caden nudged Arkane a bit closer. "Whether you will be punished isn't the point of this all, Arkane. You must enter the portal. You're not strong enough to linger here."

"I can, if I steal enough souls."

"That power is gone, along with your body. Your soul isn't strong enough to remain here, on this plane." Fate gently pushed Arkane. "If you stay, you'll observe life, be a faint breeze as people walk by. Nothing more. Then, after a time of watching and not being able to live life, you'll simply cease."

Arkane's wail came out strong and then she thrust herself into the portal. Caden and Fate watched as she blended into the neutrality of the other side.

The Prioress glided in front of them. "Well done, my

~ ☾ ~

children. Now, go, convince the others that this, the connection between you and the connection that will continue with your son and the children of the others, that is what I intended for the Soldiers and the Maidens."

She turned, as if to leave but stopped at Fate's question. "What happened to them?"

"Them?"

"The Soldier and Maiden who chose each other over the souls that were lost. Were they punished?"

Caden watched as the Prioress smiled and took a step toward the portal then pause. "They were not punished, other than to punish themselves."

"What do you mean?" Enough with the runaround speak.

"They decided on their own to separate, to never see each other. Only in the direst circumstances did they communicate with each other. Only when the future of the Soldiers of Light and the Society de la Morte became in jeopardy did Donan and Selene break their pact."

She disappeared, as did the portal, in the next breath.

Caden became aware of Fate trembling in his arms.

"Donan and Selene?" Fate's voice held wonder and a little surprise. Caden couldn't blame her though he had other things on his mind, more important to their own lives.

Their minds continued to be connected, would always be now, but he wanted to see her face. He leaned away enough to look at her.

"Did it take too much out of you?" He tilted her head up so he could see her eyes.

She lifted glistening eyes to him. "We did it. We convinced the Prioress of our connection."

He smiled, "Honey, I don't think we convinced her at all. I wonder if it was her idea from the beginning."

She gurgled a small laugh and then sighed. "We need

~ ☾ ~

to find the others."

"The others are here." Donan's voice came from the
door of the room and Fate turned in Caden's arms.
Indeed, the others were there. The large room suddenly
seemed close and tiny, as several large men she
identified as Soldiers filed in and ranged along the wall.
Jake stood off to the side as well and leveled a wink at
her as her eyes swept him.

Fate finally settled her gaze on Donan and Selene.
"Did you see?"

"We were allowed to observe, not to assist." Selene
nodded her head, a slight flush to her cheeks and her
gaze carefully avoiding looking at Donan.

Donan heaved a sigh and glanced around, taking in
all the cabinets and their contents. "Arkane never made
her presence known in the past. We suspected she
survived, but never had the means to find her." He
nodded toward Fate and Caden. "Until you came to your
power."

Fate wrinkled her brow. "But I'd come into my
powers as a teenager. Why wait until now to try to kill
me?"

Selene raised her hand to hover over the glassed in
enclosures. Now she looked at Fate. "I think she may
have stolen a touch of precognition and saw the
immediate future. Saw that you would meet Caden."

Caden stirred against Fate. "We only met because of
the threats against Fate."

"Can you be sure you wouldn't have met otherwise?"
Selene eyed them. "I have a feeling destiny would have
lent a hand either way."

The Prioress settled the fight for their future in the
instant she approved of them, yet Fate still wanted some
answers. "Our future? Did we battle, defeat Arkane for
nothing?"

Donan shook then bowed his head slightly. "I heard

~ ☾ ~

the Prioress, as did Selene. You won't be punished or
separated from the orders for your connection."

"Our love." *In for a penny.* Fate smiled.

He quirked a grin. "For your love. In fact, we will all
be working as a single unit, I think. It won't be easy; we
all have pretty concrete rules that will have to be
broken." He sent Selene a look filled with promise.

"But with your example of how the connection
functions in a couple that are committed to the souls'
care, I think the Society and Soldiers will continue and
work well." Selene finished, her blush deepened. "With
some training, of course."

Fate let herself relax and she sank a bit more into
Caden's arms. His voice rumbled around her. "What
now?"

Donan straightened, his obeisance gone. "Now, we
release the souls trapped here."

Selene bandaged Fate's arm then it fell to Caden,
Fate, and the leaders of the two organizations to lead the
Soldiers in the room to release the souls. As he worked
Caden sent Fate a puzzled question, *"How in hell do I
know what I'm doing?"*

*"You must have gotten a taste of the Maiden's
powers and knowledge when we merged skills."* She
didn't bother holding back her amusement at his shock,
but also her pride in the care he used with the souls.

In the end, Fate and Selene put out a mental call to
Maidens as well. By the time the many rooms of souls
were released and sent on to the portal, putting nearly
every Maiden and Soldier to at work, either remotely or
on scene. The men and women eyed each other with a
little trepidation, curiosity and interest. An indication of
things to come?

Fate and Caden ended the day with her arm stitched
and freshly bandaged, and in the bed at the cabin. He'd
loved her gently and thoroughly, and now she lay in his

~ ☾ ~

arms, sleepy and yawning against his chest.

"You're okay with the baby?" She murmured, her mind already comfortable with its dual home, in his consciousness and her own. This sharing of thoughts could be convenient.

"Convenient until we have an argument." He rumbled then his voice deepened more. "I'm looking forward to seeing you with our son, feeding him."

Fate got a mental picture of her with a blond baby at her breast. Her heart lurched with the love she felt and received in that moment. Caden shifted her a bit to lay on his chest. "I do have one thing I'll insist on."

"What?"

"We marry."

"No one's married in the Society or Soldiers for hundreds of years."

"So, we start another tradition." Caden nudged her head up and kissed her. Their minds melded deeper, sure in the knowledge they'd discovered their destiny.

~ ☾ ~

Kate McKeever

Kate McKeever was born and raised in the southern highlands. She spent most of her childhood exploring, woods, words and her imagination. After several jobs and further exploration of careers, she settled on working with special children and in the evenings, working on writing the stories that persist to both entertain and distract her.

CPSIA information can be obtained at www.ICGtesting.com
Printed in the USA
BVOW09s1843030314

346533BV00002B/77/P